DOWN THE COALTOWN ROAD

Down the Coaltown Road

A NOVEL

Sheldon Currie

KEY PORTER BOOKS

National Library of Canada Cataloguing in Publication Data

Currie, Sheldon, 1934–
    Down the Coaltown Road/Sheldon Currie.

ISBN 1-55263-482-5

1. Italian Canadians—Nova Scotia—Cape Breton Island—History—20th century—Fiction. 2. World War, 1939-1945—Nova Scotia—Cape Breton Island—Fiction. I. Title.

PS8555.U74D69 2002   C813'.54   C2002-903290-3
PR9199.3.C82D69 2002

The publisher gratefully acknowledges the support of the Canada Council for the Arts and the Ontario Arts Council for its publishing program.

We acknowledge the financial support of the Government of Canada through the Book Publishing Industry Development Program (BPIDP) for our publishing activities.

Key Porter Books Limited
70 The Esplanade
Toronto, Ontario
Canada M5E 1R2

www.keyporter.com

Text design: Peter Maher
Electronic formatting: Heidi Palfrey

Printed and bound in Canada

02 03 04 05 06 07 6 5 4 3 2 1

FRANCES DOLORES (DONNELLY),
SISTER OF CHARITY, LIBRARIAN AND
DIRECTOR OF ADULT EDUCATION,
RESERVE MINES,
1941–1949
Sine qua non.

My many helpful readers: Ron Caplan, Reynold Stone, Jim Taylor, Effie Taylor, George Sanderson, Gertrude Sanderson, Ann Camozzie, Sandra Coyle.

R.B. MacDonald for help with Latin, Italian and Liturgical History.

Sam Migliore and Evo Dipierro for their wonderful book *Italian Lives, Cape Breton Memories.* Esperanza Maria Razzolini for her excellent work *All Our Fathers: The North Italian Colony in Industrial Cape Breton.* Rusty Neal for her chapter on Sister Frances Dolores in her work *Brotherhood Economics.* Brian Tennyson and Roger Sarty for their book *Guardian of the Gulf: Sydney, Cape Breton and the Atlantic Wars.* Peter Moogk for his essay "From Fortress Louisbourg to Fortress Sydney: Artillery and Gunners on Cape Breton, 1743–1964," in Ken Donovan's collection *Cape Breton at 200.* Ted Jones for his book *Both Sides of the Wire: The Fredericton Internment Camp.* Ed Caissie and his students for creating the Internment Camp Museum at Minto, New Brunswick. Franca Iacovetta et al. for *Enemies Within: Italian and Other Internees in Canada and Abroad.* Salvatore J. La Gumina for *WOP! A Documentary History of Anti-Italian Discrimination.* Sharon Gibson Palermo for her children's novel, *The Lie That Had to Be.* Innumerable others.

Nelson Beaton, Italo Secco, Gino Scattalon, and Lennie Stephenson for information about Italian Cape Breton.

Marie Mac Phee for the loan of a 1940 diary.

Allister MacGillivray for his beautiful song, "Down the Coal Town Road."

Clare McKeon, sure-footed editor at Key Porter who made a novel out of a manuscript.

Dawn Currie, indefatigable, in-house editor of a thousand versions of my manuscript and my life.

Selves—goes itself; myself it speaks and spells,
Crying what I do is me: for that I came.

GERARD MANLEY HOPKINS

Language is the blood of society.

LAURIE MACDONALD

PROLOGUE

✠

JUNE 1965

THE THREE BUILDINGS stand solid, the church in the middle, flanked on either side by the glebe house and the convent. Little of significance has changed externally since the day Father Rod MacDonald came to be the parish priest in 1940. The two maple trees in the large front yard now rise to half the height of the bell tower. A paved driveway between the church and the glebe house leads to a parking lot at the back. Otherwise the parish church remains the same as the day it was completed, an immense mass of brown shingles, tall windows and doors, a medieval anomaly dominating the rows of company houses crouching in its neighbourhood like legions of urban peasants.

The glebe house is a modest two-storey building large enough for two priests and guests. It is painted blue, and a blue painted picket fence surrounds its front-yard lawn and separates it from the main street. Nothing here has changed since 1940 except that the large vegetable garden in the back yard is now a weedy lawn.

A short distance beyond the church parking lot and a safe distance before the cliffs overlooking the Atlantic Ocean, a practical, square, two-storey school houses the parish students and their teachers. Internally little has changed. Grades one to six are smaller because there are fewer children in the parish, the junior and senior high grades are larger because more students stay in school until graduation. Except for Sisters Sarah, Mary, and Helen, all the teachers are laymen and laywomen. The hardwood floors are covered with tiles. The Douglas fir walls of the cloakrooms and hallways are painted pink. Crucifixes, pictures of the Sacred Heart of Jesus and the Blessed Virgin Mary are gone from the classroom walls, leaving as the only decorations posters recommending wholesome eating from Canada's four food groups and strategies for disease prevention. "Whenever you cough or sneeze or sniff, be quick my lad with your handkerchief."

The convent, a no-nonsense rectangle beginning to deteriorate from lack of regular maintenance, houses the three nuns still teaching in the school. The chapel and music room are downstairs, as well as the kitchen, dining room, and living room. Upstairs two rows of single rooms can accommodate up to fifteen nuns. The grounds around the convent, once a highly productive miniature farm, are now, like the glebe house garden, a lawn. The greenhouse, site of many an agricultural experiment, is gone. The potting shed, still full of tools, is locked most of the time and serves as a shelter for Sister Helen's Harley-Davidson.

None of the nuns are classroom teachers. Sister Sarah, a librarian and music teacher, looks after the library and helps with music. Sister Mary teaches music and helps with the library. Sister Helen, a librarian, teaches Home Economics and Religion and helps with the library. Between 1940, when they first came to Coaltown to help Father Rod MacDonald with Confirmation, and 1965, the world of these three nuns has changed.

Sister Helen Perenowsky does not look like a forty-one-year-old nun, or even a post–Vatican II nun. Dressed in Levis and a leather windbreaker, she begins her descent. Black leather gloves dangle from her left hand. A silver helmet balloons from her left arm. Half-Wellington boots tap down the stairs and whitish-blonde hair cascades over her leather shoulders and falls to her leather belt. Her uncertain smile drops like a question mark down her long face. Her right arm extends, palm out, as if warding off attack from her two colleagues at the foot of the stairs. Halfway down she drops her hand for balance and slides it down the banister.

Sister Sarah, dressed in skirt and suit coat, and Sister Mary, in sweater and dress, their eyebrows peaking above their horn-rimmed glasses, exchange glances, clamp the palms of their hands together, and fall to their knees on the hardwood floor, in mock despair.

"Holy Mary Mother of God, pray for her," they intone in unison.

"Where in the name of God did you get those threads?" asks Sister Mary.

"Skins would be more like it," Sister Sarah adds. "Where in the name of God are you going?"

Sister Helen slows, hesitates, then plunges on down.

As Sister Mary puts it, after Pope John XXIII fired off his big round smile during Vatican II, the nuns who were ready, by dint of personality, preparation, and courage, began to trade in their habits for regular clothes. Sister Sarah and Sister Mary, both fifty years old, were more than ready. Sister Mary chose the casual dress-cum-cardigan and let her greying hair hang straight down to her collar. Sister Sarah chose the professional, all-business-looking serge skirt and suit coat. She wore her helmet of still dark hair curled in slightly below her ears. The horn-rimmed glasses, combined with her tall body and long face, give her a handsome, scholarly appearance and disguise the quixotic light shimmering in her eyes. Horn-rimmed glasses did not suit Sister Mary but the beauty of her petite, athletic body and the beautiful symmetry of her face could not be disguised.

Sister Helen, younger than her colleagues by nine years, was not ready to give up her habit. She did not know why. They discussed it freely, but could not come up with an answer. " Perhaps I'm one of those people who need a uniform," she suggested. "Identity, you know. Perhaps I'm afraid if I give it up I won't be anybody."

"You're too smart for that, Helen," Sister Sarah told her. "If that were true, you'd be the last person to think it."

To get ready, in a tentative way, Sister Helen allowed her hair to grow, hidden under her veil.

But of late they know she is up to something. Somebody delivered a letter with her name on it but no postmark or return address on the envelope. She opened it with her steak knife at supper and slid out several blue folded pages, but after one glance she slid the blue pages back into the envelope and slid the package up the sleeve of her habit. She looked up and across the table and stared through the space between the heads of Sister Mary and Sister Sarah.

She began taking taxis to unannounced destinations. She'd land back carrying parcels in anonymous shopping bags and hide them in her room. The only sister left in the convent still wearing the full habit. And now this modern apparition coming down the stairs!

"See you later," Sister Helen says, as she wheels around the newel post and walks down the hall toward the back door. The two nuns, in awe-full admiration, watch her rear end undulate until she lets the screen door slam shut behind her.

Sister Mary and Sister Sarah watch through the screen as Sister Helen opens the shed doors and wheels her Harley-Davidson out onto the lawn. She pulls her hair into a ponytail and ties it with an elastic band, straps on the helmet, pulls on the gloves, mounts the motorcycle. She sits there for a moment, staring over the windshield of the motorcycle into the distance. She takes a deep breath, her shoulders rising and falling, ignites the engine, rolls across the wet grass, down the driveway, turns at the gate, and flees down the street in a burst of noise.

"What d'ya think?" says Sister Mary.

"Hell's nuns, I guess," says Sister Sarah, her eyes twinkling.

"You don't think we should be worried?"

"No. Something is up. It must be important. Helen is smart. She's not foolish. She must know what she's doing or she'd ask for help. Maybe it's something easier to explain after it's over."

They knew about the motorcycle. She told them all about it, insisted on keeping it when she joined the convent. It belonged to her brother. He went missing in the war but she vowed she'd keep it for him until she knew for sure he was dead. She knew how to drive it, she said, but of course she didn't. Until now. But she kept it in perfect condition. She knew all about that too.

In the dim dawn light, only one jogger and a few vehicles appear before her as she moves through and out of Coaltown. Once she feels the familiar comfort of the movement, she speeds her motorcycle to Sydney, banks around Ashby Corner, and races to Whitney Pier in the pre-breakfast sun, her white ponytail fluttering like a mane in the wake of the wind behind her helmet. The rows of company houses lining the road to the steel plant, breakfast smoke rising from their chimneys, whiz through her peripheral vision like an animated cartoon character in one of the Little Big Books she devoured as a child. Every picture the same except for a slight incremental change, giving the illusion of rapidly changing shapes, colours, the flowers in the window boxes, as if the motorcycle is motionless and the houses like one house painted on a strip of film over and over with small variations.

With Sydney Harbour on her left, she leaves the houses behind and rolls across the overpass that arches above the entrails of the steel plant. She continues down into the town of Whitney Pier and along the main street. The shops are not yet open for morning business but she notices a light in the restaurant where her father used to work when she was a girl. Her memory calls up the smell and the taste of the tangy sausages he brought home for their suppers. She represses the memory to focus on the business at hand.

At Holy Redeemer Church she parks her bike by the side door and tiptoes up the side aisle to avoid the notice of the woman in the sanctuary dressing the altar. She lights a candle, kneels and prays, and endures a flood of memory.

"I need a bit of wisdom," she prays.

The road from Whitney Pier to Fort Petrie, halfway to New Waterford, is transformed from the expanse of barrens she remembers from her childhood. She never noticed during the few times she passed by in a car, but now, drifting along on the motorcycle, she realizes that what had once been deemed a windswept snowcatcher at the mercy of North Atlantic storms blown in along the funnel of Sydney Harbour, uninhabitable except by those who could afford nothing else, is blossoming into ocean-front bungalow country. Paved roads, modern cars, and efficient snow removal have transformed subsistence farms and blueberry barrens on the high hills above the harbour into prime real estate. On the low side of the highway, nothing much has changed. The space between the highway and the harbour is too narrow in most places for building, and erosion of the cliffs and shoreline makes it narrower every year. She cannot help but think of her father and mother and their basement house, the foundation for their castle.

By the time she reaches Fort Petrie, her eyes are dry. She pulls in past the open gate of the adjacent graveyard and parks her bike by the gravestone/monument dedicated to Bishop McArthur, the first pastor of the parish. She lifts off her helmet, sits it on the seat, and sets out for the cliff overlooking Sydney Harbour where a woman is picking wild strawberries.

"I know you," the woman greets her. "Helen. You got older but you look the same. I thought first you were your mother. A ghost. Scared me for a minute. You remember me?"

"I never knew your name."

"Sine," she says. "Gaelic for Jean."

"You're still picking strawberries."

"I am. Nobody else comes here, but I do, every year."

"I suppose people think nothing grows here," Helen says, "what with the wind and the salt."

"The strawberries manage. They keep low. You managed," Sine says.

"Yes, but I moved."

"It was you found that body."

"Yes," Helen replies, with a sigh. "That was me."

"Must have been a terrible fright for a sixteen-year-old?"

"Yes. It was. And then some."

"Is this your first time back to Fort Petrie?"

"Yes. I've been by once in a while in a car. But never stopped."

"Are you gonna go look down there, by the Lorelei Rock?"

"No, my God, no! I get the shivers just to think about it."

"Here, try a fistful of berries. They're sweet for the time of year. And they're early this year."

"Thank you. I love wild strawberries. And if somebody else picks them, so much the better. Thank you. I'm gonna go look over there, by the old fortress."

"Here, take the dish. Drop it off on the way back. Not much to see now. It's hard to imagine the goings-on here twenty-five years ago when the war was on. I don't know if you can get underground or not, where they used to keep the ammunition or whatever it was they kept down there."

The guns are gone, the searchlight gone, long gone, their concrete pads deteriorating into gravel and half overrun with grass. The half-hearted boards covering doors and windows of the concrete structures, over-ground and underground, plus the possibility of rats, dissuade her from trying to get inside. She would come back sometime with a friend and try to get in. She still hopes to recover a long since forgotten but now remembered rag doll that she had clung to even into her teens. Perhaps it survived the war and the past two decades. It was a

posthumous gift from her mother. Helen lost it somewhere on the grounds and perhaps a soldier had picked it
up and kept it safe inside somewhere.

From her bike she waves goodbye to the strawberry
woman and continues down the highway, following the
Cape Breton coastline, through Low Point, New Waterford,
Lingan, across the sandbar at Indian Bay, through Dominion,
Coaltown, Table Head, through the town of Glace Bay,
through Port Morien, Mira Gut, Main A Dieu, Louisbourg,
and up through Marion Bridge to Sydney, retracing her
ecstatic journey of a lifetime, her hopeless golden dream.

The sun-drenched day is calm. The ocean around the
coast from Sydney Harbour to Indian Bay is flat. The
Newfoundland ferry ploughs a gentle furrow toward its
berth in North Sydney. On this day there is no hint of menace on the surface or in the depths of the sea. On land every
reminder of former menace is gone or going: the artillery
batteries, the searchlights, the signal stations, the fortress
observation posts, anti-aircraft guns. The bunkers now
nothing but deteriorating, windowless, graffiti-bedecked,
concrete walls advertising the hopes and fears of two
decades of frustrated teenagers. And around the bunkers
nothing but the grass and the ash-covered chunks of rot-
ting and rusting gear and equipment of long-ago soldiers,
junk treasures for the archaeologists of war. Poking the toes
of her half-Wellington boots through the grass surrounding the artillery emplacement at Lingan, she dislodges one
whole thing, a soldier's mess tin with fork, knife, and spoon
clipped together inside, looking clean enough to use. She
slips it into one of her saddlebags. It could not have been
her brother's, but it is identical to the one he packed before
he departed twenty-five years ago.

ONE

I was, being human, born alone
I am, being woman, hard beset
I live by wringing from a stone
The little nourishment I get
ELINOR WYLIE

JUNE 1940

I STARTED THE WALKING *in Italy. It was the only way I could be alone. And it was the only way I could be doing what I wanted to do. When I was a girl it was okay. I could tear around, climb trees, fight, and play soccer. But when I was thirteen they made me stop. I didn't mind learning to make dresses and cooking, helping with the wine, gardening and canning the vegetables, at least it was something to do. But I soon got sick and tired of the scrubbing and washing and ironing and doing the dishes and tidying up everybody's mess.*

And they wouldn't let me play soccer. First, I thought, maybe they think I'm not good enough, though I should have known better, the signs were all there. I guess I had wood for brains in those days. But I soon learned. One time, I made myself look like a boy. I was amazed how easy it was. I just put on my father's old soccer clothes, and my father was even there and he never caught on. I just went down to the field and started playing and before anybody realized who I was I ran through their stupid defence and scored. Then some arsehole pulled the cap off me. My father had a fit. He grabbed me by the ear and never let go till he hauled me into the kitchen and told my mother to do something before I disgraced the whole family. He was a good one to talk.

My mother and I got along okay. She hugged me, but there wasn't much she could do. "Anna, you have to get ready for your life," she said. I knew what that meant. The priest said the same thing to me after Mass one Sunday. He looked me up and down and he said, "You have to get ready for your life."

That's when I started walking. Running really. I was too pissed off to walk. I'd run until I couldn't breathe and then I'd walk and think, and then I'd run again, all along the cliffs. I was doing it for months before anyone knew. I'd get up before dawn and I'd be back before anyone was up and I'd be in the kitchen getting breakfast for the family. They thought that was great until they realized I was up and gone for two hours. But once they knew I wasn't meeting somebody on the sly—well, they didn't like me out there, beyond their control, but they couldn't put a name to anything wrong I was doing so they put up with it. And they loved the breakfast. The funny thing is, even when I started, I wasn't tired. I didn't even take a nap in the afternoon. And the longer I did it, the stronger I got. My legs got hard as coconuts and sturdy as fence posts.

But then it dawned on me. One morning I stopped running and started walking and I was looking at the first streak of light in the eastern sky and a big boat on the horizon. I could just barely see the top of it and the big tube of smoke coming out, and it just hit me. The water is the way out. That's when I fell in love/hate with the sea. It stopped me from running away from home, but it was the way away from home. I realized then that it wasn't walking or running would be my salvation. Walking and running were just putting it off. I had to jump. One Big Jump. On that day I thought I would burst. My body filled up with hope. I ran all the way home and I wasn't even puffing.

"What's wrong with you?" my mother said when she came into the kitchen.

"What?" I said.

"If that smile on your face was any bigger I'd be able to tie your mouth up at the back of your head."

I just shrugged my shoulders. She didn't say anything for a while but I knew what was coming, and finally she said it.

"Are you meeting somebody out there?"

"No," I said. "Not yet." Saucy.

"I hope not. I hope I don't have to send somebody to follow you around."

"They better be able to run."

"Is that what you're doing? Running? It better not be running around."

I should have let it go at that. But of course I can never let anything go. Sometimes I think there's no valve between my brain and my tongue. Everything I think of is out past my lips before I can stop it. Yes. I should have let it go at that. My mother didn't need grief from me. But I couldn't. I didn't.

"Well, what if I was running around," I said, "at least I'm not married."

My mother's knees buckled. It's a good thing she had a chair behind her. Her face went white. And when the tears started to roll, she put her head on the table and shook. I don't know what she was thinking. The whole town knew about my father. Did she think I wouldn't know? I went to school. I had to put up with it too. But maybe it was just the cruelty of it made her cry. I don't always know when I'm being cruel.

I bided my time. After I saw the last sliver of smoke from the disappeared ship become a blue cloud over the edge of the world, I didn't mind waiting, because I had something to wait for. I wrote a secret letter to my uncle in Canada. I wrote it from my grandmother's address. My grandmother and I had lots of secrets. Uncle Pietro sent me lots of stuff and told me lots of things. He sent me a book and I started to learn English and sometimes I'd get to talk to people who came back who could speak English almost like they could always speak it. And after a while I could talk just like them. And in school I did all my projects on Canada, so I knew where it was and how long it took to get there, and after all, it was an Italian, Giovanni Caboto, who found it in the first place. I didn't mind the wait of a few years before I got my chance.

In the meantime I got good-looking, or interesting, or whatever it is they want. And soon all the young men started going out of their way to be near me, hoping I would smile. I could have had any one I wanted but I had my eye on Tomassio, because I knew he had an uncle in Canada too. And I knew it was the men who went to Canada. The women went with them, or sometimes after them. And I knew they wanted coal miners in Canada and Tomassio was very strong. My uncle told me you had to be very strong to get good-paying jobs in the mines. The trouble was, Tomassio was the best soccer player in town, and maybe he would be the best soccer player in all of Italy. So he could choose any girl in town, and maybe he would be able to choose any girl in all of Italy.

But that wasn't the only trouble with Tomassio. Tomassio was like my father. He wouldn't be satisfied with any girl in town. He wanted every girl in town. And maybe every girl in all of Italy. But I figured I could deal with that, once I got him out of Italy.

So I went to all the soccer games with all the girls. Eventually he got around to me. I caught him with his eye on me when he was talking to another girl but looking over her shoulder at me. I buried myself in the crowd of girls and watched him try to wriggle his way around to meet me. I dodged him for weeks, after the soccer matches, downtown in the square, after Mass, after school. I was always buried in the crowd or slipping away at the last minute, or not even there but across the street in a shop watching him looking for me. I wanted him to invest a lot of time in me so he'd have something at stake, and I'd have something to bargain with. I wanted him to begin to suspect the unthinkable, that I was trying to avoid him. Him! Avoid him, for God's sake!

One day I let him catch up to me. I was walking alone along the square. I could see him behind me, reflected in the shop windows. He kept his distance, trying to think of how to approach me. I could hear his step quicken when he made up his mind and I ducked into a lingerie shop. Of course he wouldn't dare follow me in there, but he dangled on the sidewalk and waited. I took my sweet old time. When I came out, he fell into step with me. Once he made up his mind he was full of confidence. He had a way of walking made people like me want to stick out my foot and watch him fall on his face. He even brushed my arm with his elbow. He was one handsome guy, no question about that. He put the big smile on me. We were coming to a corner with a lot of people hanging around with nothing to do but watch us coming toward them.

"How are you today?" he said.

"Oh, I'm fine."

"What are you doing today?"

"You mean right now?"

"Yeah. Right now. And later on?"

"Well," I said, "right now, I just came downtown to buy some underwear." Then I reached into the bag and pulled out a pair of panties and a bra and dangled them in front of him and I thought he was going to drop goddamn dead right there on the sidewalk. We both stopped dead in our tracks, with everybody laughing, and when he heard that he caught his breath and the best he could blurt out was "Mama mia," and he looked at his watch. Of course all the soccer players had wristwatches.

"I got to get to practice," he said, and he took off up the alley. I stuffed my underwear back in the bag and turned to the people on the corner and took a bow.

No wonder I got a reputation for being wild. I knew I'd be in trouble when my father found out and that wouldn't take long, so I went home and told my mother before she'd hear about it.

"I hope you know what you're doing," she said.

"So do I," I said.

"I'll tell your father we talked about it already, and you're not allowed out of the house for a week."

"What about the morning, my running?"

"Well, except for the morning. He doesn't know about that anyway."

My father was satisfied with that but he gave me an awful tongue-lashing anyway. But oh my God it was worth it. I didn't see Tomassio for over a week, but I knew he'd have a hard time getting my underwear out of his head.

After I got back out and around, Tomassio started showing up but he was pretty ginger with me for a while. Then one day after a soccer game I found an excuse to stay behind. I knew he was in charge of the equipment and he'd be in the equipment shack and when I saw him come to the door I started walking and I pretended to turn my ankle and I fell on the ground. Well, he came running.

"Help me sit on the bench," I said.

"Are you all right?" he said after he got me up. It took him a while because I didn't help much, and he had my whole weight, and he had to be careful where he put his hands.

"It's my ankle," I said.

Well, the minute I said that he was down on his knees and he glommed onto my foot like a trout on a hook. He went all over my ankle with the tip of his finger. "Does that hurt? Does that hurt? It's not swollen yet. Wait here." He went to the shack and came back with a cold, wet towel and wrapped my ankle.

"Stand up and try a little weight on it," he said. "How's that? Is it sore?"

"Just tender."

So he held my arm and I limped home. I could hardly keep from
bursting out laughing. My mother stood on the step, her doubtful face
on while he tried to explain why he had a hold of her daughter. I had
to grimace to keep the smile off my face, but I wasn't fooling her any
she nearly laughed herself.

"I'll be seeing you," he said, when he waved goodbye.

I smiled. If you only knew, I thought. If you only knew. There we
were, standing on the edge of the soccer field in Italy and Tomassio
with no idea we were standing on the edge of North America and me
with only a faint idea myself.

I did get my way. I kept Tomassio on hook and line until he didn
think he could live without me. He didn't dare even walk with another
girl for fear I'd get wind of it. He was ready to burst. But I wouldn
marry him unless he took me to Canada. He didn't want to go. For one
thing he dreamed he would get the tailoring business when his father
died. That was Tomassio, he thought he could get what he wanted just
because he wanted it. Everybody knew he was daydreaming. He was
the oldest in the family but his two brothers spent every spare minute i
the tailor shop and Tomassio spent every spare minute on the soccer
field. He barely knew his father, because old Pelegrino set foot out the
door twice a year, to go to Midnight Mass and to make his Easter Dut
at the end of Lent. He ate in the back shop and most of the time slept o
a cot there. Tomassio was the same. He never went home except to ea
and sleep. And there was no work in La Prudenza. Tomassio planned t
leave, but like most of the other young men in town he planned to g
over the Alps to Switzerland to work. When he made his fortune, h
would come back and take over the shop and his two brothers woul
work for him. That was his fantasy. And of course he could play socce
in Switzerland. He loved soccer. And no wonder he loved it, with every
body in town jumping up and down every time he touched the ball. Bu
I told him he could play baseball in Canada. Uncle Pietro told m
about it. Every town had a baseball team. And they paid people to pla

"You're an athlete," I said. "You could be a star. It's a game, like soccer, just a different ball."

"They pay people to play?" he said. "To play?"

"Yes," I said. I didn't tell him they only paid the American imports. He didn't ask.

But it was more than that. Tomassio loved adventure. He liked to take chances. It made him a good soccer player but it got him into trouble too. He wasn't scared of the ocean like me. He wasn't scared of anything. Once the possibility got into his head, it was like a dare to him. So it wasn't just that he wanted me, although I think he loved me at first. And I think he thought I loved him. I did, too, later on.

TWO

✝

Send my roots rain
GERARD MANLEY HOPKINS

MAY–JUNE 1940

FATHER ROD MACDONALD didn't lose his faith during the war. At least he didn't think so. The haunting memory of his brief war leaned in the doorway of his consciousness like a deceased spouse with a macabre smile. He imagined his faith hibernating like a comfortable frog in the pocket of the old golf bag of battered clubs his father gave him on his return from overseas.

"Here, Rod," his father said. "Had my bellyful of golf. You take them. To relax. God knows they didn't relax me. The 2 wood is missing. Don't ask me what I did with it."

Father Rod enjoyed golf but after about the fifth hole he'd start to feel disoriented. Not that he didn't know where he was, but he began to think of the war, which raged on without him, and a feeling crept over him that he should be somewhere else, the hospital, the rectory, the ball field, the house of some sick or dying parishioner. The game made him feel self-indulgent. When he returned from the war, he vowed to give up self-indulgence. After a few Saturday morning trips to the links, he banished the clubs to the glebe house attic behind a half-filled case of sacramental sherry abandoned by the former pastor. After a sample sip, Father Rod stored the wine away with other stuff he inherited. Stuff that might do in a pinch, or even return to general use, in somebody else's tenure. Into the attic it went with the golf bag, a tandem bicycle, a walking stick, and a picture of Jesus, Mary, Joseph, and a camel, enjoying a picnic under a palm tree.

Somebody stuck labels on the bottles of the Mass wine but wrote nothing on the labels. Father Rod wrote on one bottle in thick black ink and kept it in the vestry where the bishop would see it when he came to visit.

SAINT COMPOSTINA MASS WINE
Wine for the masses

He brought it over from the church to the glebe house one evening and read it to his friend as they enjoyed a glass of Harvey's Shooting Sherry.

"Who's Saint Compostino?" Father Pat asked.

"The patron saint of sewer drains. You never heard of her? Where does this stuff come from anyway, Pat?"

Father Pat Mancini was a veteran. Like Father Rod, he was missing a part, in his case his right hand. He was the bishop's chancellor. Father Rod called him the bishop's left-handed right-hand man.

"The bishop imports it," Father Pat explained, "from a wholesaler in Moncton who offers a discount for buying in bulk. So he buys it wholesale and retails it to the parishes for the regular price. The difference pays for his car, and his driver, namely me. He decreed it standard Mass wine for every parish in the diocese. The Bishop likes to standardize, Rod. You know that."

"So you're his driver. Here, have another little touch of grape. And here I was thinking you were his chancellor."

"I think chancellor is church talk for driver."

"Well, he's not gonna standardize me. Does he use that rotgut himself at the cathedral? And you, do you drink it?"

"Not bloody likely."

"Well, take it from me, Paddy, it smells like piss-flavoured grape juice and tastes worse than it smells."

Father Rod preferred Harvey's Shooting Sherry, the taste of sweet, secret extravagance, a minor indulgence he allowed himself since he came back from the war. The aggressive name suited his image of himself. The altar boys liked it too, so he kept it in the safe with his moonshine and condoms, behind the record books of baptisms, marriages, and deaths and whatever other essentials needed protection from fire and the curious eyes of housekeepers, sacristans, and altar boys.

"What are you doing with condoms?" Pat asked. "The war is over for us, buddy. We're back home. We're parish priests. We're celibate. We can't afford scandal."

"There are other wars."

"What's that supposed to mean?"

"Did you know my Uncle Mickey?"

"No. But no doubt I'm gonna hear about him now."

"He was an alcoholic. Picked up the habit in the first war."

"No kidding."

"The booze helped him tolerate the gas, he told me. The doctors sucked it out of his lungs but Mickey couldn't get it out of his head. He knew he had to quit drinking before it killed him. 'The booze is worse than gas,' he said. 'It takes longer to do you in.'"

"There is a point to this story, Rod, right?"

"Mickey had a silver flask. A gift from his wife, Sheilagh. She gave it to him when they were going together before the war, and she kept it for him till he came back. But he never drank a drop from it. Never used it until one rumsick Sunday he fetched it from her cedar chest, took it to Johnny Murphy, filled it full of moonshine.

"'What are you up to?' Sheilagh said, when he landed home sober.

"Mickey pulled the flask from his back pocket, and grinning, dangled it between them like a pendulum and said, 'I got a full load in here, Sheilagh, and I'm gonna spend every minute the rest of my life not takin' a drink out of 'er.' He called it his twin Mickey. 'You're married to two Mickeys, Sheilagh,' he said to her, 'one of us is sober and the other one is full of moonshine.' When he changed pants he transferred it from pocket to pocket like a wallet. He took it in his can to the pit. And he took it in his coffin to the grave. He wrote a note to Sheilagh on his deathbed. 'Everything else is yours, Sheilagh, but put my twin Mickey in me arse pocket, I want to give Jesus a taste of Murphy's shine.'"

"Yeah, Rod. I get the point," Pat said. "Now give me the shine. I'm sick of the sherry and I might as well stay the night. The bishop, you know, if he hasn't got a snootful himself by the time I come in, he'll be sniffing like a dog at a zoo. Got an awful nose on him. And oh yeah. You know the bishop knows the combination to that safe."

"He thinks he does. I got it changed. I can't wait till the next time he tries to poke his nosey nose into it."

Indeed the bishop came to visit, and invited himself to supper. Canned beans and wieners were not what he had anticipated, but if you drop in on a young man without a housekeeper you have to take what you get. He would announce his next visit. This was merely the obligatory drop-in on a priest with a new posting to a parish, just to make sure he is comfortable and happy and properly briefed on the recent history of the parish and fully aware of its ongoing problems and to offer guidance toward proper solutions. In other words, to show who's the boss.

"You know, Rod," the bishop said, his head down, peering at the plate as he tried to locate and set aside chunks of pork, "I do find it hard to forget, it's one of my failings. I guess I'll have to work on that, but I am quite willing to forgive, and I do feel you should admit you were wrong." He raised a forkful of beans to his mouth and stared at Father Rod's puzzled eyes while he chewed the beans to mush after extracting the fork and pointing at his dinner companion's chin as if he were exposing a clue to his meaning.

"I don't know what you're talking about, bishop," Father Rod said.

"Oh, I think you do. When we were coaching ball, remember, you were still a seminarian and I was still a parish priest. You remember that?"

"Certainly. I remember it well. We beat you. For the championship. You were supposed to win, according to everybody, but not according to me."

"You threw the ball at my boy's head."

"He wasn't a boy, he was a young man. You put on a

suicide squeeze. There is only one defence against the suicide squeeze with a right-handed batter."

"You didn't have to throw at his head."

"It's the only way to be sure not to hit him in the head. Any lower and he's liable to duck his head right into the ball."

"You were taking an awful chance with that young man's life."

"Not at all. I warned him. I told my catcher, 'Warn him, tell him to hit the dirt.'"

"You won't admit you were wrong?"

"The rules and tactics of baseball don't change to accommodate the relative rank of the coaches. That's why they write it all down. Why don't you read it?"

The bishop lost his appetite and changed the subject. "Harvey's Shooting Sherry," the Bishop exclaimed. "It's twice the price! Why? Why use that expensive stuff?"

"It makes better blood," Father Rod exclaimed. "It's Jesus' blood, after all. He deserves the best."

Unable to invent a response adequate to in-your-face insolence, the bishop's frustration boiled in his belly like molten lava. He fled the dinner table, escaped the house, jumped into his car, and drove until he ran out of gas.

When the bishop left the house, Father Rod mixed a mug of moonshine, maple syrup, and boiled water and walked upstairs to the bathroom. He submerged his body shoulder deep in his claw-foot tub of hot suds and sipped the ambrosia through his smiling lips. In moments of moonshine and sudsy ecstasy, Father Rod liked to recall his great-grandfather Rory, his grandfather Colin, and his father, Angus, who always kept him in mind of his Scottish ancestry, a topic which interested his sister Sarah but bored him when he was a growing boy. But over the past few years his interest grew and was becoming intense.

His sister Sarah, although she helped him reconstruct the past and tried to teach him to play the fiddle and speak Gaelic, scoffed at the late conversion to his heritage. "I suppose it's because you won't be begetting children of your own that you're trying to make children of your ancestors."

Of course, he knew she was pleased enough.

Their father prized two things. He called them things. "See this thing?" he said to his boy Rod.

"Yes."

"Learn to read it." The boy looked without assent or dissent.

"See this thing?"

"Yes."

"Learn to play it." The boy looked without assent or dissent.

"I'll teach you."

The boy understood. It was an invitation, not a command.

The first thing was a Gaelic bible, a huge thing, you'd need a strong lap to rest it on. The covers might have come from some ancient version of quarter-inch plywood, the parchment pages thick as lampshades. When it was out of the cupboard and in no one else's hands, Sarah would lug it over her small lap, turn the pages, and look at it with fascinated eyes.

From inside the bible, Angus frequently extracted the first of several letters written in Gaelic by his grandfather Rory, Father Rod's great-grandfather. Rory wrote them and addressed them to his friend Malcolm, whom he had left behind in the Isle of Sky when he sailed to Cape Breton.

Dear Malcolm:

It's a great place altogether, Malcolm. When we got off the boat, hauled our stuff up the beach and over the cliffs the land was nothing but trees. We cut down the trees and made a house. The cleared land was nothing but rocks. We piled the rocks into a fence. Then the winter. Thank God wood burns or we would've froze. And the ashes from the wood were like manure to us until we got the real thing with the cows. The rivers team with smelt in the spring and there's always trout and salmon, and partridge and rabbits and deer and moose in the woods. And the lakes are full of ducks and geese. We get clams and mussels at the shore. So even the first year we could always eat. And it's better now.

In spring we started to farm and it was nothing but black flies. I counted two billion myself in ten minutes. What blood they didn't take home they smeared on my face and neck. We cover our skin with clothes and axle grease even in the summer heat to keep the buggers off. It's good me and Maggie are healthy. The few sick that survived the boat didn't last long. Potatoes grow great where the spruce trees grew and fish are fond of manure worms. Thank God for cowshit. It's a great place altogether if you like potatoes and fish. The twins are born healthy. Colin and Mairi. I made a tune for them on the fiddle. Maggie was pleased, thank God. There's little enough to please her here, but at least she can sing and dance. I lost my chanter overboard. It just floated away on me and the miserable creature of a captain wouldn't turn around so I could fetch it from the water. But I met a Currie from Uist who told me how to make one out of a maple tree sapling. Anyway we got Maggie's fiddle.

The other thing Angus prized was his grandmother Maggie's fiddle. Angus would often pick it up when Roddie and Sarah were in the room and coax from it one of the many tunes hidden within it. His favourite was a birth song for the first children born in Canada: "A Song and a Jig for

Colin and Mairi, On the Occasion of their Escape from the Sea of Liquid to the Land of Air." When he put the fiddle down, Sarah would pick it up and play with it until her father took it from her. Rod, as soon as he felt his father's release, went out in the yard to play.

Now, as a man recalling these events, Father Rod wondered at his indifference, and at his sister Sarah's intense attention, which was all but ignored by their father.

Angus kept his grandmother Maggie's fiddle and his grandfather's bible locked in a cupboard. And he kept his grandfather Rory's letters to Malcolm between the parchment pages, the letters Rory continued to write on occasion but never mailed, because he intended to carry them back to Scotland when he became wealthy, and to recite them to Malcolm himself, so he could watch his reaction. But Malcolm drowned soon after the fifth letter. The news came over on the boat, but Rory kept writing letters anyway, although he had to put up with Maggie's crooked smile. The letters became a diary. When Angus realized his Roddie and Sarah would not likely be able to read them in Gaelic, he translated them and put the translation in a folder at the back of the bible. Father Rod often re-read his favourite. Now he knew it by heart and one of his bathtub pastimes was to recite to himself.

Dear Malcolm:

She's smiling at me now and who could blame her. A woman with a family to raise wants to keep her eye on a man who writes letters to a dead priest. I guess there's no doubt of it now, you would have been better off to come with us. You certainly couldn't be any the worse off. You could be the priest here as well as there. We got a pretty good priest here but he's a cranky old bugger. Rides around on his horse like he's the Lord God Himself. We built him a church and a glebe house and he lives in it with a woman who's so cross nobody would marry her, and she gets him meals and keeps the place up. Now he wants us to build him a school and get a teacher so the children can learn English and Latin.

And what would they want with that? I asked him. The language of business is English, he hissed at me through his teeth. The language of the church is Latin. If you don't want your children to be forever mosquito meat you better build me a school. I told that to Maggie and she sided right with him. Look in town, she said, everybody with a good job is either English or Protestant, or both. And they all went to school. And I guess we didn't cross the ocean to see our children go Protestant. So they better learn English. Give them half a chance anyway. You think like a woman, I told her. Yes, she said, and it's a good thing one of us does. We slept on our own sides of the bed for a week after that.

As a boy, Father Rod never asked his father to teach him either the language of the Gael or the language of the fiddle. His father's hints and prompts went unheeded, and eventually Angus gave up trying and this loss became one in his litany of laments: "The pit killed the Gaelic, and the pit killed the fiddle. The minute we left the farm the writing was on the wall."

As for Rod, he was too busy playing peggy, baseball, hockey, and milk-can cricket. Too busy going to school. Too busy reading, in English.

"Always a nose in a book, that one," Angus would growl to his wife.

"Yes. And it's a good place for his nose, if you ask me," Catriona would say.

But the priest Rod regretted his delinquency and the recollection of it soured his sudsy bath. Now he took lessons in both Gaelic and fiddle from his sister Sarah, the nun. But it was a struggle more full of hope than success. Self-doubt punctured his reverie and he rose from his clawfoot tub. Shedding suds and trailing water, he slap-footed down to the kitchen and boiled up another moonshine.

Back under the suds, Father Rod made ready for phase two of his reverie by removing his eye patch and resting it on the table next to the tub beside his glass of maple syrup nectar and his collection of Gerard Manley Hopkins.

Thou mastering me
God! giver of breath and bread;
World's strand, sway of the sea;
Lord of living and dead;
Thou hast bound bones and veins in me, fastened
    me flesh,
And after it almost unmade, what with dread,
Thy doing: and dost thou touch me afresh?
Over again I feel thy finger and find thee.

When Father Rod's parents talked about him or his sister Sarah, they spoke Gaelic, partly so he and Sarah wouldn't understand what they heard in their little house of small privacy, and partly because, for them, speaking in English was more a performance of someone else's song than a conversation grounded in reality, firm with commitment. Rod could comprehend only the tone, his own name and Sarah's, and the words that always began the current review of each child's trajectory through life, and the probable details and consequences of its likely arc:

"*Uill, a-nisd, a Chatriona, mu dheoghainn na cloinne?*"

But the children, *na cloinne*, Rod and Sarah, who paid scant attention to their parents when they spoke English, listened with rapt attention when they spoke Gaelic because they knew it was family talk and *na cloinne* were at the centre of it. By the time they were teenagers, Sarah understood nearly half the words and most of the drift of their conversations, which usually varied only enough to account for the developing maturity of *na cloinne*. When the parents were gone from the house, Rod and Sarah would take over the kitchen and, playing the parts of mother and father, they would reconstruct their parents' family talks like social archaeologists refitting shards of broken fossils. They carried on their family theatre until they went away to their separate vocations. And when they returned home for a holiday from seminary and convent, and then as priest and nun, they went for long walks together, and after catching up on the gossip they would amuse themselves by performing the latest version of their imagined conversations between their parents. Recalling one of these performances was another of Father Rod's favourite bathtub pastimes.

"Well, now, Catriona, about the children. What do you think yourself? And will you have more tea?"

"It's more than tea I'll need for that kind of talk. You know very well what I think."

"I do. And I know what I think. But I can't help thinking about it anyway."

"Think, then. Just don't talk," Catriona would say.

"I'm wondering if you're satisfied."

"With what? Satisfied with what?"

"You got a priest in the family. And now you got a nun to boot. Are you satisfied with that?"

"Yes."

"You are. And there will be no grandchild. Are you satisfied with that?"

"Well, it's not too late."

"It's too late so far, Catriona."

"Yes, so far."

"Yes. And so far can last a long time, with you so stiff."

"Stiff is it. Well, it's not me the one need be stiff."

"If you were any the stiffer, we could get Duncan the carpenter to nail you in for a floor joist."

"Yes. Very funny, Angus. Very funny. Perhaps I could try out the milkman, that young fella's bottle of Two-in-One could likely loosen up a rusty old nut like me. Anyway that's not what I mean. Sarah will not stay in the convent."

"She'll stay," Angus said. "You know how stubborn she is. If she went, she'll stick it out."

"She's not the type. She's about as holy as a spruce tree. That tea you made wouldn't support a long-legged fly on skis. Would you make some more and put in a decent fistful of tea. I've got bread to make."

"Well, you encouraged her."

"You better watch your tongue, Angus, I can use this poker for more than shaking up the fire in the stove."

"Well, did you, or didn't you?"

"I did not encourage her," Sarah would say in mock imitation of the slow, deliberate voice her mother used for such occasions, as if every word were a nail she wanted to drive home with one blow. "I told her the choice. Go to the convent. Get an education. Be the teacher, a real job teaching music. Hobnob with the best of them. Summer vacations. Trips to Boston. And all she need do is dress like a crow and mutter a few Our Fathers and Hail Marys every day.

"Or she could marry a miner. Like you. Spend the rest of her days hanging clothes on the line, wiping dirty arses, baking, cooking, cleaning. End up getting called stiff, because she's worn out from work. I did not encourage her, I told her the choice. I did the same for Rod. You can be a priest, and go right to the top in one step. Or down the pit and shovel coal all week, and drink all weekend. And what you don't spend on drink you can give your stiff wife to buy shoes for the kids.

"Neither one. Neither one did I encourage. I drew them a picture of the world. He's not the type either, for a priest, but he can still be a good one, if he can behave himself. He's as horny as you used to be, and now he's going to the war, I didn't have that in mind let me tell you. He'll get himself shot. His education will do him one lot of good then. He might just as well have got married and left a trace of himself. A dead priest is no better off than a dead husband and father, but don't you worry, Sarah will be out struttin' her stuff before too long, and at least she'll be a little older and wiser and not marry some nitwit can't even talk to his wife. She can marry somebody she'll meet in Boston or Halifax, and you can have your little grandson in fancy pants and a haircut from the barber."

"But he won't be a MacDonald, will he?" Angus always insisted.

"There's too many MacDonalds anyway. The world is full of them. But, come to think of it, she could find a MacDonald. They're as plenty as smelt in the Sou'west Brook, and surely to God they're not all first cousins. I'll tell her that. I got so much influence over the girl I'm sure she'll do whatever I tell her; although, the last time she did what I told her, I think she was three."

"He'll not get shot. After all, he's a priest, not a real soldier."

"Yes. I'm sure the Germans will be pretty careful about that. Don't shoot that one, Adolf, that's a priest, and it's Angus MacDonald's son, and he doesn't want him shot."

✝ ✝ ✝

Father Rod's war was nasty, brutish, and short. And absurd. Among the first to enlist as chaplains, he and his buddy Father Pat Mancini went to Europe with the first contingent of Canadian soldiers in 1939, to England and then to France, just in time for the retreat from the invading German army and just unlucky enough to get involved in an unscheduled firefight that never should have happened. Through some snafu, both of them were assigned to the same company, each catching up to it in separate trucks, full of replacement platoons and arriving at the same moment, confusing Captain MacQuarrie, who already had a padre in his company and was temporarily out of contact with his command, and pretty busy trying to figure out how to get his company across a river.

The bridge lay close to the water and had no railing but for a six-by-six wooden beam at either edge. From all sides it offered a clear field of fire. Bent low, Private Franco Passerello got halfway across before a machine gun sputtered. Franco fell flat while bullets tore at the wood around him. When the firing stopped, he rolled to the edge of the bridge and dropped to the water. He swam. Twenty minutes later he sat in a copse of birch and ate from his mess tin a banquet of hot stew and pulled splinters from his hands. Fear that filled his belly like a hot, soft basketball subsided. He felt plucked by God from certain death. When he finished his banquet, he picked up an ant that was grappling with one of his crumbs. He watched it run in confusion over his hand until it stopped on the heel of his thumb. With the tip of his index finger, he crushed it.

Corporal Peters came and stood beside Franco and watched him stare at the dead ant on his hand.

"The war is hard on ants," Peters said. "I guess they'd expect it'd be safe enough out here in the countryside."

"Yeah."

"Where's your rifle?"

"On the bridge."

"On the bridge. Well. How we gonna get it back?"

"Oh, why don't you just go on out on the bridge and pick it up, bring it back. I'd go myself, Corporal, but I just ate and I'm feeling a bit heavy."

"The captain wants you."

"What for?"

"How would I know? I think he wants you to cross the river."

"That's a joke, I hope."

Captain MacQuarrie sat in a tent behind a table with Franco's sergeant and lieutenant on either side of him. Corporal Peters stood at the door.

"Sit down, Private."

"Yes, sir."

"You're quite the swimmer."

"No, sir."

"What?"

"No, sir. I can't swim."

"How'd you get back from the bridge?"

"That's far as I can make it in the water, sir. That's my limit."

"You had your boots on?"

"Yes, sir."

"Your clothes?"

"Yes, sir."

"Your rifle?"

"No, sir."

"What? Where's your rifle?"

"I left it on the bridge, sir."

"I see. Well. I guess without the boots and uniform you could swim twice as fast, or twice as far. We need twice as far, so you can take your sweet old time. No hurry. Corporal, take him to the quartermaster. Staff Sergeant Starzomsky knows what he needs. If he wants to see the padre, take him—I understand we got three of them now, it shouldn't be hard to find one."

"Sir?" Franco said.

"Yes, Private."

"Sir. I'd like to see my girlfriend."

"Girlfriend?"

"Yes, sir. Back at the hospital. She's a nurse. I'd like to see her before I go."

"Not a chance. See her when you get back. Corporal, you make sure he doesn't leave the area."

"Yes, sir."

"Or you'll be crossing the river yourself."

"Just for an hour, sir," Franco pleaded.

"Yeah. I'll bet."

"What if I won't do this, sir."

"Sergeant. Take Private Passerello somewhere and tell him what'll happen if he won't do it."

"Yes, sir."

"Private?"

"Sir?"

"What's your girlfriend's name?"

"Jocelynn AuCoin, sir."

"Don't worry, Private. If you don't come back, I'll go talk to her myself."

In the stores tent, the quartermaster gave Franco a knife in a sheath, along with grenades and binoculars in a water-tight bag.

"I'll tie this stuff to your back so you can pull it around when you need it."

"What am I going for? What am I supposed to do? "

"Slip the knife in the sheath back here, see if you can reach it. Just swim over, take a look, see what's there."

"Why don't they put in artillery and we all go over the bridge?"

"Here now, hook on the grenades, there's three in there. You remember how to use them, I hope. The thing is, the Air Force took pictures and they say there's nothing there."

"Somebody was shooting at me."

"We think the bridge is booby-trapped. That's why they shot at you. They didn't want you setting it off. They want all of us on it when it blows, then they'll shoot the rest of us in the water. So...we need to know. If they got a company or more it's too much for us, but if it's just a platoon with a machine gun and a few snipers, we'll ford the river upstream and downstream at low tide and pinch them out of there. Then the engineers can clean up the bridge for the tanks."

"Why don't I wait till low tide and walk over?"

"That's what they'll be expecting."

"Won't they think we might try this too?"

"Sure. But it'll be pitch dark tonight. And we're gonna cover you with this black grease. You'll be invisible if you don't smile."

"Why don't you get Joey to do it? He's black already."

"Yeah. But he's got buck teeth."

By midnight Father Mancini realized it was his nephew Franco they were waiting for. By four-thirty he and Father Rod and the pickets were the only ones still waiting. They sat, taking turns napping on the edge of the wood near the riverbank. At four-thirty-five Father Mancini stripped to his shorts and slipped into the water. At four-forty-five Father Rod woke and, seeing his buddy's clothes on the rocks, stripped to his shorts and slipped into the water.

By the time Father Rod touched bottom on the other side it was past first light. He lay in the water behind a rock. He could see Father Pat huddled behind a mound of earth near the riverbank.

"What's the story? Where's Franco?"

"Here. Behind me. His leg's shot. He can't walk."

"And you?"

"Shot my hand. Sniper. Don't move."

Father Rod pushed off a rock on the bottom and dashed up the short beach. No sniper fire. Franco lay on the ground, staring through pain. Father Rod took the strap with the grenades, knife, and binoculars from Franco's waist and tied them around his shoulder blades and under his armpits and up around the back of his neck. Father Pat's hand was a mess of blood and bones.

"Where's the sniper?"

"Down the shore in a tree. Can't tell what he's up to. Shot me in the hand. Shot Franco in the leg. Didn't shoot at you. No time, maybe. Or he's on the move, getting closer. He can't see us here, but he's got a good view of the beach, unless he moved."

Father Rod lifted Franco to his shoulder, ran across the beach, and plunged into the water. No sniper fire. He positioned Franco behind a rock.

"Can you cling on the rock, Franco, keep your head up?"

Franco nodded. Father Rod positioned himself behind his rock and beckoned to his buddy. Father Pat dashed to the water. They huddled behind rocks and rested for a while and then started off, Father Pat first, as he began to one-hand his way through the rest of his life, Father Rod second, pulling Franco, who clung to the belt around his neck and armpits, all keeping as low as breathing would allow. As Father Rod passed the last rock covering their retreat, the compassionate sniper shot it, splintering off a chip and smashing it into Father Rod's left eye.

✛ ✛ ✛

A few months later in the glebe house in Bayport, Cape Breton, Father Rod, the twenty-seven-year-old veteran, in suds up to his chin, dreamed the hospital, while the telephone rang downstairs. All three of them safe and back from pain. Franco still had one leg. Father Pat still had one hand. Father Rod one eye. Their red badges of courage would send them home.

And the nurse was Erica, beautiful, compassionate, Danish, comical as a Newfoundlander. She dressed his eye. She squeezed his hand.

"Is the pain going away?"

"Every time you come in the room it hides under the bed."

"Are you really a priest?"

"I can't deny it."

"No difference to me, I'm not a Catholic, but why have you got a tent pole under your sheet?"

"Priest is my profession, not my nature."

She wagged her finger at him. "You're gonna get in trouble."

His reverie was interrupted when the telephone rang again, this time longer. Father Rod wrapped himself in a towel and went downstairs to answer it.

"Hello."

"Why don't you get a housekeeper?" It was Father Pat calling from the Chancery office, with his usual greeting when he had to call more than once to get an answer.

"I don't need a housekeeper. Did I mention that last time you called? It costs money. I like to cook. I don't mind dust. I got a fry pan, a roast pan, bowl, plate, fork, knife, and a spoon. I wash them once a day. Five minutes. I got two pair of underwear. I wash a pair every night. I do my pyjamas once a week. I'm independent. It's one of the few joys of celibacy. Why would I want a housekeeper?"

"To answer the phone."

"Why? It's almost always you," he joked.

"What about sick calls? Don't people get sick, don't people die in your parish?"

"If I don't answer the phone when I'm here, they do what they do when I'm at the ball field, or hearing confessions, or on retreat, or, or, or. Everybody knows the drill."

"Yeah. Well, it wasn't me who called, it was the bishop. He ran out of gas crossing Coaltown beach. Walked to Lingan to find a telephone. He sounded like his radiator was boiling over. What did you do? What did you say to him?"

"Oh, this and that. Most of it meant he should mind his own goddamn business."

"Well, I'd like to advise you to keep out of his way, but ..."

"Thanks for the warning, but is he out on the beach? Should I go get him?"

"No. He called Father 'Suckup' in Coaltown. I imagine he's picked him up by now. But like I said, you should stay out of his way. Trouble is, he'll likely be coming to see you again before too long, and he'll want to stay the night."

"What's he coming here for?"

"He's not going there, he's going to Coaltown, and that, buddy boy, is where you are going to be."

"He's moving me? He told you that? I just got here."

"Not yet. He doesn't know it yet."

"What are you talking about? If he doesn't know, how do you know?"

"What I'm talking about is it looks like Mussolini is about to take Italy into the war. And guess whose side he'd be on? Churchill? No. Hitler, what d'ya think?"

"So what d'ya want me to do. Go over and give Mussolini a good shake?"

"As you know, buddy boy, most of the Italians in Cape Breton live in Coaltown. Most of them work in the pit. What d'ya think is gonna happen?"

"So what's it got to do with me?"

"Well, let's just say you displeased the bishop and he took refuge in Coaltown with Father Suckup. And guess what? They had a chat. And guess what? Father Suckup is nervous. He's worried what the miners will do when the band starts playing. Give him till breakfast time and he'll be hinting for a move. When I suggest to His Excellency that he move him out and you in, he'll think he just thought of the perfect solution: bail out his favourite little sook, and send you, his worst nightmare, into a maelstrom.

He'll figure, well, if the Germans couldn't kill him, maybe the Italians will."

"You prick. Why don't you go? You're an Italian."

"I guess you just answered your own question."

"And this is the way you treat your friends?"

"On the one hand you're my friend. On the other hand, guess what else you are. I know, you guessed it already, you're a shepherd. And the bishop is the boss of the shepherds. And it's his job to make sure all the shepherds look after all the flocks. But he doesn't have enough common sense to know how to do it. So that's why he hired me. To make sure he gets a bright idea every time a problem comes up. I'm his left-handed right-hand man. You said so yourself. So you're it, buddy boy, I hope you have fun."

"They'll kill me out there."

"Ach, you'll be okay. They'll love you out there. After all, you're a war hero. And don't forget, Confirmations are coming up soon. The bishop will be down for that and he'll want to spend the night so he can count it as his yearly parish visit. And don't forget, he likes sirloin steak, marinated and cooked, medium rare, boiled carrots soaked in hot butter, and lemon meringue pie for dessert. He'll want two double whiskeys before supper, Ne Plus Ultra is what he drinks, a red wine, Chateau Neuf du Pape, to go with the steak, and crème de menthe to go with the dessert. Coffee. He won't drink tea. After supper he'll finish off the Scotch, so make sure you don't have any embarrassing visitors. And don't drink yourself, he doesn't like to see his priests drinking. And don't forget he's allergic to cats and dust. Father Suckup's housekeeper is his sister so she'll go with him. You find somebody to look after things, a housekeeper or at least a cook."

"Thanks."

Father Rod put the telephone on its cradle and smiled. He was pleased. Coaltown was a big parish and in ordinary times a bit of a plum usually reserved for experienced priests who were in good standing with the bishop. It looked like it was about to be a trouble spot now, certainly, and perhaps until the war ended. The yahoos were already persecuting Canadians with German names and now the Italians would be in for it. At least in Coaltown there were lots of Italians so it should be manageable. It would be difficult for the bishop to move him out after the war when things settled down. Indeed, as parish priest he could refuse to move, according to canon law. Not that he would, but the bishop might think he would and that would make him think twice. And Franco was in Coaltown. He had been drinking heavily since he came back from the war, and it would be a good idea to be close enough to keep an eye on him. He was such a good guy, perhaps he could be turned around. Father Rod thought for a moment, he might even play ball if he wasn't too busy. Well, with one eye, maybe not, but it would be nice to get to know Tomassio, who was a half dozen years or so older and his boyhood hero on the ballfield. But he would coach the kids. Get to know the people that way.

And he knew from Father Pat's bragging that Tomassio had a son who was promising to be a good ballplayer, must be close to a Junior by now. Yes. All in all, a good spot for a priest with his eye on the ball and his nose in a book. He'd start a library, get the kids reading. Sarah could help out there. Yes. Father Pat was right, the Italians are going to need a sympathetic ear, and maybe a helping hand.

THREE

Christ never asked us to be successful,
He expects us to be faithful.
MOTHER TERESA

J UNE 1940. IN THE EARLY morning two days later,
Father Rod drove his Ford into Coaltown. It was a
bright, sun-filled, not-a-breath-of-wind day. The smell
of salt and seaweed flooded through the open window of
the car. He parked by the pile of beach rocks at the head of
the sandbar and walked across the sand of his boyhood
summer days. Here he learned to swim, and meet friends
beyond the circle of his cousins and hometown buddies of
Baytown. And along this mile, a neck of land where the
water of the Atlantic Ocean connects North America to
Europe, he lounged through his teenage summers, learning
to appreciate the variety of sizes and shapes of the mysterious female, and the occasional thrill of a quick look, or
even a shy flirt.

"Hi, Roddie, how's the water? Cold, is it? I think I'm
gonna wait. Let me know when it warms up, will ya?"

Even now, in early June, encouraged by fair weather, a few little groups, teenagers, mothers with young children, and here and there a couple of young lovers, sat on blankets in the shelter of the dunes of sand and eelgrass. A few runners jogged on the hard sand of low tide along the mile between Coaltown and Lingan. Father Rod took off his shoes and socks, rolled the pant legs to his knees, and waded through the foamy after-flow of the breakers on the hard, brown sand. He loved to drag his toes along the shingled sand and feel the grains of sea-washed coal, silted from outcropped seams along the cliffs of Indian Bay and carried on the tide to the shore.

A bright yellow Harvard Trainer dropped from the sky over Coaltown and roared like an angry bee thirty feet above the water and across the bay, startled the seagulls fishing in the wake of the waves, and sent them squawking for cover in the eelgrass dunes. The pilot tipped his wings in a sharp bank to avoid the cliffs on the Lingan side of the bay and fled in a diminishing drone out to sea, practising low flying skills. When Father Rod stopped to watch, he could see the intent features of two men, one behind the other in the cockpit, student and instructor. He wondered how long before that young man would be in England, zooming off a runway in a Spitfire. How well trained would he be? Would he last beyond the first Messerschmitt to come at him out of the sun?

When he got to the black iron bridge connecting the sandbar to Lingan, he walked to the middle, leaned on the iron railing, and watched the water begin to churn, reversing its direction to rush back in from the sea. The bridge was his favourite spot. During his seminary days, he would come here on early summer mornings or evenings and meditate, his eyes focused on the roiling or rushing water.

Or he would watch the comings and goings of the fishermen along the wharf, gearing up their swordfishing boats and their lobster boats. And he and his buddy Pat Mancini would frequently meet on the bridge and chat about their vocations and their futures. After ordination they stood together on this bridge, their elbows on the iron rail, and decided to join the army. Today, he didn't want to think about the army. He absentmindedly adjusted his eye patch and straightened up to leave the bridge and walk back across the sandbar when he heard a step on the Lingan side of the bridge. A woman dressed in a paisley housedress was striding toward him, smiling.

"Hello, Father."

"Hello. You're in a hurry."

"Yes. I'm late today," she said, but she made a tentative stop. "I'm usually back home by now. It's my daily walk."

"Every morning. You're quite the early bird."

"Sometimes I go at night. Depends on what shift my husband is on. Are you the new parish priest?"

"Yes."

"Father Rod MacDonald."

"Yes. I guess the news got here before I did."

"Father Mancini told me. You're the priest that saved my cousin Franco."

"Well, I was there. So was Father Mancini."

"I know. My name is Anna. Anna Pellegrina."

"You're Tomassio's wife?"

"Yes. You know him?"

"I knew him, as a ballplayer. He was always beating us."

"You played against him? He's older than you."

"Not that much, six or seven years. Seemed like a lot more then. I was a college student."

"Funny I don't remember you," Anna said. "I go to all the games. I've got to run now. Welcome to Coaltown. See you around."

Father Rod waited and watched seagulls do takeoffs and landings along the wharf and roofs of the fishing shacks until Anna's swift pace had carried her across the sandbar. Then he left the bridge and walked quickly back across the beach. He kept going past his car, leaving it by the rocks, and walked up to the ball field and along the cliffs at the bottom of the outfield.

The baseball field. He could remember parts of every game he played here. Partly because so many Italians played for the Panthers and he enjoyed their bilingual chatter, and partly because they had so many smart players and he learned something from them every time they played, so even when his team lost he went home with something. But mostly he remembered two things. He remembered playing centre field and tracking a long, high fly, catching up with it, leaping and stabbing the ball out of the air, his back to the ocean, turning around when he landed and realizing his two heels stood on the edge of the cliff. He looked down at a set of steep, stone steps leading from the cliff to the gravel shore thirty feet below. For a dizzy moment he thought he was going to tumble off backwards and cartwheel down the steps. But he recovered and started to walk in with the ball until he realized, with only one out, the two runners were advancing. He threw the ball to the cutoff man. Too late. Both runs scored. Game over. Coaltown 3, Baytown 2.

And he remembered the time Tomassio did a cartwheel as he stole second base. He watched him closely from then on and learned his many ways of playing the game. Now he planned on coaching the children in Coaltown, for fun, and as a way of getting to know the families in relaxed, informal situations. He'd need to gain their confidence quickly to be effective in the strained and unpredictable immediate future. Father Mancini had already recruited a few boys, including Tomassio's son Angelo, to help him organize the teams. He was feeling better about the bishop sending him to Coaltown.

From the baseball field he walked the path along the cliff through the cranberry bushes until he reached the field behind the parish hall. He walked up along the picket fence to the glebe house and got the keys to the church.

The church was open. The door to the choir loft was open. The door to the bell tower was open. He climbed to the top of the bell tower, three storeys above the choir loft and connected by three ladders. The perpendicular ladders to each sub-loft rose from the floor to a three-foot-square hole in the floor above. The rope fell from the bell through the centres of the holes to the floor of the room adjacent to the choir loft. Father Rod could feel the rope rub between his shoulder blades as he climbed the ladder to the top loft, which housed the bell.

The eight arched windows on the four walls of the bell loft extended almost from floor to ceiling but were covered with wooden shutters on the inside so that Father Rod could see only by the dim light from below. He unlatched the shutters and hooked them to the walls and flooded the space with light. Out the north windows he saw Indian Bay and the beach, and beyond that Lingan and the beginnings of New Waterford. Beyond that he saw the North Atlantic Ocean to its horizon and before that, but beneath his aerial vision, he knew the coastline bent west and south through New

Victoria, South Bar, Whitney Pier, Sydney, and across the harbour to North Sydney and Sydney Mines. Through the west windows he saw half of Coaltown and beyond that miles of woods where rabbits and deer led a precarious existence, especially when the mines were not working full-time. To the east he saw the other half of Coaltown and beyond it Glace Bay and again the North Atlantic. Beyond his vision the coastline continued around the island to Louisbourg and on to the Strait of Canso. To the south and directly below him he saw Coaltown's main street, Coal Road. He was at the centre of a circle that comprised the steel city of Sydney and the coal towns of industrial Cape Breton.

When he went to college at St. Francis Xavier University on the mainland of Nova Scotia, he soon realized there are two Cape Breton islands, two cultural islands separated from the mainland by the Strait of Canso. When he heard the other students talking about home in Cape Breton, he knew it wasn't his home they were talking about. He went to the library to look at the map. The island as a whole is divided into two land masses that look on the map like two upflung arms of an exasperated Nova Scotia reaching out into the North Atlantic. The dual arms are separated by the salty inland sea, Bras d'Or Lake. North and west of Bras d'Or Lake lay Inverness and Victoria counties, referred to as "the country" by the migrants, among them Father Rod's parents, who came from their Celtic and Acadian farms and villages, the men to work in the mines, the single women to work as domestics or clerks, or attend nursing school in Glace Bay. To the migrants of the coal towns who came from Italy, Germany, France, Poland, the Ukraine, Africa, and China, "the country" was a green expanse on the map as undifferentiated as the white expanse of the Northwest Territories.

To the south and west of Bras d'Or Lake is Richmond County, also "the country." And finally, to the south and east, Cape Breton County, industrial Cape Breton, containing Sydney, the only city on the island, built around the steel plant, and Glace Bay, the largest town in Canada, the commercial centre of the half-dozen or so smaller towns built around coal mines.

Father Rod was from industrial Cape Breton. He lived in Cape Breton County but when he talked to his university companions from Inverness County, he realized that their jealous notion of Cape Breton did not include his homeland except as an afterthought of geographical reality. And by the same token he realized his own version of his homeland did not include "the country" except as a historical fact, a place where his people came from; it might almost as well have been France. Two islands on an island. One an island of farms and music and Gaelic, and the other an island of steel and coal. It occurred to him later on, after some thinking and experience, that the territorial jealousy of islanders, geographical and cultural, is a rich source of misplaced pride, and false joy.

From his perch in the bell tower of the church, Father Rod looked down on the main street of Coaltown and felt himself at the centre of the island of steel and coal. Coal Road was a wide strip of ashes and mud, full of potholes. He'd come out yesterday and walked it up and down, stopping to talk to people on the street and in the doorways of businesses. Everybody talked about the war. Everyone talked about the road. Everyone was waiting patiently for the war to end when the road would be paved and perhaps christened with a more elegant name. Along the road edge ran the tramcar tracks, which circled the wrist of industrial

Cape Breton like a dual iron bracelet, with most of the coal towns attached to it like unlucky charms. When he ran out of people to talk to, he boarded the tram. He knew the driver, Jack MacLellan from Baytown.

"If you got the time, I'll take you for a tour around the loop."

"Sounds good. My feet are weary from walking the road."

The tramcar, powered by electricity from overhead wires, ran from Sydney to Reserve Mines, to Dominion, to Coaltown, to Baytown, to Glace Bay, back to Reserve Mines and to Sydney, carrying passengers, messages, and parcels. It was the delight of dogs and kids, who challenged it to a race at every opportunity.

After the early morning rain the muddy road glistened in the sun. The rocks and puddles and tramcar tracks seemed to Father Rod, from his high perch in the bell tower, to wink like enormous jewels. Small boys and girls played in the mud in the margin between the tramcar tracks and the picket fences of their front yards. Slightly older children, free of school on a bright Saturday, wheeled old discarded rubber tires or wagon wheel rims up and down the road through the potholes and puddles. From along the side roads and the front yards of the company houses he could hear the chatter-noise of games of hopscotch, marbles, tag, and hide-and-seek. He could see some of the back yards and back streets from the bell tower, kids and teenagers played peggy and milk-can cricket, keeping busy while they waited for an end to the season that lingered while the hockey ponds melted and the baseball fields dried. Today was a drying day and hope was rampant. Even the miners trudging from day shift smiled at the prospect of seeing the sun for a few hours before they hit the blankets to rest up for Sunday, their one day off.

Now and again a car moved up or down the street and occasionally a truck hauled chuck blocks and roof timbers to the coal mine. But for the most part people walked or, if they were going a distance, took the tramcar. And if they walked they walked on the sleepers between the rails of the tramcar roadbed, the only portion of the road properly drained and maintained. Few families could afford a car or truck, and since the war began all vehicles, as well as many foods and some articles of clothing, were rationed. Only miners who transported other miners to work could buy any kind of new vehicle. Most goods, such as coal for domestic use, groceries, lumber, and produce, moved about in Bain wagons or dump-carts pulled by horses. The few pre-war cars still on the road required constant care because of the seldom-attended-to potholes and mud holes that made the road look like an abandoned ash-covered rugby field. As Father Rod watched, the only taxi from Baytown, driven by his cousin Zachary, pulled up by the Coaltown post office and a man with a briefcase got out and went in. The taxi waited. If it waited long enough, Father Rod thought he might get a chance to chat with Zack and catch up on family gossip.

It all seemed peaceful enough. But the scene below did nothing to abate Father Rod's apprehension. Looking out over the rows of company houses, he could identify most of the Italian dwellings by the gardens in their back yards. About two hundred Italian families lived in Coaltown. He knew some of them already. At least he knew about them from Father Pat, who seemed to be related to everybody. And he knew some of the ballplayers. Most of them came from northern Italy after World War One, from villages and small towns. And so, like the "country" migrants from Inverness, Victoria, and Richmond counties, second- and third-generation migrants whose parents and grandparents migrated from Scotland, Ireland, and France, the Italians were now a rural people living in an industry town. But unlike most of their English- and French-speaking neighbours, the Italians created their new-world farms "in miniature," in their back yards. They loved good wine, good food, and good music, and they provided it for themselves and for each other and for anyone else gracious enough to lean over their fences and share a bit of gossip.

Like immigrants everywhere, the Italians tended to live in clusters. But after twenty years or so, their children were integrating into the general community by virtue of a variety of melting pots: the church, the school, the beach, the ball field, the hockey rinks, the parish hall dances, and the Capital Theatre, the only place you could see a movie without the extra expense of a trip to Glace Bay, Sydney, or New Waterford. The Catholic Church, the Church of Rome, was the largest social institution in Coaltown and the only cultural institution where miners and their families were introduced to a foreign language and classical music. And like the majority of the Scots, Irish, and Acadians, the Italians were all Catholics. The parochial school was administered and taught by nuns, who by nature and profession tended toward charity, tolerance, and integration.

And then there was sex, the warmest melting pot of all. But sex aside, melting pots simmer exceedingly slow. During the twenties, work was plentiful, and people were too tired, too busy, and having too much fun spending money to worry about Italians. But in the thirties, work was scarce, and the boils of prejudice began to fester. Although the Italians from northern Italy were far lighter in skin colour than their southern counterparts who were a small minority among them, people began to talk of white women in mixed marriages. But since the war began, work was again plentiful, and people began to be busy and tired, and to have fun spending money. But now—Mussolini. Until 1935, the whole world, as well as the Italians at home and abroad, imagined Mussolini a-horse, a hero, an Italian Napoleon, the author of dependable train schedules. After 1935, the Italians of Coaltown, most of whom had never heard of Ethiopia, were among a diminishing number who might still unwittingly walk downtown in a black shirt.

In his first action as pastor, Father Rod left the shutters in the bell tower open to the flooding light, then on impulse he grabbed the bell rope in his hands, pressed the soles of his shoes into the rope, and slid to the bottom. The bell rang once as he left the top loft, and twice when he let the rope loose on the bottom floor. "That is the sound of me being here," he mumbled to himself. Everybody within hearing distance stopped and looked up at the bell they had not heard ring in a long, long time.

When he came out of the church, the taxi and his cousin Zack were gone, but he spotted Damien rolling down the road on his dump cart. Damien had been his first employer. He made his living hauling bootleg coal from his own mine and sometimes he hauled for others. Young Roddie had earned spending money helping him winch up the coal from the pit and riding with him for company to see his customers. Damien was old then, and now he was ancient and his huge frame had shrivelled, but his eyes were as lively as ever. He reined the horse to a halt beside the post office.

"Damien," Father Rod said. "Are you still hauling?"

"No, Roddie. Just use the cart to get around. How's my old slave doing?"

"I'm doing fine. And you, you're making a living?"

"Oh yes. Better than ever. I'm on the pension. I make my own booze and my daughters are always buying things and bringing them over. I think I'm gonna hafta start a store. I see you've got a new job yourself. Lot easier on the arms, I bet."

"Come and see me sometime. I'm here in Coaltown now."

"I'll bring you over a hank. Keep you warm in the winter." He flicked the reins and his horse nudged into a walk.

Father Rod walked across the yard to the school. Since Confirmation was coming up he thought he had better check to see how the instruction was coming along. He dashed up the wooden steps to the entrance but before he could put his hand to the handle the door swung open. "Hello, Father MacDonald, how nice of you to visit. Did you just arrive?"

"Yes. Today. Did you know I was coming? The appointment was kind of sudden. I barely knew myself."

"We weren't expecting you so soon. But I saw you through my classroom window, going into the church. And I saw you open the shutters. We're pretty nosy around here. And you rang the bell, and then you come over here. Come in. I'm Sister Joseph. We're a bit disorganized today, I'm afraid, but come in and I'll give you a quick tour and tell you what we're up to." Sister Joseph's genuine smile and confident demeanour failed to mask the anxiety in her eyes, and Father Rod realized he should have let them know he was coming.

"I can come back," he said, "maybe tomorrow?"

"No, no, no," Sister Joseph said. "You're here now. You must be busy trying to get acquainted in the parish. I'll show you around, you can meet the teachers and the boys and girls, and then we'll invite you over for a longer visit when you've got yourself organized." She touched his arm and renewed her smile. "It's no trouble."

"I was just thinking I should see how the Confirmation class is doing."

"Oh," Sister Joseph said. Her smile disappeared and her eyes fell to the floor. "Confirmation," she said, and she touched his arm again. "Yes, the truth is we are having a little problem."

"Perhaps I'll come back after school."

"No, no. Let's take a look. The sooner the better." She led him down the large central corridor to a classroom at the other end of the school. They paused at the door for a moment and listened to the din inside the classroom. When they entered the room, Sister Joseph shut the door with a snap. The children were scattered around the room. Some were in motion, swirling aimlessly in the aisles between the desks, some gathered in groups in animated conversation, some sat at their desks copying from the board a list of Latin phrases. A short nun was at the blackboard, her back to the class, stretching to begin a new list as high up as she could reach. With the snap of the door everyone stopped and stared at the nun and the priest with the quizzical smile on his face. Sister Joseph spoke into the silence. "Father MacDonald, this is Sister Miriam of the Temple." For a moment, Sister Miriam stood still as a startled rabbit. The chalk broke in her hand and a piece fell to the floor. She tried to smile but her face wouldn't budge. She picked up the chalk from the floor and put both pieces on the rail of the blackboard, then she walked to the cloakroom door and left the room.

Sister Joseph got the students back at their desks and assigned them some seat work to do in their scribblers. She escorted Father Rod back to the front door. She explained that the nun in charge of Confirmation had the flu and was in danger of developing pneumonia. "Sister Miriam was helping her but she can't continue by herself because she can't handle the children. Not much more mature than a child herself," Sister Joseph explained, "not to be unkind, nice woman, though, very nice. But whenever she's reminded the bishop will be coming, she's just fit to be tied. So that's our quandary. Could you help, Father? Do you have the time?"

"I think so. Would you mind if I got someone to help me?"

"Not at all. Have you someone in mind?"

"I was thinking my sister, Sister Sarah."

"Oh, that would be wonderful. But perhaps she shouldn't stay with us. She might catch the flu and bring it back to her convent."

"We'll work something out, Sister Joseph," Father Rod reassured her as he bid her goodbye at the door. Her smile was full and now her eyes were quiet.

At the glebe house he found a half jar of peanut butter and some bread and made a sandwich, washing it down with black tea, and then he called his sister's convent.

"Could I speak with Sister Sarah, please?"

"Sister Sarah?"

"Yes, my sister Sarah. Sarah MacDonald. This is Rod, her brother."

"Father Roderick MacDonald?"

"Yes. I'm looking for my sister, Sarah."

"You mean Sister St. Jude, do you, Father MacDonald?"

"Yes, Sister St. Jude, my sister Sarah."

"Oh, Sister is at prayer right now, Father. May I take a message?"

"I need her right away. It's an emergency. We need to talk. I need help."

"An emergency? What sort of emergency, Father?"

"It's a religious emergency. For the love of God, would you get her to the phone?"

"Please, Father. No need for impatience. No need to raise your voice. It's not nice. It's not appropriate. If you don't mind."

Father Rod, who had not raised his voice, was indeed getting impatient. There was something definitely not quite right about the tone of this conversation. He took a deep breath.

"Are you still there, Father MacDonald?" the voice asked.

"Yes. Look. I think it would be appropriate, Sister, for you to go get my sister, and get her to the phone."

"Father MacDonald. My assignment is to keep the sisters at prayer free from distraction by visitors and what not. That's my job. If I fail to do my job, I will be disciplined by my superior, not to mention the fact that I would disappoint my creator."

"Okay, Sister. I understand. What's your name?"

"Sister Saint Mary Magdalene of the Well."

"Well, listen, Sister Saint Mary Magdalene of the Well. I am not a visitor. And I am not a what not. I just got assigned to a new parish. I've got a problem on my hands, and I need my sister whom I know could solve it for me. I need to talk to her to ask her if she can come out and help me."

"Oh, I'm sure any of the sisters could do the job. You do have sisters in your parish. Aren't you in Coaltown now?

We have a convent there and lots of sisters. Why don't you get one of them?"

"Half of the sisters out here are sick. And the sister in charge of Confirmation is on the verge of a nervous breakdown. She needs help. I'm trying to get help. Let me talk to my sister."

"Look. The sisters are coming out of chapel now. I'll pull her sleeve and see if she wants to talk to you."

Father Rod waited. Sarah's voice came over the phone. *"Ciamar a tha thu, Rod?"*

"Tha gu math, tapadh leat, ciamar a tha thu fhein?"

"Well, I guess I taught you something after all. What in the name of God did you say to Sister Mary?"

"Sister Mary. Wasn't I talking to Sister Saint Mary Magdalene of the Well?"

"Sister Saint Mary Magdalene of the Well. Are you kidding? That was Sister Mary. You remember her, Mary Catherine, she was always at our house."

"Mermaid?"

"Yes. I guess she was putting you on, eh? She's out in the hall laughing to kill herself. She's got two sisters holding her up off the floor. What did you say to her?"

"Nothing. I asked to talk to you, and she kept putting me off with a bunch of pious drivel."

"I guess you met your match there, b'y. If anything she's worse than you. She's got us in stitches from morning till night."

"What's she doing in the convent? Didn't she get married?"

"She did. Her husband was killed in the pit."

"I didn't think she's the type to be a nun."

"Type? What are you talking about, type? Are you the type to be a priest? Am I the type to be a nun? None of us is the type. What's type got to do with it?"

"Okay. Save it. Let's not get into that now."

"So what do you want, that you have to interrupt the even tenor of my ways?"

"Are you Sister Saint Jude, the saint for hopeless cases, or not?"

"I'm supposed to be. But nobody will call me that any more, except Mary Catherine for a joke. 'We know you're a hopeless case,' she says, 'but I don't want to be reminded that you're hopeless every time we talk.' Anyway, Rod, what did you call for? Have you got a hopeless case?"

"Well, not hopeless. I got a bunch of kids for Confirmation and they don't know what to do, or what to say, or what to wear, or when it is, or where to go, or how to get there."

"Who's looking after them?"

"Sister Miriam of the Temple. Where in the name of God do you people dredge those names up from?"

"Now Rod, you know better than to end a sentence with a preposition, especially two prepositions."

"If Winston Churchill can get away with it ..."

"It's a damn good thing he's running the war and not try-ing to teach grade eight."

"I guess he'd do a better job of it than Sister Miriam of the Cathedral or whatever ecclesiastical edifice she's the Miriam of."

"Oh my God, that poor thing doesn't know which one is her elbow. Crazy as a flea."

"Be charitable now."

"And she'll drive you crazy, flip-flitting around jibber-jabbering away to herself in French; she got a tongue on her like a loose board on a dump cart, until you try to talk to her. She is a nice person, but the poor thing is not well. Not all there. You can't put any pressure on her."

"Can you get here and help me, or they'll be hauling the both of us off to Sydney River."

"You know I just can't jump on the tramcar and take off to anywhere I feel like. But I'll tell you what. You call Sister Marie, the superior, and explain the situation. But listen here. If I do go out there, I'm not staying in the convent. Tell her you need me to stay at the glebe to organize the bishop's visit because you don't have a housekeeper. They got the flu in the convent out there anyway. And I want Mary Catherine with me. I can't go without a travelling companion anyway, and I don't want Sister St. Agnes, who I know she'll send with me just to get under my skin, so you make up some reason why the two of us have to go and stay in the glebe. Hey, I got it, listen, get your buddy Pat to do it. If he calls she'll think it's the bishop himself is asking."

"Can you come tomorrow?"

"If you can arrange it from your end."

"Consider it done. Pat owes me a favour. He'll get it done."

"Good enough. Here's Mary Catherine, she wants to say hello."

"Hi, Rod, I got ya going, eh?"

"I guess you did. But listen here, Mermaid, if you come out here with Sarah, you better behave."

"Don't worry about me, Rod. I just wanted to see if you were the same pushover you were in grade seven. I guess you haven't learned a thing."

On the baseball field overlooking the ocean, Gelo fielded a practice ground ball during his team warm-up, and distracted by the thought that he was due for Confirmation practice in an hour, soared the ball over the first baseman's leaping glove and into the seats, just missing Sadie, his girlfriend. He didn't know she was there until he saw her duck. Then he saw her worried smile. She'd said she'd be shopping with her mother.

"Play ball," the umpire yelled and the game began.

Confirmation practice was going better since Sister Sarah and Sister Mary took over a couple of days ago, but he still felt foolish. The other kids were younger, some half his age. He had missed Confirmation with his classmates because he was in bed with "a touch of T.B." His friend George had died with it, so he was glad he had stayed in bed. But now he was older than his classmates in school. All the friends his own age were ahead of him, and now because he missed it last time, four years ago, he had to make his Confirmation with little kids, and Sadie was teasing him about it, and now he almost hit her in the face with the ball. It's a good thing she was paying attention.

Crack. He heard the crack of the bat and took his eyes off Sadie just in time to see a line drive zooming at his head. He lifted his glove and caught the stinging ball. He winced and stood for a few seconds in shock, not so much from the impact of the ball as the realization that he had almost got hit between the eyes with the ball.

"Wake up, Gelo," he heard from somewhere, and he bent his knees and touched his glove to the ground.

Into the batter's box stepped Paul, a habitual bunter and a fast runner. The third baseman cheated up the line so Gelo cheated to his right. He couldn't keep his mind on the game. Sister Miriam of the Temple told them Confirmation would make them "Soldiers of Christ." He tried to imagine himself a Soldier of Christ. What would he wear? Where would he go? He asked Sister Miriam of the Temple if a Soldier of Christ would carry a gun and she told him, "Don't be ridiculous." He was trying to be a smart aleck, but all the other kids laughed at him instead of her so he felt foolish.

Paul popped up to the catcher. Two out.

Gelo thought he wanted to be a soldier for Canada like his cousin Franco, but when Franco came back with his leg shot off, Gelo began to think second thoughts. He wanted to talk to him about it but every time he saw him Franco was drunk. Shell-shock, everybody said. Poor bastard. Once, when Gelo and Sadie were walking up Commercial Street, coming from a movie at the Russell Theatre in Glace Bay, Franco was step-dancing on his one leg and crutches, whistling a jig in the middle of the intersection at Senator's Corner, traffic backed up in all four directions.

"Wake up, Gelo."

The right-handed batter took up a closed stance so Gelo cheated a bit to his left, staying deep.

Crack. The ball skidded under the pitcher's glove and scooted toward the outfield, but Gelo dashed and dived, knocked it down with his glove, picked it up and fired to first. Easy out. He took three small rocks from his back pocket, scattered them between shortstop and home plate, and ran off the field. Once on the bench he looked over his shoulder at Sadie. Why is she here? She loves to go shopping. He told her he might skip Confirmation practice so maybe she came down to change his mind. When he told her that yesterday, she gave him a dirty look. He waved. She gave him a little wave and a worried smile.

"Are you on sleeping pills, Gelo, or what?" Jake elbowed his ribs.

"What?"

"You're up next. Get going."

There was nobody on base so he didn't expect the pitcher would give him much. The ball came in at his ankles.

"Strike one."

Gelo looked at the catcher, who shrugged his shoulders and lobbed the ball back to the mound. Gelo watched the pitcher; he could see the two fingers on top of the ball as the pitcher's hand arched over his head—fastball. The ball came in hard but too high, and the catcher had to stand up to take it. Whop, Gelo watched the ball slam into the catcher's glove and saw him wince.

"Ouch, I bet that hurt," Gelo said.

"Strike two," the umpire yelled.

"Ouch," the catcher smiled. "I bet that hurt."

Gelo looked at the umpire. He knew him. He played on the senior team with his father and he was his father's boss in the pit. And he was Sadie's father, Wilfred MacLeod. He ignored Gelo's outraged gaze.

With two strikes on him, Gelo knew he'd get a bad pitch now. He'd have to swing if it was hittable at all. He watched the pitcher's hand turn over, curve ball. It came in under his elbows, too tight to hit.

"Strike three, batter's out. Three out. Side retired."

The catcher stood up, rolled the ball out to the mound, pulled off his mask, and stood for a moment with a funny look on his face. Gelo knew him, Peter Christmas, an Indian from Eskasoni. They often chatted during games.

"Hey, Peter?" Gelo said.

"Yeah."

"You got a dog?"

"Yeah."

"Is it a bitch, or a son of a bitch?" Gelo said, and glanced at the umpire, whose eyes flared behind the bars of his mask. Gelo smiled.

"Take the field, Dago . . . for now," Wilfred growled.

Gelo and Peter froze together in a frieze of space and time, the umpire hovering like a malign, detached creator. After a few seconds, Peter's face renewed its funny look.

"You'll get used to it, Gelo," he said. "It's only scum. It scrapes off, and it thickens your skin."

They stepped off toward their different dugouts. Gelo ran to get his glove and hustled onto the field, picked up his rocks, and slipped them into his back pocket.

"Play ball," the umpire yelled, but immediately called time and beckoned Harry and Chris, the managers, to the plate.

"Harry, call in your shortstop," Wilfred demanded.

"What for?" Harry asked, but the umpire glared and waited until Harry yelled at Gelo and called him in. "Here he is," Harry said. "What is it?"

The umpire put his hand palm up in front of Gelo and demanded, "Give me those rocks. In your back pocket."

Gelo ignored the umpire's hand. He put his ungloved hand into his back pocket but left it there and looked past the umpire's shoulder at Sadie, sitting by herself in the stands, staring at them, wondering what was going on between her father and her boyfriend. Nobody was moving.

Wilfred turned and looked over his shoulder just as Sadie lifted her hand in a faint wave. He turned to Harry in a rage. "You want me to call the game, or would you rather I threw you out of the game?"

Gelo pulled out three rocks and, ignoring the umpire's hand, dropped the rocks on the ground.

"He throws them on the field when he comes in," Wilfred explained, "so maybe they'll cause a bad bounce for the other shortstop. His father does the same thing."

Harry looked at Wilfred, still glaring in anger behind the mask. He looked at Chris, the opposing manager.

"Okay, Ump, so tell him to stop," Chris said. "And let's play ball. We got a long drive back home in an open truck and it looks like rain."

"It's not up to you, Tonto, it's up to me. First of all, Harry, he called me a son of a bitch. I let that go, but enough is enough—he's out of the game."

Harry watched Chris's face go as white as an Indian face could go, as blood, supercharged with adrenaline, drained from his head and surged into his heart. His spine coiled for flight or fight. Harry put his hand on Chris's arm. "Take it easy, Chris."

But for Chris it was a familiar scene and he knew his role. He entertained a wave of rage full of interesting possibilities for a few seconds, with Harry's soothing hand on his arm, and Wilfred's watchful eyes on his clenched fists, and he smiled the way his father taught him, the smile of insolent retreat.

"For the love of Christ," Chris said, pointing to Gelo. "He's only a Jesus kid. We're winning the game anyway. It didn't change the game any. Let him play. He's a kid. It's a game."

"You can curse all you want in Eskasoni, Tonto, but in my back yard, if you take the name of the Lord God in vain, in English, you'll be gone too."

Chris looked at the sky, pursed his lips, made a two-note sound through his nose, put his chin in his hand, and turned and looked at Harry. Harry looked at the sky, pursed his lips, made the same sound through his nose, put his chin in his hand, and turned and looked at Chris. They cocked their heads and eyed each other with a skiff of a smile.

"Better go sit on the bench, Gelo," Harry said. "We'll give Gerry a try at short."

"Can I sit in the stands?"

"Sure."

Sadie sat with her head in her hands away from the small gatherings of people in the stands and watched him climb the stands and sit beside her. They sat in silence for a while and gazed across the field. The day was darkening. It was hard to distinguish sea from sky over the cliffs, beyond the outfield. Seagulls glided in from the fog, wheeled with a squawk or two over second base, then landed on the outfield to yank worms from the ground through the short grass, stubbled from the salty ocean air. Drizzle leaked from the low clouds.

"How come you're sitting back here by yourself?"

"So he can't see me through that pole."

"He saw you anyway."

"I know. When he turned to see who you were gawking at. He said I can't go with you any more. He hates you."

"Oh God, that's great. I just told him off for calling me out. He kicked me out of the game."

"I know, I saw him at it. But no difference. He hates you 'cause you're Italian. Not bad enough you're a Catholic. At least you can stop being a Catholic. Not much you can do about being an Italian."

They sat in silence for a while and thought about their situation while they watched the game. It was almost dark now, although only a little after four in the afternoon. The clouds looked like they had picked up a blanket of soot from the smoke stacks of the coal mines and the chimneys of the innumerable company houses and dragged them in bundles across the sky.

"Hey. I could be a convert," Gelo said. "I could become Irish or Scotch. It can't be much harder than changing to a Protestant."

"Yeah, that's funny. But who's laughing? What are we gonna do?"

"We'll just have to break up, I guess."

"Oh yeah. I guess you'd just love an excuse."

"I'm kidding, Sadie, for God's sake. So what d'ya think. What can we do?"

"We'll have to hide is all. Sneak around. We'll meet inside the show and stuff. But he better not catch us, he'll be wild."

"Will he beat you or anything?"

"No, he wouldn't beat me, like, beat me. But he's not beyond giving me a good backhander if he loses his temper. He's got a short fuse on him. I can just imagine him, no trouble at all, grabbing me up by the clothes and the scruff of the neck out of a seat in the movie and marching me up the road dangling like a mouse in the mouth of a cat."

"What did you say to him—anything?"

"Say to him? I didn't get a chance. I just said, not to him, to my mother, but him there, I said, 'For two cents I'd get pregnant, just for spite.'"

"What'd he say?"

"What'd he say? Nothing. Blew his stack. Got red in the face. When I saw smoke coming out of his ears, I ran to my room and locked the door, him pounding up the stairs behind me. Stood outside my door and yelled, 'If you think you're gonna bring a goddamn grandchild of Mussolini into this house, little miss, you got another think coming.'

Then he took off his shoes and sneaked off in his sock feet so I'd think he was waiting outside the door. I'm up to his old tricks. I didn't care anyway, I just went out the window, down the porch and over to June's. Then I came here."

The drizzle became rain and fell straight down from the hovering clouds. The wind stopped completely like a held breath waiting to explode, and in its silence they could hear the rain hitting the puddles and the stands.

"Who's Mussolini?" Gelo asked.

"Who's Mussolini! Who's Mussolini? Are you kidding?"

"How am I supposed to know? I'm just asking. It's just a name to me."

"Don't you ever listen to the radio?"

"All the time."

"Yeah. Ball games, you and your father." Sadie grabbed him by the elbow and looked him in the face. "Don't you ever listen to anything else?"

The ballplayers' sneakers were sinking a half-inch into the mud so the umpire called the game in the seventh inning. The Indians threw their equipment into the box of their half-ton truck and fled home through the rain. The wind was rising. The ocean had disappeared from the horizon but they heard it crashing over the rock at the base of the outfield cliffs, and growling up the sand at Lingan Beach. The little groups of people were gone from the stands. Sadie and Gelo sat, soaking, alone in the empty stands on the top seats, holding hands across their laps. Wilfred appeared at the bottom.

"Oh-oh. He's here," she whispered. "Don't move. Yet."

"You fly the hell out of here and leave my daughter alone."

"You're not the umpire of the field, you're the umpire of the game. The game's over. And I'm not in it, anyway."

Ump stared at him, but before he could answer, Sadie said in the flat voice she reserved for her father, "The game's over, Daddy. Take off the mask and chest protector. You look like a turtle."

Ump turned his gaze to Sadie. Even through the mask he managed to reveal a look of pained betrayal. His rage grew. "Didn't I tell you to stay away from him?"

"Just came to say goodbye. Polite thing to do. Goodbye, Gelo. Nice knowing ya."

Sadie moved off. Ladylike and provocative, she stepped down benches made of unfinished two-by-fours in high heels and a tight skirt. The seams running up the back of her black-market nylons lengthened the look of her prematurely voluptuous body and shortened the length of her father's premature fuse. When she disappeared around the corner of the dugout, Wilfred, still behind the mask, aimed his florid attention at Gelo.

"She's too old for you."

"Yeah. Well. Some things I'm too old for. Some things I'm too young for. I'm too young to play on the junior team, but I'm playing on it anyway. If you can do it, they let you do it."

"Well, you're not gonna do it with my daughter, you little wop."

"Kiss my arse."

"I'll kick your arse up around your ears. Is that the way you talk around her? I wouldn't be surprised."

"It was her taught me how to talk like that. Told me she learned it from you."

"You little shit. For two cents I'd go up there and wring your neck."

"I guess you and your family come cheap, eh? For two cents you'd do anything."

Gelo cranked up an insolent smile, impelling Wilfred up the stands until he slipped on the wet boards and went face and chest first into the edges of the seats, as if it were precisely against this eventuality that he'd kept wearing the face mask and chest protector. Gelo jumped off the top seat to the ground behind the stands and sauntered off.

"Might as well go to Confirmation practice now," he mumbled to his sneakers.

✝   ✝   ✝

Sister Mary and Sister Sarah, with the co-operation of Sister Theresa, the Domestic Science teacher, soon established an orderly step-by-step march toward Confirmation Day. First order of business, finding a straitjacket for Sister Miriam of the Temple, whom they found on their arrival to be a woman fit to be tied, on the precipice of a dissolving universe. She was not a person to whom you could give three projects with three different deadlines because she could only do everything she had to do all at once. Sister Miriam of the Temple was Aimée LeBlanc. She had come to Glace Bay from Grande Étang with her sister Térèse to go to nursing school but the noise and chaos of the streets scared her and she fled to the convent. The sisters decided to keep her until she became fluent in English but by then they realized she had problems more serious than a French accent. So they gave her a habit and a list of chores.

"She's like a flea flitting on a bed sheet," Sister Mary said, "so what I'm gonna do, what I'm gonna give her to do, is the most important part of the operation, and a nice cozy corner to do it in."

Sister Miriam of the Temple was a witless ninny but she could do many things to perfection. She could knit, for example. In her spare time she was knitting socks for soldiers and she knit hundreds of them, and most of her sins, venial of course, were committed after she went to bed and imagined all those soldiers doing things in the comfort of her socks. One sock of every pair contained a card with a message, inscribed in perfect penmanship: "Knit by Sister Miriam of the Temple. I hope that God will keep you safe when you are wearing these socks. And even when you are not." She printed her address on the back. Some of the soldiers wrote her thank-you notes, which made her feel as warm as if she were wearing wool socks herself. Every time she got one she read it, palmed it, and rubbed it up and down the top of her thigh, from her knee to her belly, until it got so warm she thought it might catch fire, and she put it under her mattress with the others.

One soldier's letter Sister Miriam kept on her person. She safety-pinned it to her bloomers and no one knew about it except Sister Mary and Sister Sarah because Sister Miriam of the Temple showed it to Sister Mary, her best buddy, who told Sister Sarah, her best buddy.

Dear Sister Saint Miriam of the Temple,
I am well. I hope you are the same. Thank you, thank you, and thank you for the socks. We have lots of socks in the army. But the army socks are as hard as barbed wire compared to your socks and your socks are soft as hair. I never wear them because they might wear out. But I take them to bed with me every night, be I in a trench or be I in a bunk, and I think of you. I love your socks. In the morning I wash them out, in a sink, or in a river. We always seem to bivouac by a river. We always seem to want to cross a river. After I dry them out, I

keep them in my mess tin, where they cuddle up together like two
pussycats in a basket. While I'm using my mess tin to eat my meals, I
sling them one over each shoulder so they can chat. Oh, thank you,
thank you, oh, thank you, oh, oh, oh, thank you for your socks.

Yours Truly,
Archie MacLean

When Sister Miriam of the Temple showed it to Sister Mary, she said, "Isn't that nice?"

When Sister Mary told Sister Sarah, she said, " Isn't that nice."

"I know," said Sister Mary. "And you know what? She reads herself to sleep with that letter every night, a smile on her face, I imagine, and as innocent as the Infant Jesus."

"Anyone as stunned as that must be a good person," Sister Sarah said to Sister Mary.

Sister Mary set Sister Miriam of the Temple up in the Domestic Science room walk-in closet behind the clothes racks where they kept the costumes for the Christmas and Easter concerts and pageants. She provided her with a student desk from the Domestic Science room, a pen with a handful of fancy nibs, two colours of ink, red for the capital letters and black for the others, and lots and lots of cards, so even her tiny mistakes she could redress by starting afresh with a pristine rectangle and scratch on it her perfect scroll and script.

"There's lots of cards, Sister, so don't be afraid of making mistakes," Sister Mary told her.

"But what will I put on them?"

"The boy's or girl's name—here's the list. And here, I'll write something out for you," Sister Mary said, and she grabbed a page from a scribbler inside the desk and wrote:

Dear Jesus, help me to be a Soldier of Christ. Help me to bear the storm and strife of bearing your cross down the road of life.

"And put on the bottom, 'Souvenir of Confirmation.'"

"Good God," Sister Sarah said when she read one of the cards, "couldn't you do any better than that?"

"Well, I only had a minute. It was all I could do to keep from gawking it up altogether."

"It's a bit of a gawk as it is, if you ask me."

"Well, Sarah, if you get a bit of a gawk to do the work, you know what you're gonna get."

By the eve of Confirmation Day the sisters had established the dress code, white shirt and the best pair of pants they could find in the house for the boys, and a bow tie made by Sister Theresa. For the girls the best dress possible without buying anything. Polish the best pair of shoes in the house that fit. Everyone memorized the sequence of events for the ceremony and proper responses.

The children and Gelo knelt in a row along the wall. "So pretend I'm the bishop," Sister Mary said. She picked up the long pole with the hook on the end of it, used for pulling down the high windows. "This is my crosier," she said, holding it aloft. "The bishop is a shepherd, you know, and he carries a staff, we call it a crosier, just like an officer in the army carries a swagger stick. You will kneel down at the altar rail and I'll move from one to the other and I'll say, '*Signo te signo Crucis*,' which means, I sign you with the sign of the cross, and I'll put my hand on top of your head and anoint your forehead with a bit of chrism and I'll say, '*Et confirmo te chrismate salutis, in nomine Patris, et Filii, et Spiritus Sancti*' and that means, and I confirm you with the chrism of salvation, and you say ..."

Sister Mary signalled with the open palm of her free hand, and all but Gelo chanted in unison: "Amen."

Gelo knew she favoured him. He knew it right away. He could feel it when she swept the room with her searching gaze. She reminded him, when her chin arced the room, of the searchlight at the airport which he watched through his bedroom window at night until he fell asleep under its hypnotic regularity, momentarily highlighting clouds drifting across the sky, and sometimes aircraft approaching runways to land, or scooting off runways to hunt for submarines out over the Atlantic.

"*Pax tecum*, peace be with you," Sister Mary said. "Any questions?"

"Yes, Sister?"

"What is it, Iris?"

"What's a swagger stick?"

"Gelo, can you tell Iris what a swagger stick is?"

Gelo was trying to keep his participation down to a minimum, but he couldn't resist appeals to his superior knowledge of the world because it created the impression he was more allied with the teachers than with the learners. "Officers in the army carry them," he said. "It's like a short stick about a foot and a half long, covered in leather. It means they're the bosses. The soldiers have to do what they say." By the time he finished his little speech, he was facing the children as if he were the teacher. Some of the children's faces clouded in doubt or puzzlement, and Sister Sarah gave him one of her sideways looks. Sister Mary beamed.

In class, when Sister Mary's chin arced and circled the room, her eyes stayed focused on him, perhaps because he was in the front seat, perhaps because he was so much bigger than the others, perhaps because of his potential for creating chaos. They were always watching to see if he would turn out to be a "chip off the old block." But perhaps he was in the centre of her circle simply because she was depending on his performance to show off to the bishop. She had selected him to deliver the Latin responses. He had a knack for language, his mother, Anna, told him that, just like her. He was a natural mimic. The others were supposed to chant the Latin responses too, but they were young and their memorized responses were as interchangeable as they were unintelligible. Gelo understood Latin and pronounced it properly. When the group faltered, his sweet baritone rose above the babble. The bishop would realize that in Coaltown the sisters and priests knew how to get things done.

"Amen," Sister Sarah said. "Any more questions? Yes, Iris."

"What's chrism?"

"Okay. Does anyone remember what Sister Mary said chrism is? Yes, Gelo."

"It's a mixture of axle grease and horse manure," Gelo explained. The lie was out of his mouth before he could stop it. He looked up, startled, and stared at the door as if he were about to flee. But the children were laughing. Sister Mary was laughing. Even Sister Sarah was concealing a smile.

Father Rod arrived as the gale of laughter began to subside. He was pleased to see everybody in a good mood.

"Good afternoon, Father," all but Gelo sang in unison.

"Good afternoon, boys and girls. Hi, Gelo."

Gelo raised his hand in a faint wave. He and Father Rod were acquainted. Both spent a lot of time on the ball field, and now Gelo was helping the priest organize and coach the younger players.

"So, everything okay, Sister Sarah, Sister Mary? Where's Sister Miriam?"

"In her cocoon," Sister Mary said. "Yes, everything is okay. Well, we've got one little problem. With Angelo."

"With Gelo?"

"Yes," said Sister Mary. "Angelo, could you come over here a minute."

Gelo sauntered over, trying to give the impression to the children that he was being singled out for some sort of award, but in spite of his friendship with the priest, he was a bit worried. The two nuns and the priest joined Sister Theresa in her little cubicle office and along with Gelo they formed a circle around her desk.

"Okay," Father Rod said, and looked at Sister Mary.

"Your buddy Father Pat told us that the bishop has taken to making the children take the pledge not to drink any alcohol until they are twenty-one. He lines them up and he asks the question, and they have to raise their right hand if they agree to take the pledge."

"So?"

"In Gelo's family they have wine with supper every day."

"Okay," Father Rod said. "Ah, hah. Okay. Ah, Gelo?"

"Yeah . . . ah, yes, Father."

"How much wine do you drink with your supper?"

"Half a glass."

"Okay. Tell you what. When the bishop asks the question, you put your hand up halfway."

"There you go," said Sister Sarah, "problem solved."

"Good," said Father Rod. "But we do have another problem."

"Oh-oh. What is it?"

"The bishop is postponing Confirmation."

"What? Why? Until?"

Father Rod explained that the bishop had a heavy schedule, that he had to go to Toronto, he had to go to Montreal, that he had to see the apostolic delegate. He could delegate Father Pat to do the Confirmation, or even the parish priest, but that would be unusual, and unfair because every parish wants the bishop to come and make a fuss over the children, it's good for their formation. The litany of the usual reasons. "But I think we all know what's up," Father Rod said. "He's a bit leery to come to Coaltown because of the Italian Thing."

"The Italian Thing?"

"Yeah. The Italian Thing. It's only a matter of time until Mussolini brings Italy into the war. The day it happens will be an interesting day in Coaltown and everywhere else in the country. The newspapers are already filling up with hostility. You remember what happened to people with German names last year. He'll want to wait until it happens and see if it settles down. Politics, you know."

"How do you know all this?" Sister Mary asked.

"Well, we could guess easy enough. But Father Pat heard him on the phone to Montreal. He didn't hear much but he did hear 'the Italian Thing.' So I am awfully sorry. I know you'd like to get it over with."

"Are you kidding?" said Sister Sarah. "This is wonderful. Now we get to stay in the glebe house until he does come. The convent is great, but it's always nice to get a break. He'll be away, so Pat will be running things. We'll have to keep things up to scratch here until he gets back, keep the kids tuned up, otherwise they'll forget everything and we'll have to start over. Pat will have to make the case with Sister Superior."

"Yeah, come to think of it," Father Rod said, "you're right. This will give me time to get some cats. Gelo, do you think you could round me up some cats?"

"Sure."

"Don't bring them over yet, just get them lined up, and I'll tell you when I want them."

"Sure. How many?"

"Oh, two or three would be enough."

"Kittens okay? With the mother?"

"Perfect."

With everyone pleased, the three sisters, priest, and Gelo stepped out of Sister Theresa's office and into the Domestic Science room proper. The children were scattered all over, rooting into cupboards and drawers and spreading stuff all over the place. Every child was eating a cookie and carrying a fistful of replacement cookies. They waited and watched until one by one the children saw them watching and settled down.

"Father is going now," Sister Mary addressed the crowd. "Does anyone have a question before he leaves? Yes, Iris?"

"What's a wop?"

FOUR

Thou hast bound bones and veins in me,
fastened me flesh.
GERARD MANLEY HOPKINS

REE FROM CONFIRMATION PRACTICE, Gelo slammed the ball into the palm of his glove as he walked along the tramcar tracks down Coal Road. He stepped on every second sleeper but managed to maintain the rhythm of his saunter, a walking style he copied from his father. It oozed arrogance and a clear message: "Anything you can do, I can do better." Gelo smiled. He'd redeemed the time lost in Confirmation prison by blurting out his flippant chrism joke. Why didn't the sky fall? Was it a venial sin, a mortal sin? Something else he could tell in confession? He should have buttoned his lip, maybe, but rage and frustration had pushed him over the edge. The nerve of Ump calling him out on three straight balls. And then throwing him out of the game. And coming over and making a fool of himself in front of his own daughter. Good thing Sadie was gone before he told him off. And to top it off to be called a wop twice in the same day. Once by a man too big to beat the shit out of, and once by a girl too small. And even if she were big, honour and pride would have tied his hands—he couldn't very well hit a girl. But nothing could tie his tongue. Oh well. He had to go to confession anyway. It was always better with a half-decent sin to confess.

But anyway, nothing happened. Nothing bad. They all laughed. They all laughed. Not at him this time but at his joke, at his daring. For a moment he owned the room. And the one who laughed the loudest was Sister Mary, the one he tried to put the blame on for making up the joke in the first place. He was in love with Sister Mary. It started yesterday in the classroom going over the Latin for Confirmation.

"*Spiritus Sanctus superveniat in te, et vertus Altissimi custodiat te a peccatis*," Sister Mary chanted, and the boys and girls began to babble.

"No, no, children, that's the bishop's part, you just say 'Amen.'"

"Amen," they chanted.

"Can you tell them what the bishop's words mean, Angelo?"

"May the Holy Spirit come down on you, and the power above keep you out of sin."

"Good," Sister Mary said, and she went to the board and underlined the response. "This is the part everybody says. Look at the board and listen to Angelo. Then we'll try it without the board. Now. Let's try that again. Angelo, be the bishop, say the bishop's words—who knows, maybe someday you will be the bishop. Here's the book, you can read the words, you needn't memorize that part," Sister Mary said in her teacher's voice. She came back from the board and hovered over him like a large bent blackbird and lay the book down on his student desk, holding it open with the thumb and little finger of one hand and running the index finger of her other hand along the passage in big black print.

"*Spiritus Sanctus superveniat in te, et vertus Altissimi custodiat te a peccatis.*"

When he finished the chant, Sister Mary straightened up and beckoned the class with her open palms. The ample sleeves of her habit fell like wings from her raised arms and the margin of white starched linen surrounding her head reminded him of a hovering eagle poised to drop from the sky.

"Okay, class," she pleaded, "after me, when my hands come down say, Ah—men."

"Aaaa—men," they chanted.

"Very good. Very good. Thank you, Angelo." She bent, scooped the book up with her fingers, and stood back a few inches from his desk.

"Now," she said, "let's do the next one. We're having a little trouble with it, so let's try hard. *Domini, exaudi orationem meam.* That means 'Oh, Lord, hear my prayer.' Look at your booklets and read along."

Even the children were startled with the emotion Sister Mary managed to get into her plea. It was only a practice after all. They chanted, trying to imitate her intensity, "*Domini, exaudi orationem meam,*" or variations thereof, and Sister Mary swayed back and forth with the music of it.

"*Et clamor meus ad te veniat.* That means 'And let my cry come on to you.' Look at your booklets and read along."

And the children chanted, "*Et clamor meus ad te veniat,*" with variations, and Sister Mary swayed back and forth with the music of it.

Angelo's desk top was a two-foot-square slab of maple with rounded corners at the front and as Sister Mary swayed back and forth with the chant, her forward motion brought her body into contact with a corner of the desk and pressed the folds of her habit between the tops of her legs. Angelo was no longer chanting. His thumbs were under his chin, and the tips of his fingers touched his temples, and the palms of his hands shaded his eyes like the blinkers attached to a horse's bridle to prevent peripheral distraction. And his head began to sway in sync with the folding and unfolding, the tightening and loosening of Sister Mary's habit, and in a trance he dropped a hand and wrapped its fingers around the corner of the desk and Sister Mary's black crotch came roaring down upon it.

"*Domini, exaudi orationem meam.*"

"*Et clamor meus ad te veniat.*" Angelo's hand vanished into the black garment. Engulfed. His heart rattled when his knuckle fitted into her crevice through the innocent cloth. He tried to retrieve his fingers but for a few seconds of eternity they were locked onto the maple arc, until Sister Mary's rhythm pulled her back and he hauled his sweaty hand away and hid it inside its innocent twin.

"'O, Lord, hear my prayer, and let my cry come to thee.' Don't forget what it means, children, and memorize the Latin. Angelo, you better come back after school and we'll take up where we left off. We still have a thing or two to straighten out."

The children, puzzled and awed by the drama of the afternoon, filed quietly from the room and went to their regular classrooms. Gelo went upstairs to the physics lab where his classmates were trying to make needles float on the surface of glasses of water.

Angelo showed up after school, but Sister Mary did not. He found Sister Theresa in the Domestic Science room in her flowered apron full of cake flour, and she gave him some gingersnaps and scones made by her grade eleven cooking class.

"Here, take these. I'd give you more but we have some families to feed that are a whole lot worse off than you. Sister Mary likely forgot. She's got a lot on her mind these days. Sister Sarah is in the library, you could ask her."

"Thanks for the cookies. I think I'll just go home. And *pax vobiscum*."

"*Pax vobiscum*, you little scamp," Sister Theresa called after him, laughing, shaking her head. "Chip off the old block, I hope not," she mumbled into her sink.

Gelo went to his classroom and got his ball and glove out of his desk.

Sister Mary did not go to her meeting with Angelo because she so sorely wanted to go. Flesh said go. Bones said go. Blood said go. But Brain said no. No. *No*.

She flew out the door, not waiting for her buddy Sister Sarah, and, leaning against the wind of desire, walked the two miles to the school where she taught elementary children how to tie shoelaces, button coats, pull on overshoes, add, subtract, divide, and read sentences like "Here I am, My name is Nan, I have a dog, I have a cat too."

Declan and Currie Smith, bachelors, identical twins, carpenters, retired from forty years working in the mines, spent their time in good weather sitting on the veranda of the house they built themselves. They watched the tramcar make its routine trips and they watched people and the occasional car and truck pass along the roadway. Each knew everything the other was liable to say so there was little to stir them to articulate their thoughts. But the wonder of a nun, out alone, walking the tramcar tracks three sleepers at a step, her habit flapping in the wind behind her heels, was more than enough to stir them to brief conversation.

"If the tramcar is behind her, she's safe," Declan said. "It'll never catch up to that one."

"Yes," Currie said, "but pity the poor tramcar that's heading her way."

When she got to the school, she completed her class register, prepared the room for the next day's lessons and walked back. There was nobody in the glebe house when she got there. She put a pot roast on the stove, she peeled potatoes, carrots, turnips, and put them in pots of water to boil; she peeled apples and made a pie and put it in the oven. She swept the house from attic to basement, took out the pie, and washed windows until the roast was cooked. Still nobody home. She covered the roast and the pie with dishcloths against houseflies. She grabbed Father Rod's trench coat and a peaked cap from the hall-tree, shut off the back porch light, and entered the dark night. A crescent moon blinked briefly through a fissure in a dark cloud and reflected a sliver of light off the white cowl of her hood and then she vanished.

She headed for the ocean, following a path behind the company houses and using the picket fences as a guide. After the last picket, she knew she was on the barren cranberry land and she could hear the roar of the Atlantic hurling waves against the cliffs. She walked until she felt the spray on her face spewing over the edge of the cliff, then walked along the edge to the middle of the outfield of the ball field. She descended the stairs of boulders to the gravelled shore.

A cloud fled and the moon grimaced through the mottled sky. Sister Mary shed her clothes, piled them in a little tower at the base of the cliff, Father Rod's peaked cap and trench coat on the bottom, her bloomers and brassiere on the top, and she waded through the frigid water that swirled and eddied around the boulders that the ocean waves had wrenched from the cliff and rolled down the slope of the strand. Once beyond the boulders, Sister Mary dived, and when she surfaced she put into motion the rhythmical Australian crawl she had developed during the endless summers of her teenage youth, when she clawed her way through breaking waves on the way out, and skimmed over the menacing undertow on her way back to shore. In those days, nobody could swim with her. Nobody would dare. Her parents, even, gave up trying to dissuade her. She would start on the day school stopped, along with a few others who could stand the frigid June Atlantic Ocean. But every day as the water warmed and she got used to it, she swam farther and farther and before long she was beyond where anyone else would dare. Now, in June 1940, she found it worse, colder than she remembered.

Now, as then, she could feel her bone-blonde hair on her neck. Even after she had entered the convent, she kept her hair as long as she could get away with. She headed for Europe. But long before she reached her imagined destination, she stopped, let her feet fall, and treading water, she rode the swells and troughs. She waved to the lights of a ship steaming away from land, perhaps the ferry to Newfoundland, perhaps a boat heading for Labrador for a load of iron ore for the steel plant in Sydney, perhaps a coal boat heading for England. Good luck, she thought.

She knew there were German U-boats lurking in the near North Atlantic. If she were a spy, she'd go back to the glebe house and call her contact in Berlin on shortwave radio in the attic, like a resistance fighter in France. She recalled her favourite movie in which a French nun ran an orphanage by day and sent messages to England at night on a radio transmitter in the attic of the orphanage. She carried a hunting knife strapped to the calf of her leg; it came in handy when a German officer tried to rape her in the cattle barn of the farmers' market in the town. Sister Mary often wondered if the image of that nun stabbing that German officer nudged her into her vocation. She could be a spy. No one would suspect a nun in Canada. No one knew that her father changed his name from Bauer to Bower. When anyone asked him his national origin, he always said Irish, from County Lyre.

She rolled over on her back and her feet rose to the surface. She floated easily on the dense salt water, so easily she could clasp her hands behind her neck and lie back like a Saturday morning sleep-in the way she used to do day after day in the hot summers, sometimes an hour at a time, letting the daily doses of sunshine transform her white skin to a light mahogany. Eventually she had to lie on her belly on the beach and give her back equal time in the sun because the boys started to call her Two-Tone Tony.

Now, her body was blonde like her hair. White. She watched her breasts sprawling and lolling over her chest and she couldn't help but smile at the only two brown spots she could boast about, staggering around like two orphans let loose and free after two years of solitary confinement. Only God can see me here, she thought. She closed her eyes and imagined herself back in the classroom, back standing in front of Angelo's desk, and she raised her arm, letting the sleeve of her habit fall back, and she brought down her hand and rubbed the knuckle of her wrist along the down of his cheek, and when he looked up at her, his mouth opened, and letters, like smoke rings, came silently out, forming the bold black Latin words he had read from the *Collectio Rituum* this morning at Confirmation practice, the startling words so full of unintended meaning: *Domini, exaudi orationem meam. Et clamor meus ad te veniat*—Lord, hear my prayer. And let my cry come on to you. *Spiritus Sanctus superveniat in te. Vertus Altissimi custodiat te a peccatis*—May the Holy Ghost come down on you. The power above keep you from sin.

And Sister Mary raised the skirts of her habit and tented him in his desk. She opened her eyes and looked up at the cruel sky. "You're right," she said to God. "Better to think about it than to do it."

Sister Mary took a bearing on a lighthouse winking through the mist from a faraway cliff, and using her practised backstroke, rowed herself to shore.

Sister Mary was wrong about God. Indeed, God could see her and watched with interest. But not only God. Three sets of eyes, only one of them aware of the others, watched with interest. One set of eyes watched from the top of the stairs of boulders, waiting. Another set, farther along the beach, watched from the shadow of a ragged tree for a while and moved on when she saw the swimmer near the safety of cliffs. Another set of eyes stopped quickly and retreated when he saw the figure at the top of the stairs.

When Sister Mary rolled over to one side and side-stroked her way through the scattered boulders near the shore, Sister Sarah stepped down the bouldered stairway and waited. The moon reappeared for a moment and put down a carpet of white light, and Sister Mary rose from the water like a white goddess, laughing and crying, and splashed up the foaming slope and into the arms of her buddy, Sister Sarah.

Only one set of eyes watched with interest as the two women whirled together for a moment in the dance of those who dance because they don't quite know what to say or do, and then they came to a clinging halt. A black and white conundrum. Only one set of puzzled eyes, besides God's. But then God, being a spirit, would not, strictly speaking, have a set of eyes. So, just one set of eyes, although God's spiritual, virtual eye was cocked, so to speak. A cloud closed over the moon like a winking eyelid.

"Do you realize, Sister Mary, that you are naked?"

"Yes, I do. Can't you feel me shiver?"

"But why are you naked?"

"Well, I couldn't go swimming in all that regalia."

"But why did you go swimming?"

"Oh my God. Because I touched that boy."

"What boy?"

"Angelo."

"Angelo. From Confirmation class, Gelo?"

"Yes."

"You touched him?"

"Yes."

"You touched him where?"

"On the finger, on his knuckle."

"What? You touched him on the knuckle?"

"I touched his knuckle."

"You touched his knuckle. So you went for a swim in the North Atlantic Ocean. Alone. At night. That certainly makes sense to me. Anybody would do the same thing. What are you talking about?" Sister Sarah reached down and pulled Father Rod's trench coat from under the pile of clothing and pulled it cape-like over Sister Mary's shoulders. She picked his peaked cap from the gravel and put it on her head. They had been friends since childhood and she knew she would get a satisfactory answer sooner or later. She embraced her for warmth and let her garments soak up the water dripping from her body. "Why in the name of God didn't you bring a towel? We have to get you dry and get your clothes back on."

"I feel terrible," Sister Mary said.

"You feel terrible. You touched his knuckle and you feel terrible. I feel like I'm talking to a pupil in grade two. So. There's more to this than meets the eye."

"His knuckle touched me."

"He touched you, with his knuckle."

"Yes."

"Where?"

"My thing."

"What thing? This thing?"

"No. The other thing."

"The little brat. I'd like to touch him with some of my knuckles."

"It was my fault. No, not my fault I guess but ..."

"But," Sister Sarah said, "but what?"

"I liked it," Sister Mary said.

"You liked it. What does that mean? Are you telling me he came right up and grabbed you and you liked it?"

"No. It wasn't like that. It might have been an accident. But I liked it. I felt like touching him back."

"But you didn't."

"No. I sent him out. But I told him to come back after school. Oh my God. I told him we had to get something straight between us."

"Mother of God, Mary, do you know what you're saying half the time?"

"Yes. I'm afraid I do."

"Put your clothes back on. We have to get back to the warm kitchen." Sister Sarah picked the clothes up from the gravel strand one at a time and handed them to her until she was fully clothed. With her habit and Father Rod's trench coat on, her shivering stopped. After exposure to the cold air and the colder water, she felt relatively warm and except for her hair she was dry. They climbed the stone steps together.

"So did he come back after school?"

"I don't know. I imagine. But I took off. I went back to our school and did my work and came back and put supper on, and cleaned the house. Then I went for a walk. Then I went for a swim. And I'm still not tired. That poor boy."

"Poor boy, my arse. He probably loved it. It's poor you I'm worried about."

As they walked up the boulder steps, a pair of eyes retreated into the cranberry barren. When she saw the two nuns come over the edge of the cliff and walk back along the edge, their arms over each other's shoulders, she followed them until they entered the back door of the glebe house, and she turned around and continued on home, wondering at the things she never expected to see when she left Italy and came to Canada.

FIVE

Were man never to fall,
he would be a God;
were he never to aspire,
he would be a brute.

WILLIAM LYON MACKENZIE KING

ONCE WE GOT ACROSS THE OCEAN, *Tomassio never once brought it up I lied to him. He played baseball but he never got paid because he was a local. Maybe he forgot, but I doubt it. I think what it was he just liked it here so much. Just like me. Once I got across that water, I said to myself, I'm here. This is where I am. I could already speak English okay, and before anybody ever heard of Mussolini I was talking like a Cape Bretoner. My friend Ceit taught me. I never learned her Scottish brogue, but I lost my Italian sound. I never joined the Italian Association. I never hung around with the Hall crowd. They coaxed me but I said, "Look, I didn't come to Canada to be an Italian." Of course, I couldn't stop talking with my hands. I could never talk like Ceit. The only thing moves on her is her mouth. And even her mouth is near closed. Even when she laughs. Inside her mouth, her tongue jumps around like a loose board on a dump cart once she gets it going. But me, I can't talk without even my toes are on the go. And Tomassio was the same. We got talking in the kitchen, we looked like two windmills on a trampoline. That's what Ceit said.*

Once the war started the mines were going full tilt, day and night, and Tomassio's buddy in the pit was just as strong as he was so they made good money loading coal. But even before the war, with the men getting maybe two or three shifts a week, money was scarce, but he could play baseball on the days off. He'd help with the garden if I asked him. He'd hunt. He'd fish. We always had rabbits or deer or moose, or trout or smelts. We'd salt the meat and the fish. We could keep our potatoes and carrots in the root cellar through most of the winter. We could buy blueberries and strawberries and raspberries from the children who came around selling them to make movie money. We never had a problem getting a bite to eat. So we got along fine. Some people didn't like Tomassio's arrogance. I didn't like it myself. But he was such a good baseball player, just as good as the American imports, and such a good man in the pit, they didn't call it arrogance, they called it bravado, because he pleased them. Of course, the women loved him, and I kept a sharp eye out but I never saw anything to make me suspicious except twice. The second time didn't leave much room for doubt.

The first time happened in the Co-op. He was in dry goods, Cathy in there with him, and he was chatting her up and she was laughing, having a good time. He was always doing that to some woman or other so I was only half on the alert. But then I was pulling bananas from the banana stock hanging in the corner and I could hear them and at the same time I could see Ump, her husband, watching from another part of the store. His real name was Wilfred MacLeod, but everybody called him Ump because he was so serious about his job as a baseball umpire. Sometimes even off the ball field he'd wear a baseball cap backwards on his head. It was like he was ready to call a ball or a strike on somebody every minute of his life. Cathy and Tomassio couldn't see him. They didn't know he was watching. He was livid. When she came to the counter, she had a pair of gloves and when the cashier picked them up to check the price, Ump stuck his arm over her and grabbed the gloves from the cashier and put them in Cathy's hand.

"Put them back."

"I need gloves," she said.

"Put them back." His face was red, puffed up.

She threw the gloves on the floor at her feet and ran from the store. Talk about embarrassing. I felt sorry for her. Of course, I was quite interested in this go-ahead, but I knew Ump hated Tomassio and he was the type of person who liked to hit things he didn't like. And when he hated somebody, he hated everything connected to them. I know he picked on Gelo on the ball field, and Gelo was going out with his daughter, or at least he was until Ump put a stop to it, though I didn't think they'd be stopped for long. So I was more worried than suspicious. To this day I don't know if they were carrying on at the time. Maybe that day was the start of it.

It was Tomassio's bravado that put Ump off. To him it was nothing but arrogance. And once Tomassio realized that Ump minded him, he taunted him. He'd brag about it to me in the kitchen when he had his tea after work. I didn't like it. Tomassio and his buddy always loaded more coal than anybody else. When they came up, Tomassio would wait until they were all under the showers in the wash house and he'd say, "Hey Ump, how much you guys load today?"

"Oh about ten, how about yourself?" Everybody waited for the answer.

But the answer never came. I could just picture it. All those men standing around in their bare bums, dripping soap and water, waiting for the answer that would never come. Everybody knew the answer, it hung in the steamy air like the smell of sour milk.

"You're building up for a payback," I'd say, but he'd just laugh and go upstairs for his nap.

Then when Ump became a shot-fire, he'd find every kind of excuse to delay shooting Tomassio's coal. But even so Tomassio and his buddy would load more than anybody else. It just took a little more time. His buddy was Jim McMahon. Ump hated him too. Not just because he was Tomassio's buddy. Jim was a big union man, and of course Ump was a company man. Jim was a great talker and nobody could beat him in an argument. He talked very quiet so people had to lean in to him to hear him. And after he got the last word, he'd smile. He had a smile like Tomassio's walk. Between the two of them, they could make a lot of people mad.

But it was on the ball field that Tomassio really made Ump furious, because the whole town would be watching. I don't think Tomassio would have done it in public if Ump didn't treat him so bad in the pit. I went to all the ball games. I loved baseball. But of course I couldn't play baseball in Coaltown any more than I could play soccer in Italy, except in the street or somebody's back yard with the kids. But I went to all the games and I saw it all. Ump was an umpire but sometimes he was a catcher for the New Waterford team. Tomassio was nearly always getting hits and when he got on first base he always stole second. Ump could never throw him out. That was bad enough, but Tomassio would taunt him, taking too big a lead off first when the catcher had the ball, and if he threw to first base Tomassio would run to second. Sometimes Tomassio would beat the throw to second with so much time to spare he'd stop a step before the base and step on it just as the second baseman caught the ball. Once he did a cartwheel on the way to second and still beat the throw. The manager benched him for two weeks and that cooled him down quite a bit. But nobody ever forgot that cartwheel, especially Ump. And every time after, when Tomassio got on base, the whole crowd waited for him to do it again. He never did. But he always stole second base when Ump was catching. And to make matters worse, Ump got so frustrated and nervous every time Tomassio got on first, he'd throw the ball in the dirt, or over the player's head at second and into centre field. Then Tomassio would steal third and sometimes come all the way to home plate and slide in, and there he'd be, right under Ump's nose, the umpire with his arms spread out like wings calling him safe, and him with an arrogant smile all over his face. I asked him once, "How come

Ump can never catch you stealing? Other catchers do now and again."

"After you jump across an ocean, Anna," he said, "stealing second base is not a big problem. And Ump, well, he's not like the others. The others, they love to catch me stealing, they love to throw me out, but Ump, he needs to, he wants to so bad, way too bad, because for him it's more than baseball. For the others, it's only baseball."

But there was a lot more to it than baseball.

When Ump was the umpire, Tomassio would never do any of those things because he knew if it was close Ump would call him out, even if it wasn't all that close. And Ump never once, not once ever got the chance to call him out. So it's no wonder he hated him.

Of course, by then I was in love with Tomassio myself, even though I only married him to get to Canada. Like me, Tomassio was a much better Cape Bretoner than he was an Italian, even though, not like me, he looked and talked like an Italian, and shot his mouth off like an arrogant Italian. But we were a happy family. And we loved our boy Gelo.

But of course. Well. It was predictable enough, I guess. I was hoping it was just an Italy thing. I was on my walk across the beach, my shoes in my hands, enjoying the splash and suck of the waves breaking on the sand and foaming back to the sea. It was warm and hazy but I could see everything clearly and I saw a car. On the opposite side of the beach from where people swam there was a wide stretch of flat sand and the water was warm and shallow. People dug clams there at low tide, and mothers took little kids and let them wade in the water, and people parked their cars there. The sand was always wet and hard and you could drive a car to the end of the beach where the bridge crossed the channel to Lingan. I never before saw a car there that early in the morning. I worried maybe somebody died in it overnight. So I went down off the ridge. When I got to it I recognized the car. It was Ump's car. And there in the back seat were the two of them, sound asleep, Tomassio and Cathy. I thought he was at work. He was on back shift. His lunch can open on the front seat. My sandwiches and date squares gone. The tea bottle half empty. A Lover's Moonlight Feast.

I climbed back up on the ridge and kept walking. I could feel my chin tightening. My heart felt like a fist full of knuckles. I could think of nothing to do but what I always do. Walk. I walked to the end of the beach and over the iron bridge and up along the wharf on the Lingan side of the channel. Only a few fishermen were still around getting their boats and gear ready because they always went out early in the morning. Mostly lobster boats and swordfishing boats. The swordfishing boats had a little platform sticking out over the bow where a fisherman would stand with the harpoon ready to spear the swordfish. I always thought, if only I didn't mind boats, that's the job I'd like. I could just see myself out on that platform, flinging the harpoon, the line flying after it, singing past my ear.

On that morning, scared or not, I would have braved the boat ride if it would have given me the chance to harpoon who I felt like harpooning, a creature with a stiff sword out the front that I'd like to puncture and deflate.

At the end of the wharf I turned to walk back. I realized right away that scared or not, I would just as soon get on a boat and ride the ocean as walk back over that beach. A fisherman looked up at me out of his boat and called out. It was Kurt. Normally he wouldn't be there that time in the morning. He'd already be out fishing. But since the war started, he never went out until daylight. They were watching him because he was a German. So he wanted to make sure they saw every move he made. They watched him from the artillery post out on the Lingan headland.

"Hello, Anna," Kurt yelled, sticking his head out the doorway of the boat's cabin.

"Hi, Kurt, how's the fishing?"

"Pretty good. We're keeping alive," he said. I knew by the look on his face that he knew something was wrong with me.

"Here, Anna, take these lobsters home, you and Tomassio have a feast."

"Thanks."

"Where's your smile this morning, Anna?"

"I left it on the beach."

"Well, pick it up on the way back, you look even better when you got it on."

"Thanks, Kurt."

"Here. Have a snort of rum. It'll keep you company on the way back."

"Thanks."

"Go ahead, take another one. It's a long way back."

He was right. It was a long way back. The rum was good company. My chin loosened up, and my heart unknuckled, for a while. The edge of the sun came up and I could see clearly, but I noticed nothing except that the car was gone. Maybe the waves were gone too because I never saw or heard them. Maybe the Atlantic Ocean itself was gone for all I knew.

I was in the kitchen at the ironing, doing yesterday's sheets and shirts when my husband landed, his pit can under his arm.

"You look rested," I said.

"Easy shift," he said. "Ump finally blasted the coal the way I want it. Maybe he's changing his attitude toward me."

"And no wonder," I said. He was right beside me but he was poking and clanking at the stove to hurry up the kettle and he didn't hear me or wasn't listening.

"How did you like the date squares?" I said.

"Delicious."

"I hope you ate them all yourself and didn't feed them to your rat."

"Now, Anna, you know I don't have a special rat. A rat's a rat."

"That's not what I heard. I heard the miners can tell one rat from another, and they all have a special rat they feed the ends of their sandwiches to."

"Who told you that?" he said, pouring a handful of tea into the pot and filling it with boiling water.

"Ceit told me that."

"Oh yeah. Joe. Yeah, he got a special rat. Feeds all the rats but he saves the sweets for his pet." He shook the teapot a few times to hurry up the steeping.

"*That sounds more like you than Joe. And does his rat like date squares?*"

"*Oh yeah. Rats, they love date squares.*" Tomassio poured his tea and took the cup and headed for the stairs. "*I'm a little pooped,*" he said. "*I think I'll take my tea and go up for a nap. I'll take the storm windows off this afternoon.*"

"*You're pooped,*" I said. "*I'm not surprised. Yes, the storm windows can wait. And you never know, we might be in for another storm.*"

"*Where'd you get the lobsters?*" he asked, as he turned to go up with his hand on the newel post.

"*Lingan,*" I said. "*I took a walk across the beach.*"

"*Are they for supper?*"

"*I was planning them for supper,*" I said, "*but I might make sandwiches for your can. Lobster goes good with tea. Does your rat like lobster?*"

I listened to his steps up the stairs. Halfway up he stopped. I heard his teacup crash. I could see his legs through the struts of the stairs and his hand with the saucer on his knee. Then I could almost hear the silence of him stopped on the stair. I could see his free hand grip onto the banister, then slide up the rest of the way out of sight. I listened to his slow steps down the hall and our bedroom door shut behind him. I hung over the stove and boiled the kettle for more tea, the palms of my hands on the warming oven above the stove, the steam from the kettle wetting my face, the water mixed with tears dropping from my chin, sizzling on the stove covers. All I could think of was my mother bawling and shaking, sitting with her head on the kitchen table. It was the only way I remembered my mother ever since I left her in Italy. I tried to get her to come to Canada. I thought if I could see her every day for a while maybe I could shake her out of my head. Of course, once the war started she couldn't come, even before Mussolini.

For the rest of the week I set the breakfasts out before I went for my walk and I stayed away longer. By the time I got home Gelo was gone to school and Tomassio was in bed. I couldn't bear the sight of either one of them. On Saturday night Tomassio got in bed behind me. He put his hand on my hip. That was our signal. If I was in the mood, I would take his hand and pull it in front of me. If not, I would just rest my hand on his and leave it there. On that night I took his hand and pushed it back until it was on his own hip. I took my hand back. We both lay rigid for a long time. Then I said: "I think one woman should be enough. Even if you do have to share with her husband."

Our marriage was torn apart. I think we could have mended it. Why did it happen? I don't know. I could understand her, married to that brute. It was all he could do to be civil to his own daughter, God only knows what he was like to his wife. Even the bit of him I saw in action in the Co-op was bad enough. But Tomassio? He didn't spend a lot of time at home but that wasn't unusual. When he was home, we always got along great. We enjoyed ourselves alone together. He was nice to me, and I loved him now, and I'm pretty sure he loved me. And Cathy, it wasn't as though she was something different. She was the same size as me, she even looked like me. What was it? Did he feel sorry for her? Sometimes I wonder if he suspected I married him just to get to Canada. If that bothered him. But I was always good to him. And once we got here, once I didn't need him, I did fall in love with him. He was a show-off but he was a good man. Or maybe Cathy in her loneliness just presented herself, and maybe once the possibility presented itself it was a dare he couldn't resist. I don't know.

Yes, I think we could have mended our marriage. But then Mussolini butted in. The Mounties just came and took him. I was never so cross at myself in my life, just sitting there almost speechless and totally useless. It's a good thing Ceit was there, at least she gave them some lip. But what could I do anyway? Even the priest could only soften the situation. He couldn't stop it. I liked him though, that priest. Perhaps a little too much.

SIX

✠

…some countries have too much history,
we have too much geography.
WILLIAM LYON MACKENZIE KING

GELO WALKED THE TRAMCAR tracks after catechism class at school and turned the corner
where the main street, Coal Road, intersected
with his street, Belgium Town Road. It was a narrow length
of cinder ash, lined on either side by an open drain, a picket
fence, and two rows of duplex company houses. The drain
took water from the road and the waste from the kitchen
sinks. In front of each house, two wooden bridges crossed
the drain to gates in the picket fence. The cinder road
drained well, and since only an occasional truck or a horse
and cart drove over it to make a delivery, it served as a dry,
mud-free playground for innumerable cohorts of children.
The road was hard on the hands, the knees and elbows, but
kinder than muddy Coal Road to the grateful mothers who
did the laundry by hand and tried to dry it on backyard
clothes lines, on sunny days, during the few hours when a

lucky wind blew soot from the colliery smoke stacks in somebody else's direction.

He stopped for a moment to watch the parade of human horses. Two groups of children, with their feet jammed into empty condensed-milk cans so that the top and bottom of the cans glomerated to the bottom and sides of their sneakers and gumboots. For the sake of symmetry and distinction, the six boys wore Carnation Condensed Milk cans sporting a bouquet of carnations on the label, while the six girls wore Borden Condensed cans with a white contented cow on the label. Beneath the cow, the label proclaimed that the Borden Company took its milk only from contented cows. The label didn't say why the cow was white. The horseshoe cans transformed the children into stallions and mares. On the ashes the metal sounds were little more than scrapes, but once up on the tram tracks, the children mounted the steel rails, mares on one, stallions on the other, and they clanged along, tin against steel, sounding and looking like a double team of circus ponies on their hind legs, dressed in skirts and pants. When they got the rhythm right they started to sing.

> She'll be riding six white horses when she comes,
>   when she comes
> She'll be riding six white horses when she comes
> She'll be riding six white horses, she'll be riding six
>   white horses
> She'll be riding six white horses, when she comes.

They continued down the tracks, doing their best to stay on the rails. When the tramcar turned the corner at the bottom of the street, heading toward them, they began to chant.

Oh, we'll all go out to meet her when she comes,
    when she comes
Oh, we'll all go out to meet her when she comes
Oh, we'll all go out to meet her, oh, we'll all go out to
    meet her
Oh, we'll all go out to meet her, when she comes.

They continued their dance until the conductor braked to a stop. He was used to this forbidden performance and greeted it with benevolent annoyance.

Gelo left the tramcar tracks and turned down Belgium Town Road, slamming the ball into his glove to the rhythm of his walk. He was content. Because Sister Mary, with her big laugh, forgave him for his joke at her expense, he thought it might be all right to absolve himself for tricking her into touching him. Still, the sisters decreed confession before Confirmation to be compulsory and the two sins would come in handy. But he decided to downgrade the seriousness of the sin. Mortal sins involving body parts invited probing questions for embarrassing details and required awkward explanations and the use of words not sanctioned in conversation with priests. He would confess to an impure thought rather than an impure touch. After all, it was Sister Mary who touched him. He knew that impure thoughts were common fare in confession and would likely be passed over as routine. Impure thoughts didn't hurt anybody. He wouldn't be surprised if Father Rod himself didn't have a few now and again. He was content.

Gelo had never heard of the War Measures Act. Even with his Italian heritage, he had barely heard of Mussolini. He had heard of Hitler and he knew the war was on and that his cousin Franco, who got on the train to go to college to be a priest, didn't get off in Antigonish, but kept on to Halifax and joined the army, and went to war instead, and now he was walking around on crutches, drunk and talking to himself and yelling at people.

Sometimes Gelo would drop by the barbershop when it wasn't busy and read the newspaper. Some Saturdays he would sneak into the wash house between shift changes and take a shower and read the papers if there were any lying around, but he'd only read the sports pages or if he had any money he'd look to see what was on at the movies in Glace Bay. If they could find a seat at the back of the theatre, Sadie would let him put his arm around her shoulders. Last Saturday night they were watching some movie and some woman was singing and he wasn't paying much attention, wondering if he should go out for popcorn, and Sadie turned to him. "Listen," she said. But he only heard two lines, "I'd rather be lonely than happy with somebody else," because she was looking straight into his eyes and his hand on her shoulder started to sweat. And then she almost let him kiss her. She turned away but she put her hand up to her shoulder and took hold of his and pulled it down to her bare arm. If her father came into the theatre, he wouldn't be able to see them at the back, or if they were in the balcony at the back, they could see him come in the door and duck down.

Gelo had noticed on the front page of the *Sydney Post-Record* the maps of Europe with the names France, Belgium, Holland, Germany, Norway, and Denmark on the front page with little pictures of tanks and planes and ships lined up in groups and little flags stuck in the middle of them, but he never paid enough attention to figure out what it was all about. In the evenings at home he would sit on the floor by the radio doing his homework, listening to "L for Lankie," and following the serial exploits of the Lancaster Bomber crew, young men not much older than himself. He held his breath as the bombardier in the nose turret of the plane guided the pilot over the target while the tail gunner and the top turret gunner fended off Messerschmitts and Stukas. As cool as icicles. "A bit to the left . . . that's it . . . hold it . . . hold it . . ." and then, "Bombs away, okay, skipper, take 'er up and get us out of here. I've got a date with Rosie at eight in the Sergeant's Mess and if I'm late I'll put the blame on you."

"Well, you might be late, bucko, the flack took out my right port engine, we'll be limping home." And then, "Dive, skipper, dive, two Gerries on our tail."

Machine gun fire, roaring engines. Silence. "Are you okay, Pete?"

"I'm okay. I got one. But the other one's underneath us."

"Oh-oh. Hear that. Starboard engine gone. It's on fire. Chart us a straight trip home, navigator Joe, and Sparky, contact the base, tell them where we are. If we don't make it we'll have to ditch."

"Mayday, mayday, this is L for Lankie, L for Lankie, mayday, mayday. Over and out."

And then the theme song. "Coming in on a wing and a prayer, coming in on a wing and a prayer/Why, we've one motor gone, but we'll still carry on/Coming in on a wing and a prayer . . ."

And then the commercial with Sad Sam the B.O. Man or Sad Sadie the B.O. Lady, achieving social acceptance by virtue of their conversion to the right soap:

Singing in the bathtub, singing for joy
Living the life of Lifebuoy
Can't help singing 'cause I know.
Lifebuoy really stops B.O.

And then. Wait for next week; will they ditch or will they make it back to England?

Had Gelo visited the wash house today he wouldn't be able to miss the front page of the *Sydney Post-Record* which someone had nailed to the wall:

IL DUCE PLUNGES
ITALY INTO WAR

ROME, June 10—(AP)—Italy joined Germany tonight in war against Great Britain and France.

Premier Mussolini made the announcement to Fascists gathered throughout Italy, that the fateful declaration had been handed to the Allied ambassadors.

The formal welding of the Rome-Berlin axis in the steel of war was set officially for tomorrow, but Berlin reports claimed Italian troops already had entered France through the Riviera.

Gelo was never in the house when the news was on the radio. Like his father, he visited the house for bed and board. He saw the Newsreel Movietone News at the theatre but he paid little attention to it. Sadie berated him for his inattention but he didn't care. He was called wop, Dago, and bohunk more often now, and not so often in jest, but he brushed it off. He learned from his Indian friends how to deal with it. It was only scum. It washed off. It thickened your skin. He was content. He was not prepared for the shock of the afternoon. The shock of his life.

Gelo kicked open the gate with the toe of his gumboot, strode through the picket fence surrounding his front yard, up the path between the rows of marigolds, climbed the front doorsteps on his side of the company house, and as he pushed it open with foot and hand, caught a glimpse of an RCMP car turning the corner at Coal Road, rumbling over the tram tracks, and heading down the Belgium Town Road. He needed a bite to eat. Then he'd head for ball practice. But he'd check out the Mounties first.

When the front door burst open, Anna looked up from her task in the kitchen, beating egg whites and dropping them into gallon hanks of red wine. She was in a temper. In most Italian families the men made the wine. But her husband, Tomassio, as she often complained to Red Ceit, her next-door neighbour and best friend, couldn't or wouldn't stand still long enough to make a milkshake let alone spend the time to see wine from grape to bottle. In fact, complaining to Red Ceit is what Anna was doing when Gelo flung open the front door.

"And the few times he did make the wine it tasted like paint."

Anna knew the secrets of making good wine. She had learned from her mother, who had also married a man who couldn't keep still or stay in the house any longer than it took to tie his shoelaces. The secrets of making good wine were simple, but you could not get them past a deaf ear. From her position in the kitchen, she could see Gelo burst through the front door.

"What'd I tell you a thousand times? Don't use the front door. Get those gumboots off right there or get out and go around to the back."

"I'm going right out. Chuck me an apple."

"Chuck me an apple," she mimicked. "Chuck me an apple," she repeated to Ceit, who was standing warming her hands over the kitchen stove. Giving her son a stern look, she said, "You get in here and eat, and don't you dare track mud over my clean floor. Wait till I get newspapers."

"I gotta go. The Mounties are up the street. I gotta go see what's going on."

"Eat first. Spaghetti. In the pantry. I told you not to use that door. Go around."

"I forgot. I haven't got time for spaghetti. Gimme an apple. I haven't got time to go around."

"What did I do to deserve the likes of this child?" Anna was looking at Ceit but she was addressing the gods. "He talks back to his own mother. I spend half the day cooking and he wants an apple. You forgot. You forget everything. You forget that I have to spend all day working so you won't starve to death. You can't be bothered, that's what your problem is. If I have to wash that floor again I'll scream."

Suddenly the back and front doors burst open and RCMP officers filled the doorways. Anna, Ceit, and Gelo froze in their spaces. Anna, one knee on the floor, half a broken egg in each hand, was in the process of separating the white from the yoke and letting it flow down to one of the cereal bowls by her knee. She looked over her shoulder and stared agape at the uniformed presence in her back doorway. Ceit froze over the stove, the boiling water she was pouring into the teapot filling it, overflowing it. The overflow danced and sizzled on the hot lids. Gelo, halfway across the front room toward the kitchen, stopped, then stepped back as if pushed by the uniformed man in the back doorway. Instinctively, he turned to run and again froze at the sight of the officer filling the front doorway.

The officer at the back door crossed his arms over his chest as if to further bar the door. His mouth twisted in a derisive grin, his head swung slowly, eyes scanning in mock wonder, the rooms, the domestic paraphernalia, the creatures, framed in their fear.

"Get in here and sit down," he ordered Gelo. "At the table."

"You, off your knees and sit at the table. And Ceit, you get on the couch there by the stove."

"Gelo, go get the priest," Anna said in a stage whisper.

"Nobody goes anywhere. Sit and stay put." The officer's menacing eyes and mouth forced Gelo to a chair at the table.

"Where's your husband?"

Anna stared. She'd heard rumours the Mounties would "round up Italians" after Mussolini got into the war with Hitler. Was this it?

"Who wants to know?" Ceit shot at him from the couch where she'd sat herself down in an uncharacteristic moment of intimidation.

"I want to know," the officer replied with an extra surge of menace.

"And who are you?"

"You know perfectly well who I am."

"Yes. I know who you are, you big tub of lard. You're the brave man that beat up that boy at the rink last Saturday. I suppose I should be scared too. I wouldn't put it past you to beat up on a woman, if she wouldn't be too big and tough for you."

He turned to Anna. "Where's your husband?"

"I don't know."

The Mountie put his hands on the table and leaned over Anna. She put her hands over her face, her elbows on the table. "Was he home today? He's not at work."

"He went to work."

"You just said you didn't know where he was."

"I don't know where he is. Did you try the Italian Hall?"

"What do you think?" the Mountie asked.

Ceit twisted her face in derision at his sarcasm. "Nice talk," she said.

"What did he do?" Anna said.

"Nothing, yet, I hope."

"Nothing—what do you want with him?" Ceit demanded. "Did you come bursting in here for nothing?"

The officer ignored Ceit. The second officer at the front door stood with his hands behind his back, barely able to conceal his embarrassment. He straightened up, pursed his lips, and looked at the floor.

"If you know where he is, you better tell us. If not, it'll be so much the worse for him if we have trouble apprehending him. We've come to put him under arrest," the first Mountie said to Anna.

"What did he do?"

"Nothing that we know about yet."

"What are you doing here then?" Ceit demanded again. The officer ignored her.

"He's under arrest for nothing?" Anna said.

"Suspicion," the officer said.

"Suspicion of what?"

"Espionage."

"What's that?"

"Spying."

"Spying? Tomassio? A spy?"

"Of course he's a spy," said Ceit. "I heard him just last week, on the phone, down at the Co-op. He was calling Mussolini. He was giving him the names of all the ballplayers on his team. And their middle initials. Come Christmas, Benito's going to send them all a card."

"That's enough out of you, Ceit. Shut up."

The noise from Anna's breathing was beginning to get their attention. Her breath was rasping over her throat on the way into her lungs and moaning through her nose on the way out. She put her hand over her heart. "Gelo," she gasped, "go get my pills in the pantry."

Gelo leaped from his chair and dashed to the pantry. He knew his mother had no pills in the pantry or anywhere else in the house. "Spaghetti is my pill," she told Ceit whenever her friend urged her to make the whole family take cod liver oil. "Olive is my oil," Anna would say, "just like Popeye."

Gelo slipped the hooks off the window screen in the pantry, straddled the windowsill, dropped to the ground, and ran to the ball field. Except for Ceit's laugh, silence filled the kitchen while they waited for Gelo not to come back with the pills.

Tomassio had learned he was fired when he went to pick up his check number at the check-weighman's wicket at the beginning of his shift, and he was in a foul mood.

"Sorry. Your check number's reassigned."

"What?"

"Sorry," the check-weighman said. "Don't blame me. I just do what I'm told."

"What are you talking about? What does this mean?"

"I guess it means you're fired."

"Fired? For what?"

"You better talk to the underground manager."

"Where is he?"

"He's underground. What do you think? Now, if he was the overground manager he'd be someplace else."

"That's very funny, Joe. I'll laugh when I get my job back."

Tomassio took the rake down and scoured the levels but could find the manager nowhere. He could find nobody who'd tell him where to look. He went home.

When Tomassio's shadow fell through the kitchen window and onto the floor as he approached his back door, the officer moved forward a step, the door opened, and Tomassio entered, the edge of his swagger somewhat blunted. He saw Ceit on the couch by the stove. He saw Anna in a chair at the table. Then he saw the officer at the front door, and he felt the hands from behind on his shoulders, and he knew, and he began to turn and to swing when the hands came down and the officer's arms encircled his body, trapping his arms against his ribs.

But Tomassio's arms, strengthened by fifteen years of loading coal with a pan shovel, flung off the officer's arms like two noodles of spaghetti. Then he reached back and wrapped his hands around the officer's neck and somersaulted him to the floor, straddled him, and sat on his chest, pinning his arms at the wrists to the floor. The other officer jumped on Tomassio's back.

Father Rod arrived, wearing a sweatshirt and the pants of an old ball uniform. He came in the front door with Gelo. His black eye patch and Boston Red Sox ball cap combined to give him the look of a jaunty pirate in a movie for children. Gelo jumped the officer on Tomassio's back and started to pull him off, but the officer turned on him and pinned him to the wall with his billy club. He stared Gelo in the eye and said, "This is bad enough, son, don't make it worse."

Father Rod put his hand on Tomassio's shoulder.

"Let him up, Tommie. Let's get this straightened out."

"I think Tomassio got him straightened out pretty good already, Father," Ceit said.

"Let's keep it calm and cool, Ceit. Don't fan the fire."

The officer's face was crimson. The menace in his eyes turned to frustration and rage.

"*Och s'bochd sin*, Dick," said Ceit.

"Let the boy go," Father Rod said to the other officer, whose billy club was still under Gelo's chin, pinning him to the wall. The officer backed away. "Sit on the couch next to Ceit, Gelo. Tomassio, you get up and sit with Ceit and Gelo."

Everyone obeyed the priest. His authority restored order and calm to the kitchen and seemed to promise a solution, but everyone remained poised and apprehensive. He put his hands in his back pockets and heaved a disappointed sigh, as if he were dealing with a schoolyard brawl. "So, officer, what's going on?" he asked the senior Mountie.

"We have orders to arrest this man."

"On what charge?"

"Yeah, well, now the charge is resisting arrest."

"What charge did you come here with?"

"Suspicion of espionage."

"What? Tommie?"

"If you want an explanation, you'll have to ask my superiors."

For the first time in his life Tomassio looked defeated. He turned to Anna, "they took my check number today and now they're taking me."

"Where are you going with him?" Father Rod asked.

"Right now, we're taking him downtown to the detachment."

"I'll follow you down in my car. Tommie can ride with me, if that's all right."

"You'll guarantee to deliver him?" the Mountie said.

"Yes. And don't worry, Anna. We'll get this straightened out."

"And when we get this straightened out," the Mountie said, "we'll be back to see about bootlegging. If I'm not mistaken, we've stumbled onto a wine-making operation here."

"Come on, officer, why don't you limit yourself to one rotten project a day," Father Rod said. And they were gone, and Anna got up from the table and began to tend her wine.

"My God, Ceit. What will I do if they take him? I got no money of my own. And that Mountie is gonna come back and take my wine, which I could sell if I had to. Where's Gelo?"

"He went out. Maybe he went with them. Give me the wine, Anna. I'll take it to my sister's place in Reserve. They'll search my place next if they can't find it here. You say you got scared and spilled it out. I don't think it's against the law to make your own wine anyway. He just gets a kick out of scaring people. But he might take it anyway. Looks like they can do anything they want these days. You better give me Tomassio's gun too. I heard they're confiscating guns from all the aliens."

"Aliens. Is that what they're calling us?"

"You know Jim D'Angelo. He was born in New Waterford. I just heard someone the other day saying, 'Take Jim now, he said. 'He'll have to go. He's an enemy alien. Poor bastard. Oh well.' He said, 'It'll clear off a good job for somebody. I wouldn't mind it myself.' Can you imagine that?"

"I can now." Anna said.

"It's our own people saying it, not just the Mounties," Ceit said. "That's the worst of it. It's people's own neighbours. If you can imagine that. They're bothering the kids at school. They're bothering the ones that own stores and they're bothering the miners in the pit. But don't worry, Anna, we'll manage."

"Thank God you're here, Ceit. But what can we do? Your own man is laid up hurt."

Ceit said, "You've only got the one child, thank God. Think of the ones with half a dozen or more. Quite a few like that. I got none home myself now, and the boys are working, they'll help out."

"Maybe Father Rod would give me a job, Ceit."

"Housekeeper. He doesn't have a housekeeper?" Ceit queried.

"No. The housekeeper went with Father Chaisson. I guess this one didn't have a housekeeper to take with him. Father Pat told me he's never had a housekeeper. Doesn't want one. Father Pat said it's always the ones that need them the most that don't have them."

"Isn't that the way of it," Ceit said. "You can imagine what he eats. And wears, for that matter. Did you see what he had on today?"

"I'll ask Father Pat. Maybe he can talk him into it."

"And if he wouldn't, maybe he'd buy your wine. The church uses up a bit of wine."

"Maybe I'll get Gelo to take it up to the glebe house. If he won't buy it, he might keep it for me so the Mounties won't get it."

"Who knows, though, maybe Father Rod will fetch Tomassio back."

"Even so, then what? You heard him say he was fired."

"I hear some of the men started a bootleg pit over behind Cohen's store. Perhaps he could get on with them till this foolishness blows over."

"You think it'll blow over?"

"Surely to God they're gonna wise up soon. There's some people will use any excuse to lord it over the rest. It makes cowards feel like heroes, I guess. If they want to fight Mussolini, why don't they join the army and go to where

Mussolini is, like Franco did, instead of picking on poor coal miners. Why do they do it, Anna?"

Anna could not answer the question, but she began to think about it.

✝   ✝   ✝

"Why are you doing this?" Father Rod asked the RCMP officer in charge of the detachment.

Sergeant Archimbault sat behind his desk, leaning back in his chair, his elbows on the armrests, the thumb of his left hand under his chin, his left forefinger between his teeth. He levelled a look at Father Rod as if wondering how frank he could be. After a long silence, he said, "Between you and me, it's crazy, but I have no choice. Yesterday Prime Minister Mackenzie King broadcast a message on the radio about Italy entering the war. Did you hear it?"

"I heard about it."

"He said that the Minister of Justice authorized the Royal Canadian Mounted Police to intern all residents of Italian origin if there is reasonable suspicion they might endanger the safety of the state. Personally, I don't suspect anybody in Coaltown but Ottawa gave us names. We have no choice but to—round them up—is the term they used."

"Round up who?"

"It's supposed to be Fascists, but I can't find any Fascists."

"So what's the point?"

"We have our theories. They've got fascist organizations in Montreal and Toronto. The leaders are well known. I suppose if they're going to intern people from Ontario and Quebec, they figure they have to treat the rest of the country equally."

"You believe that?"

"Who knows? Probably a bit of envy in there too."

"Envy?"

"All the real action is on the coast, submarines sinking ships in the Gulf, convoys shipping out from Sydney, coal production, steel production in the news every day, they want to get in on it. And I suppose they figure if there are Italians in Cape Breton, there must be Fascists there too, just like in Toronto, Montreal, and Ottawa. Sometimes the farther away from a situation the more clearly you think you can see into it."

"They should come down and get in on it then. The pits are short of coal miners these days."

"Good idea, Father, I'll give them a call."

"So Tommie is one of the token Fascists in Coaltown?"

"No. He's not. He wasn't on the list. He's a special case. He was reported locally."

"By whom?"

"You know I can't tell you that."

"Why not?"

"For the same reason you can't report to me crimes you hear about in confession."

"I see."

"Perhaps you do see," the Mountie said.

"See?" Father Rod said. "In the confessional? It's pitch dark in there."

"Of course."

"I've never been in, mind you, but I imagine sometimes you can tell who the people are by their sins."

"Sometimes. You can guess. But we're drifting a bit here," Father Rod said. "How could Tommie be a spy? He's a ballplayer. He plays cards at the Italian club. I know he's a show-off."

"And he's a tomcat," the Mountie said.

"A tomcat?"

"Yes. You know tomcats and police have at least one thing in common. They prowl at night. They usually don't meet but they see each other."

"Suppose he is a show-off, and suppose he is a tomcat. So what? Nothing to be arrested for."

"Look at it this way," the Mountie said. "He's been shooting off his mouth in the pit about Signor Mussolini, as the prime minister calls him—'Production would be sky high if Mussolini were the underground manager,' stuff like that. You know what he's like. You've seen him play ball. See him walk down the street for that matter. Sometimes I feel like taking a shot at him myself just to see him fall. People don't like show-offs and they don't like tomcats, especially if they think they're pissing on their gateposts."

"Whose gatepost is he pissing on?"

"I can't tell you that. You'll have to wait until he comes to confession and tells you himself."

"We're talking about spying?"

"Yes, we're talking about spying. And we're talking about a man who has been reported to us. And we're talking about a man who is working at the production end of an essential industry. And I hate to confess this to you, Father, and remember, I said confess—sooner or later my superiors will ask me who we've rounded up on our own intelligence, and sooner or later I'll be looking for a promotion. It's got to be somebody. It might as well be Tomassio."

"I see."

"But let me tell you, Father Rod. That's not the worst of it. The worst is yet to come."

"What?"

The Mountie stood up and paced a few steps. "You know," he said, "I can't see us grabbing too many Italians. For one thing, most of them are coal miners and with the war on, the country is depending on coal. We can't do without it. But our information is that the other miners in Coaltown are going to refuse to work if they let Italians down the pit. Then we'll have a mess. Because we need the coal and the mines can't work efficiently without all the men. A lot of them are joining the army and that's making things worse. It's impossible to find experienced miners. Funny thing is, a lot of the Italians are joining the army, as you know. Think of that, Father Rod. The son joins the army and goes off to fight in Europe, and we put his father in jail because someone in Ottawa thinks there is a reasonable suspicion he might be a danger to the state. And here we haven't enough miners to do the essential work for the war effort, and the men they've been working with for years suddenly decide they don't want them in the mine. And they're ready to stay home to prove their point."

"Why would they do that?"

"Why? Well, the why of that, Father MacDonald, and your experience with confession should help you understand this, the why of that is the foundation for all police work. People will do all kinds of bad things unless somebody stops them. We both do that. Isn't it interesting that we both wear uniforms. Isn't that why people go to confession, so they can promise not to do it again, and again."

"That's a bit cynical."

"You think so. Let me tell you this, there are a lot of Italian spies in this little town if you go by telephone calls, the anonymous telephone calls we get reporting them."

"Why would they be doing that?"

"How long have you been a priest? Oh well, I suppose they don't tell you that sort of thing in confession. They think they're doing their patriotic duty. Wouldn't be a sin.

You keep your ear to the ground for a day or so. And be just a little cynical."

"By the way, Sergeant. You know that Tomassio's cousin was wounded in the war?"

"Yes, I know. Leg shot off. I wish I could help. How's your eye?"

"I can see."

"Probably one eye is enough for a priest. He doesn't need to see both sides of everything." Sergeant Archimbault laughed but immediately jumped up and excused himself. "I can't seem to resist a cheap joke. I'm glad it's not a crime. But perhaps it is a sin." He walked to the window. "Do you like cheap jokes?"

"From time to time," Father Rod said. "Tell me, Sergeant. Are you promising not to do it again?"

The sergeant unbuttoned his coat. "I feel a little over-dressed," he said. "Do you always walk around looking like that? Never mind. Yes, Father, I promise not to do it again. I hope it is a promise I can keep. If not, I'll come back next time and promise again."

"So what's to happen? After the round-up?"

"Come." Sergeant Archimbault beckoned. He threw his coat on his chair. "Take a look."

The window opened to the ocean. On the horizon several barely visible ships seemed motionless. It had been a beautiful day, hot for June, but the sky was filling up with angry-looking clouds. There was no wind and the sea was flat but looking dense and grainy. They were looking east but the sun, setting in the west, reflecting off the few white clouds left in the sky, was glinting a faint rose colour off the water. Father Rod came to the window and stood beside Sergeant Archimbault.

"What are we looking at, Sergeant?"

"I suppose you're used to it, the ocean. I come from Quebec and I thought the St. Lawrence was big. The detainees, we'll keep them in the county jail, temporarily. Then they go to internment camp. By train, I imagine, to Minto or Petawawa."

"How long?"

"Who knows? Till somebody in Ottawa with the big stick smartens up."

"Does this make any sense?"

"See, the sunset is red, you can tell by the colour of the water even though you can't see the sunset behind us. I spend a lot of time at this window, thinking. The sea is calming, even when it's angry, as long as you're not out on it. I was stationed for a while on the prairies. It's flat, like the sea. But it's not the same. If you turn around, it's still flat as far as you can see. But here if you turn around, you see rolling hills. It's like living in two different countries at the same time. I used to live in Vancouver. There you have the sea but you never seem to see the whole thing as you do here. And when you turn around, you see the huge mountains with the white shoulders on them. I could feel them there even when I wasn't looking. I felt like God was watching me. Do you believe in God, Father Rod?"

"That's an interesting question."

"You want to know if what's going on makes sense. Everybody where I lived was a Catholic, except my father. I'm an atheist. Nothing makes sense to me. In Minto, New Brunswick, there are several huts full of internees living behind barbed wire. They're German Jews who escaped Germany to England just before the war. Mr. Churchill didn't know what to do with them, so he sent them to Canada. We locked them up. We guard them day and night. Why? Are we scared they might escape and find their way back to Germany to fight for the Nazis? Does that make any sense? When people get excited, you never know who they'll be putting behind barbed wire. Mr. Churchill must be a smart man, but he seems to think that some of those German Jews might be Nazi spies. Should we be surprised if some civil servant who's never been far enough away from Ottawa that he could breathe without smelling the Rideau Canal thinks there might be some Fascists among Cape Breton Italians?"

Father Rod smiled. "And you want me to do something about it?"

"You can help a lot. You're the shepherd. It's your flock. And by the way, you are good friends with Tomassio's pit buddy, Jim McMahon?"

"Yeah."

"Maybe you better keep an eye on him."

"Why, what's he up to?"

"He's not a Catholic or a criminal, so I guess neither one of us knows his little secrets. But you know he hangs around with that UMW crowd. Big talker at union meetings. A student, you might say, of McLaughlin. Getting a reputation as a communist is not going to be helpful. And this is the point: McMahon has been shooting his mouth off about the Italians."

"Half his friends are Italians."

"I know. He's defending them. I don't blame him. But you know the pit in Coaltown is a flashpoint. He works there. That's where most of the Italians work. And a few nasty people who are not Italians. Tell him to be careful."

SEVEN

✠

The lover thinks more often of
reaching his mistress than does the
husband of guarding his wife;
the prisoner thinks more often
of escaping than does the jailer
of shutting the door.
STENDHAL

A T FIRST GLANCE the wall enclosing the county
lock-up looked like a serious wall. It was tall.
Bulges at intervals along its white stucco length
and width, and at the corners, suggested reinforcing steel
bars. It was thick. Along the wide top, steel posts, rising two
feet above the cement and angled in at thirty degrees, were
designed to carry strands of barbed and vicious wire,
intended, no doubt, to retard the progress of fleeing enemies of society while guards shot them in the back and
watched them plummet to the ground. That no prisoner
ever tried this route to freedom was a grievous disappoint-
ment to some of the old guards, whose eager expectation
far exceeded their training.

But a second glance revealed that the strands of rusty
wire, most of their barbs fallen to the top of the wall or to
the ground below, sagged like clotheslines without props.

Indeed, since the last and final public recreational hanging had faded from memory, the entire structure seemed to sag like a prominent citizen caught performing indecent acts.

Beside the wall, guarding the driveway to the administration building located behind the walled-in yard, a gate hung on one hinge. An empty sentry box guarded the gate.

In a field beside the driveway, a half dozen inmates dug into the ground with garden forks or chinked the rocks with hoes. They were trying to follow instructions from the Department of Agriculture to create a Victory Garden to provide enough vegetables for their own table and a surplus to sell and buy Victory Bonds to aid the war effort. Providing their own food would free up a few ration coupons so the inmates could enjoy a little butter on their toast. After that, any surplus would be donated to the churches to help them feed the destitute. If the garden project succeeded, the state promised to reward the men with a coop full of turkey chicks to raise for meat, half to be consumed by the inmates themselves and half for destitute families so they could eat donated meat with their donated vegetables at Christmas dinner. It was a noble plan.

At the moment the rate of progress suggested a projected surplus of minus X. Once in a while one of the men dropped his garden tool, straightened up, pressed the small of his back with the palms of his hands, and looked wistfully at the poisoned trees bending like sick sentries over the half-hearted fence intended to dissuade him from running home to his domestic care-giver.

Soon, when they exhausted the energy ingested with their late coffee and dry toast breakfast, these involuntary monks would retire to their cells for an hour of meditation before lunch. In the meantime a prison guard, armed at the belt with a flashlight, fired the occasional glance at this band of apathetic farmers from the window of the staff coffee room. As a group, these drunk-tank habitués, panhandlers, and rock-throwers-at-windows exhibited an extraordinary dearth of cohesion. They stood at random in the field in a variety of static positions, like dysfunctional robots. They peered at the future through a fog of fatigue, sickness, and yearning for alcohol, able to perceive neither vegetables nor turkeys on the horizon of their amblyopic vision.

Serious dangerous criminals, dedicated to the destruction of society as we know it, or wish it: murderers; rapists; public batterers of women, children, and small men; draft dodgers; unsanctioned thieves of legal tender or goods of less than a million dollars; tax-evaders with annual salaries of less than $50,000; labour leaders seeking to enhance the lifestyle of drudges and undermine the authority of the state; journalists, cartoonists, and left-wing politicians who criticized the government, and other such bad people, might be held overnight, or during a trial, before they went off to serious prison in Dorchester where serious prison guards knew exactly how to deal with them. While incarcerated in the county jail, serious prisoners were not expected to work in the garden. And the county did not confiscate their ration coupons.

The surface of the wall offered visual intimations of the situation behind it. Artists, some with talent and half-decent equipment and material, others with reasonable facsimiles, covered the white walls, over the years, with portraits, murals, and stick people. Some of these artifacts depicted what the artists knew from experience of the misery hidden on the other side of the wall. Some artists, without the experience, like theologians of incarceration, depicted what they imagined the wall obscured from their vision. Other artifacts seemed merely the artist's attempt to mitigate the brutal ugliness of the white expanse.

Several writers took advantage of spaces unclaimed by painters and filled them with words. Some collections of words were merely awkward sentences suggesting that certain citizens perform unmentionable acts. Others were products of more sophisticated minds wielding more experienced pencils. But most of it was faded, seared, bleared, smeared by the careless toil of time and weather and the splash from potholes in the nearby highway. Only one piece of work remained clear and legible, a poem:

ODE TO AN INCARCERATED ANCHORITE
Oh I couldn't afford to pay the rent
Or put the butter upon the table
Oh, I wasn't able to buy the coal
To comfort the boards of my bungalow.

I couldn't afford to buy the drink, and
Drinking is my life. So I threw a knife
On Charlotte Street. I cracked a pane of glass.
Alas, I missed the mayor by half an inch. Now

I've got a concrete tent. A lock to keep
the neighbours out. I'm warm as roast. The toast
Is fine. Water's my substitute for wine
It's always exactly zero o'clock

I'm knitting myself a tartan bonnet
withearlugschinstrapandbuttonsonnet

On June 11, 1940, a half-ton truck with a covered-in box pulled up at the crippled gate. A man in coveralls emerged, opened the wooden doors at the back of the truck, extracted a tool box, and addressed the hinge problem. He replaced the broken hinge with a new one and oiled all the hinges. He changed the useless lock and chain that purported to hold the double gate together. He swung the two wings of the gate back and forth 90 degrees of arc. Not a squeak. He drove his truck through, came back, and closed and locked the gate. Then he drove it to the administration building and, tool box in hand, he mounted the concrete steps, paused at the top, and looked back at the gate and gave his head a quick shake of approval and satisfaction, then disappeared inside. Even the lugubrious farmers found energy enough to interrupt their meagre motions and stare in wonder.

Later in the day, a corporal and a private stopped at the gate in a jeep. The canvas top of the jeep was folded and stored in a box at the back of the vehicle, and the two men wore their berets pulled down tight to their eyebrows so the wind wouldn't dislodge them in their haste to get to the jail.

Although they were too skinny for their new uniforms, their puttees and combat boots looked convincing enough. The corporal unlocked the gate, closed and locked it behind him, and walked to the administration building. The private entered the sentry box that looked a little less official than it should because, except for its doorless doorway, it looked like a neglected outhouse. He sat on its little bench. He opened his lunch box and took out *The Adventures of Superman* and dedicated himself to reading about the superhero defusing a saboteur's bomb in a coal mine in West Virginia and flying Lois Lane back to the *Daily Planet*.

The corporal returned to the gate, interrupted Private AuCoin's reading, left the key with him, and drove away in the jeep.

All afternoon the sun tried to burn through the damp air turned red by the gravity-chained smoke from the smoke stacks at the steel plant. The tradesman's truck waited like a faithful horse by the step of the administration building. The tradesman sat in the coffee room drinking tea and chatting with the guard.

"I can't do nothing 'less they get that junk out that cellblock," the tradesman said.

"We can't put them in with regular prisoners. No room anyway," the guard said.

"I'm not hauling junk. I got a sore back," the tradesman said.

"I got a sore back myself," the jailer said, and to illustrate the point he placed his two hands on the top of the table and levered himself up until his legs straightened and he let himself go and sat back in his chair. "I couldn't get out of this goddamn chair if I didn't have the table."

"What about those galoots in the garden?" the tradesman asked, pointing his chin at the window. "They're not doing much out there but rolling rocks around with their hoes."

"Are you kidding? Tough enough job to get those guys to stand up in the sunshine ten minutes at a time. Unless you want to buy them a quart of shine. That might gas them up."

"Not my problem."

"Me neither. I'm just the watchdog."

"Who we making room for anyway?"

"Dagos."

"What? Italians?"

"Yeah."

"What they do?"

"Nothing, far's I know. They think some might be spies."

"Spies. Isn't that kinda stupid?"

"Well, Mussolini's in the war now."

"Yeah. Mussolini lives in Italy, last I heard. It's stunned."

"Did you see the paper?"

"I heard it on the radio. It's stunned."

"Yeah," the jailer said. "Stunned as it gets. My next-door neighbour, Joe Baloney I call him, I can't figure out his last name, works at the steel plant. His boy Joey's in the army. Got on a boat for Europe yesterday. Too bad he didn't wait a day. Could have spent the war in jail. Lot safer."

"So when do they get here?" the tradesman asked.

"Today, so they tell me. I got no place to put them, just the yard. I hope it don't rain."

Residents across the road from the jail, alerted by the afternoon activity, watched from behind their blinds and curtains when an RCMP vehicle drove up through the red air and in through the gates opened by the dutiful Private AuCoin. The car stopped at the concrete steps of the administration building, and an RCMP officer and a man in a civilian suit went in through the doors. After a half-hour they left.

During the after-supper evening, four RCMP officers in two cars delivered four prisoners for temporary incarceration: Balboa Passerello, a shoemaker, carrying a beat-up duffel bag; Danny Piva, a musician carrying a black case with a clarinet in it; Pete DiVito, carrying an ancient suitcase; and Tomassio, carrying nothing.

"No room in the inn," the guard said, "so I'll have to put you in the courtyard. I got Hudson Bay blankets if it gets chilly. If it rains, which it looks like it is, I'll bring you into the coffee room and somebody is gonna have to stay up all night to keep an eye out on ya. You'll be gone tomorrow." He lifted the lid off the stove, stirred up the fire, and scooped some coal from the scuttle and dropped it on the hot coals. He filled the kettle full of water and put it on the stove to boil.

"Where we goin'?"

"Petawawa."

"Where the hell is Petawawa?"

"I'm not sure. Somewhere near Ottawa. Or maybe it's in Quebec."

"Why can't we stay here?"

"This is a jail."

"Well, what's Petawawa?"

"It's an internment camp."

"What's the difference?"

"Jails are for criminals. You guys didn't do nothing."

They all thought about it for a while. When the kettle boiled, the jailer made tea and served them all a mug and put a can of Carnation condensed milk on the table. "You fellas want to play cards?"

"You got a cribbage board?" Balboa asked.

"'Fraid not."

"That's okay. We'll play scopa. Maybe later."

"So what's the story here?" Danny asked. "Because we're not criminals they can lock us up and send us away—if we were criminals they'd have to give us a trial."

The jailer shrugged his shoulders.

Once in the yard, Balboa, Danny, Pete, and Tomassio sat together against the far wall near the roadway where they could hear the car tires slap the potholes. They tried to stare into the dim future through the wet, red, darkening air. At dusk they heard the gates open and a car drive down along the side wall to the administration building. Soon, the steel-barred door between the yard and the cellblock clanked open, and four new prisoners stepped into the dim courtyard. They huddled together near the door and talked in whispers. The Italians listened but could make out nothing until one of the new prisoners yelled out a message clear enough.

"Hey, Dagos, how's Mussolini doing? Ya call him up lately?"

"Who are those guys?" Pete said.

"I know one of them. I fixed his shoes. He's a moonshiner from Coaltown."

"I think I know who you mean. He just got out of jail, didn't he?"

"For moonshining?"

"No. Him and his buddies beat up on some gypsies. They say he shot one but they couldn't pin it on him. Couldn't find the gun. After they let him go somebody slashed the tires of his car and he blamed it on the gypsies and he went back after them and that's when the cops nailed him."

"Hey, Dago, got any spare spaghetti?"

"Do we have to put up with this?" Tomassio asked.

"You better put up with it, Tommie, they're trying to goad us into a fight."

It was getting darker, and the menacing figures at the other end of the compound, all wearing dark clothing, were almost invisible and indistinguishable. They gave up their taunts for a while but the Italians could hear them mumbling among themselves and knew it was only a matter of time before they would be at it again.

"There's four of them and four of us," Tomassio said. "We might be better off taking them on."

"Okay for you maybe. Me, I'm a clarinet player," Danny said. "I've never been in a fight in my life."

"Hey, Dago, you got any cheap wine?"

"Well, I can't put up with this," Tomassio said and stood up.

"So what are you gonna do?" Pete asked. "Take them on yourself? Somebody slipped those bastards in here with us. They might have a knife or something."

One of the men separated from the group and walked toward them. The yard was about a hundred yards long, and when the man was halfway in their direction they could see the smirk on his face from the glimmer of a streetlight shining over the wall behind them. He folded his arms over his chest and cocked his head.

"Hey, Dago, you got any brown women for sale?"

Tomassio pushed himself off the wall and began walking toward the man, but when he had covered half the distance between them, the man retreated, and when Tomassio reached where the man had been standing, he stopped and waited a few minutes. Then he went back and joined the others.

"This is gonna get worse," Balboa said. "You can see how it's going."

"Could we talk to them maybe?" Peter suggested. "Let's go over and talk to them."

"Talk to them. Sure," said Danny. "You can hear the kind of talk they got. Listen, if you go over there, go over to fight because that's the only thing you're going to get. And since you haven't got a hammer or a hoe, you can take my clarinet, put it together and use it for a stick, and be ready to win or be dead."

"Well, I'm getting out of here," Tomassio said. "I haven't even got a toothbrush or a change of socks."

"Sure. Walk over the wall."

"That's exactly what I'm gonna do."

"Sure. How?"

"See that clothesline down there, the other side of them, way to their left?"

"Sure," Balboa said. "You're gonna cut down the clothesline, make a lasso, catch something on the top of the wall, shinny up and away you go. I'm sure those guys will be down at their end cheering you on. Us too. Maybe Danny could play some escape music on the clarinet."

"That's a pretty saggy clothesline, I bet there's a clothes prop somewhere down there. Do me a favour. You three go down the other side and distract them. It's dark enough now. They'll think I'm with you. Keep together. Talk to each other or mumble to keep their attention."

"Sure, you're gonna leave us here, at their mercy. You're the only one of us with even a hope of handling them."

"If I get out, I'll try to get help."

It was a hope. Perhaps their only hope. The jailer had promised to take them in if it rained and the rain was holding off for the moment. But it was getting colder, and the jailer had not yet appeared with the promised Hudson Bay blankets.

Looking like an official delegation, the three men walked with what appeared to be purpose and intent down along the wall to their left. Tomassio, with his dark clothes and Mediterranean face, melted into the dark red air and sidled along the right wall toward the clothesline.

By the time the hoodlums twigged to his movement, Tomassio was running with the clothes prop in hand and was halfway up the length of the courtyard, streaking for the wall. While they watched, he pole-vaulted to the top of the wall, let the clothes prop fall to the ground, turned, and waved a flamboyant goodbye to all and dropped to the ground beside the highway. He ran toward downtown Sydney because he knew they would expect him to run in the opposite direction, toward Coaltown. He turned off Prince Street and ran down George until he reached the steps of the cathedral. He doubted they would look for him in church, so he went up the steps and, once inside, sat in the last pew, in front of the confessional. If someone came in the church he could kneel and put his head in his hands and pretend to be saying his prayers in preparation for confession.

The last penitent had departed five minutes earlier and Father Pat Mancini, the bishop's chancellor, was waiting in the confessional for late arrivals. When he opened the confessional door a crack and saw that the man was sitting and not apparently preparing for confession, he removed the stole from around his neck and came out and shut the door.

"You don't want to go to confession?" He addressed the back of the man's head.

Tomassio turned. "No, Father, I . . ." They recognized each other then. They were second cousins.

"Tommie. What are you doing here?"

"I'm hiding. I just escaped the county jail."

"Okay. You better go to confession."

"It's a sin to escape from jail? I didn't commit a crime. They put me in for being an Italian."

"Yeah, I know. But if you got anything to tell me, perhaps I can help you, and if it's confession I won't be able to tell anyone about it."

"All right. Let's go in."

"No, this is fine." He turned, headed back to the confessional. "I'll get my stole. Nobody can hear us here. So what happened?"

"They just came to the house and grabbed me. I flattened the Mountie. So they charged me with resisting arrest. They said they didn't come to arrest me. Detain me, they said. But after I floored the Mountie, they arrested me for resisting arrest. But after that they said detained again."

"They likely intend to forget about the arrest or they wouldn't put you in the county jail. That means they'll send you to Petawawa with the others."

"Yeah, if they make it through the night. They put a bunch of tough guys in there with us trying to goad us into a fight so they could kick the shit out of us."

"What?"

"Yeah. You know that MacNeil, the moonshiner from Coaltown."

"What?"

"Yeah. Him and his buddies. The boys are trapped in there with them. Can you do something about that?"

"Come on, let's go. I've got to make some phone calls. Then we'll see about you. Come on, we'll go to the Chancery office."

Father Mancini called the RCMP. Then he called his Member of Parliament. Then, keeping the stole around his neck, he drove Tomassio to Coaltown and let him off where the road came adjacent to the ball field.

"Are you sure you know what you're doing?" Father Mancini asked.

"I'll be fine, Father."

Tomassio crossed the road by the light from Father Mancini's car, and watched the tail lights of the car disappear into the mist. He walked to the beach, then across the ball field and along the cliffs and up the field to the rows of company houses and near enough to Ump's house to watch and wait until he saw him leave in his car. He waited ten minutes and walked up and knocked on the back door. Cathy opened the door a crack but when she saw him she opened it wide and pulled him in.

"What are you doing here? I thought you were in jail."

"I escaped. Is Sadie home?"

"No. She's never home if she can help it. She told me she went to June's, but I don't really know where they go from there. They haven't got a phone. What are you going to do?"

"I got to hide. For a while."

"Here?" Cathy asked, panic in her eyes. As brave as she was, Cathy was as wary of her husband as anyone, and since the incident in the Co-op with the gloves, she'd been wondering if suspicion of their affair was thickening.

"Nobody would ever think I'd be here. I'm a dead duck if they catch me."

"You'll be a dead duck if Ump catches you here. And what about me?"

"Well, where am I gonna go?"

"Come in then, I'll put you in the attic. But you can't make a sound."

"By tomorrow night they'll think I've gone away. I'll get my gun and some money and some food and I'll go to the woods until I can figure out what to do."

"How you gonna get your gun?"

"I'll get Gelo to bring it. Sadie could get the message to him. Don't you think?"

"Oh, I'm sure she would. But she'll have to get around her father. He told her never to see Gelo or talk to him again. Not that she'd pay any attention. Not that I blame her. If it wasn't for her, I'd wish I hadn't paid any attention to him myself. But she'd have to be careful. Get up in the attic and I'll get you something to eat. He's on day shift tomorrow.

He'll be gone most of the day. You better not snore up there," she insisted. And then to herself, "I must be crazy."

Father Mancini sped back to Sydney. The rain was pouring down now through the red air. Private AuCoin was comfortable in his cozy little sentry box, and he didn't much like being interrupted from his reading when it was still up in the air whether Archie would get to take Betty or Veronica to the prom. Betty didn't know if she should spend her last cent on a dress, and today was the last day of the sale. She didn't want to spare the money if she'd end up going to the prom with Jughead. Private AuCoin's sister Claudette was having the same problem. Her high school graduation was right around the corner and it looked like he was going to have to take her to the prom. She said to her mother, "If I have to go with Michel, at least it'll be a man in uniform, but I'm not going to the prom with that bohunk, Leonard Wojeck, even if he asks me, it would be the last minute now anyway, who does he think he is?"

Réjeanne rolled her eyes. "That bohunk's father is in a hospital in England with six machine-gun bullets in his leg."

"I don't care. He's not popular. He's got thick glasses. He wears diamond socks his mother knitted."

By the power of his collar, Father Mancini persuaded Private Michel to put aside the comic book tribulations of Archie and Betty and open the gate. He found the Italian prisoners in the coffee room under the watchful eye of Réal Roache, guard/administrator/janitor, armed as always with his trusty flashlight. The prisoners stood in their underwear, bent over and laughing around a small coal-fired furnacette, their hands wrapped around cups of steaming tea, their wet clothes hung suspended from chairs and cupboard doors.

Father Mancini came in on the end of Réal Roache's story to find his Italians bent over the stove, laughing to kill themselves.

"Are you guys all right?"

"We're warm now, and safe, and our clothes are drying. But they're shipping us off tomorrow, to Petawawa, or Ottawawa, or some wawa. Can you do something about that?"

"I'm gonna try."

"What? Is there something you can do?"

"The apostolic delegate is in Ottawa. He's an Italian. From Italy. Surely he can do something. I'll get the bishop on it tomorrow."

"Tomorrow we'll be gone. What about our families?"

"We'll look after the families. Somebody will. Réal, where are the other prisoners?"

"They're gone. The Mounties called. Let them go, they said."

"What were they in for?"

"Vagrancy."

"Who arrested them?"

"That's the big mystery. I haven't got the faintest idea."

"What are you talking about? What'd they do, just come in and offer to stay in jail?"

"No, no. Somebody brought them. I don't know. Never saw the guy before. Military looking guy, but no uniform. Flashed a badge. 'Be back tomorrow,' he said, 'to do the paperwork. Lock them up, vagrancy.' Anyway, the Mountie said to let them go. He didn't sound any too happy."

EIGHT

The Government makes paper airplanes
out of our lives and files us out the windows.
JOY KOGAWA

I WAS HALF EXPECTING *the Mounties, truth be told. There was
a lot of talk. The rumours were flying. But then everyone said
they wouldn't take the miners because it was always coming over
the radio that the miners were the backbone of the war effort. Cape
Breton was producing half of Canada's energy, they said. There's no
war without steel and there's no steel without coal. And I knew my husband Tomassio and his buddy Jim were the biggest producers in the pit.
And they worked in the biggest pit. But I knew too that Tomassio was
strutting around like Mussolini himself, he even walked down Coal
Road to the Italian Hall wearing a Mussolini shirt until I burned it in
the kitchen stove. He'd be down at the hall talking about the Sons of
Italy instead of just playing cards and shutting up like everybody else,
and him with relatives in the army, some of them already fighting in
Europe and some of them back already wounded. Even the Italians at
the Italian Hall were embarrassed with him, not to mention nervous
he might get them all arrested and the hall closed.*

Of course, some people hated Italians and loved the chance to jump on them for something, for anything. Bad enough we were Catholics, but foreign Catholics to boot, and from Italy, the Pope's back yard. But what could I do? Me, like I often said, I didn't come to Canada to be an Italian. That's why Ceit and I are such good friends. Listening to her is how I came to talk like a Canadian. She's as Gaelic as they come and she married a Polish guy and he talks just like a Cape Bretoner too. Everybody calls him Joe because they can't be bothered learning how to pronounce his name. It's her voice, I think, her talk, you can't help listening to it. When I told her I loved her MacDonald tartan kerchief, she took it right off her head then and there and gave it to me. I wore it to church, getting a whole lot of people cross at me, but I didn't care. I told Tomassio he should wear it, it might keep him out of jail. "But the least you could do," I warned him, "is keep your lips together. Loose lips sink ships and loose lips will sink you if you're not careful." He wouldn't listen to me, so what could I do? I could burn his shirt, but I couldn't zipper up his mouth. So they gave him a good excuse and they came and hauled him off. It was quite a shock. We always thought of the Mounties as protectors. If something bad happened you called the Mounties, and now they were hauling off our men who did nothing but go to work every day and come home to their families. And then the other miners, their own buddies, wouldn't even let the ones not hauled off work in the pit. It was a shock. I wondered if Gelo would ever get over it.

When he was a bit younger he used to talk about joining the Mounties. And he idolized his father. And no wonder. From the minute Gelo could sit up on the floor and stretch out his legs, Tomassio was down there with him, rolling a baseball between his legs until he could grab it and roll it back. Tomassio couldn't wait for him to walk so he could get him out in the yard where they had their tiny ball field. The three of us would play, someone to pitch, someone to catch, and someone to hit. Once Gelo was old enough to get out of the yard, they were gone to the ball field and in the fall and winter gone hunting and in the spring fishing. When the pit wasn't working, they'd be gone every day. We were always giving away meat and fish.

But when Gelo got older he picked up his own buddies for fishing and hunting and he was on his own ball team and then he got the girlfriend, Sadie. Tomassio didn't say anything but you could tell he was disappointed. Is that why he drifted away from us? Was Gelo the glue that held us together? I hate to think that. I thought we were a close family. A family has to learn to live with change. Was everything a game with Tomassio, even his family? I could see why Cathy would go for him, but why did he go for her? Was it just a new game? Another risky adventure? I wanted him back.

That night, after they took him away, the night he escaped from the jail though I didn't know that then, I took my last walk along that unforgettable stretch of cliff and beach. After that God-awful night I walked in town where people could see me. They called me the wandering widow, but I didn't care, I had to feel safe.

That black night I felt safe. I couldn't see the path and I couldn't see the edge of the cliff. But I could feel the branches of the cranberry bushes on each side of the path, and I could tell the edge of the cliff because the blackness was a little different where there was no land under it. I couldn't even see a glint from the wedding ring on my finger if I held it in front of my nose. Where there was a tree or a bush I could see a shadow, especially if it moved in the breeze, but I couldn't see the bush or tree itself, just know it was there. I always knew exactly where I was every step of the way no matter how little I could see. I'd done the walk so many times. I think maybe some part of my brain counted the steps and always knew how many I took to get to every spot on the way. I felt safe.

I was just at the top of the rock stairs leading down to the gravel beach where a few nights earlier I'd seen the nun waiting for the other nun to come in from her swim and for some reason or other I stopped to listen. I heard nothing. I decided to have a pee. I hiked up my skirt and lowered my bloomers to my knees and squatted. I just started to pee when I felt the two hands on my bum. I froze in terror. He grabbed the back of my hair through my kerchief and pushed me until my hands were on the ground and with his other hand he pulled the bloomer off one leg. It was like slow motion, and by this time I was getting my senses together. This is not going to happen, I said to myself. I could feel his penis searching between my legs. I was so scared I couldn't stop myself and I pissed all over it.

When he realized what was happening, he let go my hair and I twisted over on my back and kicked him between the legs and when I heard him make that weird noise I knew where his head was and I aimed my two feet for it and I missed and he came down on me and tried to grab my hair, but all he got was the kerchief and I grabbed it too so I'd know where to kick and I pulled my two legs back, they were like iron pistons from all my walking, and this time I caught him in the chest and he was gone. I heard him tumble down the stone steps to the gravel beach. When I heard the splash, I pulled up my bloomers and ran home.

I wanted to tell Ceit the first chance I got, but before I got the chance, she told me she'd met Cathy, who told her Ump was missing. He was missing at work and he never came home. Well, that shut me up. I had to keep quiet and think about it. My God. Would he do that to me just to get back at Tomassio? Did he know about them?

NINE

✝

If the world were perfect,
it wouldn't be.
YOGI BERRA

T HE MOUNTIES KNEW ABOUT Cathy's affair with
Tomassio, and they knew that Tomassio was on
the loose. Life went on. Ump was missing. Gone
from the house one black night and never came back.
Never showed up for work.

The Mounties organized a search party to look for Ump
and Tomassio, both, and called on Search and Rescue at the
RCAF station in Reserve Mines. They found nothing. They
didn't tell Cathy what they knew, but they questioned her
often and persistently, and they carefully searched the yard
and the outhouse and the coal house and even parts of the
house. She thought her heart would fly apart every time
they went upstairs, but they never went to the attic. They
didn't know the house had an attic because it was not an
ordinary company house. It was one of the company houses
built for officials, a single dwelling and a little bigger than

the ordinary duplex company houses and it had an attic. But you would never guess because the ceilings upstairs were made of strips of Douglas fir, varnished over, and it was impossible to see the break in the strips that marked the attic hatch. The Mounties assumed that a hatch would be in the closet but they found no sign of a hatch there.

Finally two Mounties sat with Cathy at the kitchen table and one of them said, "Okay, Cathy. Where is he?"

"I honest to God don't know, and I'm going crazy, I'm fit to be tied, but I don't know, and I can't even imagine. He never goes anywhere but I know where he is." Cathy was telling the truth but she felt as if she were lying because, distraught as she was, she was never sure who they were talking about, Wilfred, her missing husband, or Tomassio in the attic.

"Where's Sadie? We'd like to talk to her."

"Well, good luck. I'd like to talk to her myself once in a while."

The Mounties left with the feeling they were leaving something behind.

Life went on. Tomassio was missing. Leapt over the wall of the county jail one black night and never came back. The Mounties investigated and found their first clue. A couple who had been walking the beach said they saw him get out of a car at the corner of the road where it turned up from the beach road and went by the top end of the ball field. They recognized him because the car waited with its head-lights on until Tomassio crossed the ditch to the ball field. The Mounties felt grateful. Something, at least, to fill the empty feeling they'd carried away from Cathy's kitchen.

"What kind of a car?" the Mountie asked the man.

"Ford," the man said. "One of the new ones."

"Who's got a new Ford?" the Mountie asked the other

Mountie.

"Every parish priest in the diocese. And we have two. Other than that, not too many. You can't buy them without a permit. You have to be doing something for the war effort, or an essential service."

Life went on. The pit never missed a beat. The underground manager replaced Ump as shot-fire with another white Anglo-Saxon Protestant and promoted a non-Italian miner from a maintenance job on the surface to loading coal with Tomassio's buddy, Jim McMahon, who was not pleased. And Jim McMahon's pay envelope lost some bulk, and Cape Breton's contribution of coal tonnage to the war effort diminished.

Baseball too went on. Gelo was back at centre field. A different face behind the mask behind the catcher. A beautiful day. Seagulls gathered at the edge of the cliff or flew circles over the rocks below, diving and squawking like well-fed coal company officials. The Eskasoni Junior Arrows were back on the field.

Since the coach had moved Gelo to centre field, he had made no errors, made several spectacular running catches, one of them a foot and a half in the air with his back to the ball, and robbed several teams of certain victory. His position was every big hitter's favourite spot because it was possible, though it was a rare achievement, to hit the ball right into the Atlantic Ocean, a feat referred to as "sending one home," as if the Atlantic Ocean were a mere river full of trout and smelts and a rocky floor separating pseudo-nostalgic Europeans in North America from their homelands. The Italians, the largest group of recent immigrants to Cape Breton, had started the chant at ball games, "Send one home, Frankie. Send 'er home. Send one to Italy." But other European groups soon followed suit. "Send one to Poland." "Send one to France." "Send one to Germany." "Send one to Ireland." A student could hook off school, go to a ball game, and still learn a bit of geography. When the war had started, the Germans gave up the practice. When Mussolini saluted the Führer, most Italians lost enthusiasm. The Indians, with no mother country across the ocean to be lonesome for, did not participate in these patriotic choirs, but some of them smiled.

Today Gelo couldn't keep his mind on the game. Gerry was pitching a great game. He had allowed only two runners, one with a broken-bat single, one on an error. The catcher threw out both runners trying to steal second. Gelo ran in to cover the throws to second, but other than that there was nothing for him to do. He couldn't stop thinking about his father. Where was he? If he went to the woods, he'd need his rifle and his fishing gear. Gelo moved in and out, right and left, depending on the batter, but his mind was in the woods and along the streams.

For Tomassio, hunting and fishing were primarily games, secondarily a source of food, and he had taught Gelo from the time he was ten to think and to hunt and to fish the way he did. By the time Gelo was twelve he could use a rifle like a surgical instrument. They had built a rough camp in the woods near their favourite fishing pool and set up a target-shooting range with stationary and moving targets. They used a .22 for practice because of the cheaper bullets and a .303 for hunting. Either one could shoot the tipped-up bottle cap off the top of a moving pint beer bottle eight times out of ten on a bad day.

Top of the ninth. Coaltown ahead by two. Two out. Gerry walked the next batter. To tie the game, Eskasoni needed both runner and batter to score. Their long-ball hitter was at the plate, and Gelo knew he'd try to pull the ball but he could see the catcher calling for an outside fastball just above the knees. If he hit it, unless the pitcher made a mistake, it should come out to straightaway centre. It should be a line drive so he didn't want to play too deep. He could barely hear the water washing over the rocks near the cliffs behind him. He struggled to keep his mind off his father. The arrest had shocked him. The escape from jail excited him. He knew his father could survive in the woods. He must have gone to the woods. The third-base coach was yelling, waving frantically for him to play deep, but Gelo never noticed.

When they needed meat for the winter, they would lure the deer with apples in the fall. But they preferred to stalk them, outwit them, sometimes tracking the same animal for days, stepping silently through the woods, talking quietly only when they stopped for lunch. Talking baseball. They netted smelt and sometimes trout for food, but they preferred to fish them one at a time, outwitting them with flies they put together themselves, leaning against the wall of their camp in the shade of their makeshift canopy.

"Gelo, wake up."

Gelo looked up and saw the third-base coach waving. He was waving him back but Gelo moved in and focused on the batter. Two balls, no strikes. "He's going to get a fastball," Gelo mumbled to himself, "why did Jimmie wave me in?"

Tomassio had taught him everything about baseball. He was practically uncoachable in the sense that it was hardly ever necessary to tell him where to position himself, what to expect from a pitcher, where a batter was most likely to place the ball. And like Tomassio, Gelo could play any position on the field.

"Gelo," somebody yelled. He looked up, alert. The

pitcher was in his windup, the wind was rising, he could feel it on his face. I should be back farther, he thought, and started to back-pedal. Too late.

Whop. The ball arced over his head. Big mistake. He should have played deep. He ran back but knew it was no use, the ball landed twenty-five feet in front of him on the edge of the cliff, scattering the seagulls as it rolled down the stone steps. Gelo went to retrieve the precious ball. Good baseballs were hard enough to come by.

Halfway down the stone steps, he could see the ball at the edge of the narrow gravel strand still uncovered by the rising tide. The swirling foam made his head swim but he stopped and closed his eyes for a moment and then he continued down backwards on all fours until he reached the bottom with both feet on the gravel. He fished the ball out of the lapping water and as he straightened out he saw his mother's kerchief twisting like a tartan fish in the foamy bubbles. He stepped into the water, grabbed it, and pulled the kerchief and Ump's bloated body out of the purging water and up the gravel shore.

He tried to avoid looking at the blind sockets that once housed Ump's eyes while he pried open the fingers of the clenched hand and pulled free the kerchief and stuffed it down his pants. He was baffled. But he knew he had to keep going until he figured it out.

By the time he climbed back up the stone steps, the players of both teams, alarmed by how long he'd been out of sight, were standing at the top of the cliff. When they saw his face, they knew something was wrong.

"What is it?" someone asked.

"Ump is down there. He's dead. Drowned."

✢   ✢   ✢

Life stops. Wakes and funerals are difficult at best. Cathy and Sadie decided that Gelo should not go to either the wake or the funeral, even though he had discovered the body. It was a Protestant funeral anyway, and everybody knew Ump hadn't approved of Sadie's involvement with Gelo. Even without that complication, Gelo could not represent his father as Ump's co-worker because everyone knew Ump had hated Tomassio.

Tomassio's son could not be at the church; it was out of the question. Even going to the wake would be awkward and in poor taste. Sadie said, "I want you to stand across the street from the church and look at me when I come out so I'll know you're there. This will not be easy."

"Okay."

"And put a necktie on."

Cathy had told Gelo to tell his mother not to come to the wake. She didn't give a reason. "Why would she tell me that?" he asked Sadie.

"How should I know? Either my mother's going crazy, or something fishy is going on."

"What d'ya mean?"

"Our two fathers were both missing. And the Mounties were half the time questioning my mother and snooping around. In the house, in the yard, in the outhouse, in the coal house. What did they think? That if my father was missing they'd find him in his own house? His own wife wouldn't know? His own daughter wouldn't know he was there in the house? And your father missing at the same time. What? They think they were gonna find him in our house? Are the Mounties stupid? Am I stupid? Are we all crazy?"

After the funeral, life went on. "Sooner or later," Cathy said to Tomassio in their attic retreat, "you got to get out of here, and, as far as I'm concerned, the sooner the better."

"What, don't you love me anymore?"

"Somebody's gonna find out you're here."

"I don't see how. I could stay here forever."

"Sadie is gonna know. She's not stupid. I think she half knows now, the way she looks at me. And even if she can't figure it out, sooner or later she's gonna catch me up here, or coming or going. She's home no more than she has to be, but when she is, her eyes are everywhere."

About a dozen wide boards lying loose on the joists formed a partial floor of the attic. Cathy had brought up a kitchen chair she'd found in their shed so Tomassio could sit and read the few magazines she could find. She provided a few blankets from her cedar chest to serve as a mattress over the hard, uneven boards. The only natural light came from a vent in the attic wall.

"Well, I can't stay cooped up all my life anyway. I'm getting shack-happy already. Maybe I'll just go and join the army."

"You *are* shack-happy if you think you can join the army. You think they're gonna want a spy in the army?"

"I'm not a spy."

"They're calling you a spy. They put you in jail for it, remember. You think they're gonna put you in jail for a spy one week and put you in the army the next? I hope you don't think they're gonna admit they made a mistake."

Cathy stood in the centre of the attic, where the pitch of the room offered enough room for her to stand almost erect. She held on to two rafters and leaned over Tomassio like a shadow in the dim light.

"Never mind," Tomassio said. "Get me my rifle and ammunition, a fishing line and hooks, and lots of bread and some cans of Spam. I'll live in the woods till she blows over. The war shouldn't last too long now, with Mussolini in it."

"Very funny. If you didn't have that mouth on you, you'd still be in the pit making good money. And if they see you with a rifle they're liable to shoot you. Probably get a medal for it. I lost one man already this week."

"Don't worry, they won't see me." Tomassio, like Gelo, was dreaming of the woods. He had no wish to stay confined to an attic, getting cramps in his muscles and lectures from Cathy. He knew he could survive indefinitely in the woods and they'd never be able to track him down. They knew where his camp was, but he didn't need the camp.

Cathy struck a match and lit a candle she had brought to the attic and placed it on an ashtray stand. She was getting desperate and she wanted to look into his eyes so she could impress upon him their dilemma. She didn't see how he could stay and not get detected sooner or later, and she didn't see how he could leave without getting caught. She bent and put her hands on his knees, bringing her eyes level with his.

"How are you gonna get out of here? I hope you don't think they haven't got a snoop watching this place. They know something is going on. I could tell when they were here. They were too sure of themselves. I wouldn't be surprised they've seen you prowling around. Anyway, I don't know how to get your rifle. I'm not gonna get Gelo or Sadie in on it. I don't want them to know we're carrying on, although God knows they'll probably find out someday."

"Unless we stop."

"Stop? It would've been easier not to start. What about the priest? Do you go to confession? Never mind. I don't think I want to know. Who can I trust to get your rifle?"

"My buddy, Jim. I can trust him with my life. I've been doing it for years."

"Did you hear that?" she whispered. "Listen. Is that the door downstairs?" They heard a bang. They waited. Another bang. Then another. "Never mind," she said, "it's the shed. I must have left it open when I got the chair. Look. I'll talk to Jim. Maybe he'll be smart enough to get away with it. One way or another, you have to get out of here. This is getting very scary. I don't know what's going to happen to me if Anna finds out we've been carrying on."

"She knows."

"She knows? Why didn't you tell me?"

"I didn't want you to worry about it."

"What are you telling me now for?"

Tomassio took her two hands from his knees and held them to his face for a moment. Then he turned her around and sat her on his knee, wrapped his arms around her midriff, and leaned his head between her shoulder blades. She held his arms by the elbows, and they remained locked together while he rocked her for a moment.

"If I get locked up, or worse," he mumbled into the back of her sweater, "it'll be you and Anna. Gelo and Sadie are too thick to separate. You'll have to deal with it. I'll be all right, but you might as well get ready for what could happen."

Cathy froze their rocking motion. She let go of Tomassio's elbows and put her hands to her face, bent and rested her elbows on her knees. She stayed there like that for a while, staring through her fingers at the makeshift attic floorboards. When she finally spoke, her voice was full of resignation, a realisation of the implications of their brief affair. "I can't believe this. All I wanted was somebody to be nice to me for a change."

✠　✠　✠

The Mounties, energized by the escalation of their investigation from hunting a harmless, if arrogant and mouthy, alien to tracking a murder suspect, a crack shot, known to own a rifle, upgraded their search strategy. They decided to follow the rifle. But first they had to find it. They could not find it at the house. And so, they concluded, it must be somewhere else. They sat with Anna and Gelo at the kitchen table.

"Where's Tomassio's rifle, Anna?"

"I don't know," Anna lied.

"He didn't have it with him in jail. Did he come home and get it when he escaped?"

"No, he didn't come home. I don't know where he is. I don't know where the rifle is."

"Gelo?" the Mountie said. "Have you got the rifle?"

Gelo opened his arms as if to demonstrate the fact that he didn't have the rifle. "Maybe it's at the camp."

The Mountie smiled. "You expect me to believe that your father would leave his rifle at the camp."

Gelo shrugged his shoulders. "What do you want his rifle for anyway?"

"We have orders to confiscate the weapons of all aliens. But in your father's situation, he'll be considered dangerous if he's got a rifle on him because he's wanted on suspicion of murder. He might get shot."

"Murder," Anna said, startled. "What are you talking about, murder? What murder?"

"Ump's murder."

"Dada was in jail," Gelo said.

"No, he wasn't in jail. Ump was killed a few hours after your father escaped. Two witnesses saw your father get out of a car and walk across the ball field toward the cliffs. That'd be about two hours before Ump's estimated time of death."

"That doesn't mean he did it." Gelo said.

"No, that's true. But it means he had the opportunity, and on top of that the motive. Ump was his enemy."

"Yeah. In the ball park."

"Well … there's more to it than that," the Mountie said.

"What?"

"We won't get into that now."

When Gelo came home after the ball game the day he pulled Ump out of the ocean, he went to his mother's room and put her MacDonald tartan kerchief on her dresser top. They had not spoken about it, but at this point in the interrogation the tartan garment and its implications were in their minds. Anna knew that Gelo and Sadie were putting on a good front, cool as ice. She knew their hearts were crying. She didn't know what secrets they kept from each other.

"Who said anybody murdered him?" Gelo demanded. "Everybody said he likely tripped and fell off the cliff, it was black dark that night."

"He was killed by bumping his head on the rocks on the way down …"

"There you go," Gelo said.

"But he had two boot heel marks on his chest. Somebody booted him pretty hard and sent him flying."

"So it could have been anybody."

"That's true, but it couldn't have been anybody's boots. We got casts of the boot marks on Ump's chest. We got casts of the boot heel marks along the path. We got casts of the boot heels."

The Mountie opened his satchel and pulled out a pair of boots. "We found these boots over there in the corner. Are these Tomassio's boots, Anna?"

"Yes."

"If you see him, tell him not to carry that rifle."

The Mounties left. Anna and Gelo sat in silence at the table, across from each other, looking at their hands. After a while, Anna locked her hands in Gelo's.

"I might have to confess," she said. "Does Sadie know?"

"No. I never told Sadie. Nobody."

"I have to tell you what happened. It's not very nice. Okay?"

"Yes, Mama."

"If it comes to court you'll be called. I want you to know the truth. I want you to tell the truth. I'm not going to tell you everything right now. Just what you need to know. Sooner or later you'll find out everything."

But for Anna confession soon became optional. Anna was not the confessing type. Reluctantly, every year she "made her Easter duty" to fulfil the requirements of church law. Because she thought church was good for kids, she didn't want to be excommunicated. She thought her example would be good for Gelo. Perhaps help him avoid some of the bad habits of his father. But now the situation was serious. She did not want Gelo to be known as the son of a murderer. If the Mounties caught Tomassio and pinned the murder on him, she would have to confess. Then everyone would know. No help for it. But if not, there would be no need. She was not a murderer. She protected herself, that was all. She pushed him off. Gravity pulled him down. She didn't find it easy to feel sorry for him. She couldn't even feel sorry for Cathy because she was pretty sure she was still screwing Tomassio. She felt sorry for Sadie. If Sadie found out...

The little door of the confessional slid open and Anna could see Father Rod, his chin in his hand, his ear at the screen. "Bless me, Father, for I have sinned," she began. "It is two months since my last confession. I accuse myself of—" she ended the ritual opening with a deep significant pause worthy of the revelation to come, giving herself a moment to change her mind. But she needed someone to know Tomassio didn't do it. It was pitch black in the confessional, but even if he didn't recognize her he'd know it was a woman and he'd know Tomassio didn't do it. He's a priest, he couldn't tell who had confessed to him, but he could say he knew who did it and it wasn't Tomassio. She took a deep breath, let it out, then she said, "I killed Ump MacLeod."

"What?" Father Rod said, startled.

Anna remembered the priest in Italy, the one she overheard telling her parents, "Anna is a good girl. You can take it from me," he had said and winked. They couldn't see her but in a mirror in the hall she watched him saying it. She remembered the look on his face. What a slimy bastard. She knew Father Rod wasn't like that, thank God. "You didn't hear me?" she asked.

"I heard you. Does anyone else know about this?"

"Gelo." Now Father Rod was bound to know who was confessing.

"You told Gelo."

"No. Gelo found him in the water. He had my kerchief clenched in his hand. He grabbed it off my head and it stayed in his hand. That's how come Gelo found him. He noticed the kerchief and when he pulled it out of the water, he dragged Ump up the sand."

"Okay. Tell me how it happened."

"I was walking along the cliff across the bottom of the ball field. He jumped me. I kicked him off. He fell over the cliff."

Father Rod gave himself a moment, then he said, "I have to ask you a few questions. I know this is uncomfortable, but I have to ask. It'll only take a minute. Okay?"

"Yes. That's okay."

"He attacked you?"

"Yes."

"Was it a sexual attack?"

"Yes."

"You're sure?"

"He pulled off my bloomers. He put his hands all over me."

"You kicked him off?"

"Yes."

"He's a big man."

"Yes. My legs are strong. Because of all my walking."

"You kicked him off and he fell. Did you see him fall?"

"It was too dark. I heard him falling. Down the stone steps. I ran home. I didn't know who it was until Gelo found him."

"How did Gelo know it was you? Because of the kerchief?"

"Yes. Because of the kerchief. He knew it was mine. So I had to explain to him what happened."

"What happened to the kerchief?"

"Gelo hid it in his pants and took it home and put it on my dresser. He never said a word, but I knew he knew so I had to bring it up. I don't know for sure how he's doing. He seems okay, but it must be an awful shock. He's just an innocent boy. And his father is gone missing."

"Did he tell Sadie?"

"No. He said he didn't. I hope not. Think how she feels already."

Father Rod did think about it. He wondered how much

of this he would have to explain and to whom, once it all came out, as it surely would.

"Well. Look. What happened is terrible. It's not a sin. There was a sin going on there, a terrible sin, but not yours. I'll give you absolution anyway, but you'll have to confess something else, something in the past if you like, even if you confessed it before .... It's just that I can't give you absolution unless there's a sin, something you did that you think you shouldn't have. Can you do that?"

"Yes. I was cruel to my husband."

"Just once? I have to ask how many times."

"Well, I'm thinking of once."

"Okay. *Ego te absolvo ab omnibus, et peccatis, in nomine Patris, et Filii, et Spiritus Sancti, Amen.* Go in peace."

Follow Tomassio's rifle and the Mounties knew they would find their man. If it wasn't in the house, someone had taken it from the house. Had taken it somewhere. If Tomassio lent the rifle, he'd likely lend it to Jim McMahon, his buddy. If Ceit took it from the house after Tomassio's arrest, she'd bring it to a relative. She had one relative, her sister, also Ceit.

Ceit and Ceit had a mother so frugal she allowed her daughters only one short name between them. More generous with herself, she indulged two lovers, both poor in devotion but rich in hair, a black-haired man and a red-haired man. Their bequest to their daughters rendered them easy to distinguish. "We were Ceit Dhubh and Ceit Ruadh," Ceit told Anna.

The Mounties figured that if Red Ceit took the rifle, then Black Ceit concealed it. Black Ceit never left her house so if she harboured the rifle somebody had to go get it. Tomassio would trust only one man. Jim McMahon.

It didn't take long. McMahon led them to Black Ceit. With the rifle down his pant leg, he limped along to Cathy's house and the Mounties trailed behind.

After Tomassio left Cathy's house at three in the morning, he was free for two minutes. She watched him through her kitchen window. They jumped him as he walked between her coal house and her outhouse. They disarmed him and took away his fishing gear, his bag of bread, and the cans of Spam. It was a day to rejoice for sea trout on their June "strawberry run" up the streams from the sea, and for the rabbits who had survived the winter.

The Mounties put Tomassio back in the county jail, this time with no ticket to Petawawa. The keeper's function was upgraded from guard to warden. He knocked open the rusty padlock on a coffee room cupboard door and, on the advice of the Mounties, armed himself with a shotgun and a pocketful of shells. He was now in charge of an about-to-be-convicted murderer. He put Tomassio in a cell along the hallway to the courtyard. He locked the barred door between the hallway and the coffee/guard room.

"How long will he be here?" he asked the Mountie.

"Until the trial, likely. We'll send extra rations."

"Why do I need the shotgun? He can't get through that door."

"We're not worried about him getting out. We're worried about goons getting in, like the last time. This place is a sieve. There's a guard at the gate, but who's gonna wake him up?"

"Do I get extra pay?"

"We'll see."

"When's the trial?"

"Don't know. He'll be here a week, anyway."

So they thought. The warden didn't get extra pay. He didn't ask, especially once the authorities found out he hadn't locked Tomassio's cell door.

By dark, the warden was asleep. Tomassio quietly left his cell, walked down the hall and through the gate to the courtyard. When he got to the far wall, he picked up the clothes prop from where it had fallen when he vaulted to the top of the wall on his previous visit. He walked back the necessary steps, ran toward the wall, and vaulted a second time, landed on the top of the wall, letting the clothes prop fall behind him, and jumped to the ground.

Four men who had been waiting, shivering, pressed against the wall, seized him. A car pulled up and the four men encouraged Tomassio to get into the back seat with two of them. One man drove while another man in the front fondled a baseball bat. They drove to Ashby Corner, turned right, and sped along, between the rows of company houses, crossed the overpass, by the steel plant, through Whitney Pier and out along the highway beside the outer reaches of Sydney Harbour toward New Waterford. After they passed Fort Petrie, they turned down a dirt road and drove through the woods to the harbour.

Father Rod was soaking under the suds in his claw-foot tub. His eye patch sat next to his moonshine and maple syrup comfort drink. He scanned his volume of Gerard Manley Hopkins for a poem to suit his mood and settled on "Thou Art Indeed Just, Lord, If I Contend." He didn't like the poem. It was full of uncomfortable lines, such as "Oh, the sots and thralls of lust/Do in spare hours more thrive than I..." But he read it often for the sake of the last line, "Oh thou Lord of life, send my roots rain."

He licked his lips and was reaching for his first sip when he heard a foot on the stair and realized once again that he had forgotten there were other people in the house, women at that, and he hadn't bothered to shut the door. His sister Sarah, in full habit, entered the bathroom.

"Hello, Tarzan," Sister Sarah said. "There's a telephone call for you. Father Pat. He wants you to call him right back. And you have an interesting female visitor."

"Who?"

"Anna."

"Gelo's mother?"

"Um-umh." Sister Sarah smiled her knowing smile.

"What?"

"You'll see."

"All right. I'll be right down. If I can't lie back and enjoy my bath, I'd just as soon have no bath at all."

Anna was standing in the kitchen so he brought her to the living room, which did duty as a business office and library. Anna appeared to be dressed up for the occasion, but what was the occasion? She sat in a stuffed chair upholstered in clamshell-coloured leather and he sat across from her on the sofa. She crossed her legs and aimed her knees and her eyes at him.

"What can I do for you, Anna?"

"Tomassio is out of work. They put him in jail and he escaped. They captured him and put him in again and he escaped again. Nobody knows where he is. That is clever of him, but I have a house to run, if they don't boot me out

of it because I don't have a man in the pit. I'm sure somebody will soon be looking for it—the company houses are
hard to come by and people are asking why the Italians
should get company houses. The Mounties think Tomassio
murdered Ump, so even if they find him it'll be worse than
if they don't find him. The next thing you know my Gelo is
going to be looking for a job. I don't want that. Gelo is a
good student. I want him to finish school. I want him to go
to college. If he gets a job he'll get married and that will be
the end of that. Eventually he'll end up in the pit. I don't
want that."

"What can I do for you?"

"I need money. I have wine to sell. The church uses wine.
Perhaps you could buy my wine."

"Yes, Anna. I could do that."

"Thank you. I didn't think it would be that easy."

"I have to buy wine anyway," Father Rod explained. "I'll
pay you what I pay for it now."

"That's lovely. And," her eyes brightened, "I was going to
ask …" She stopped. "I need a job. And Father Mancini said
you need a housekeeper."

Father Rod was silent while the wind of her suggestion
blew over him. Her unflinching eyes held him steady while
he reviewed the reasons, one by one, to explain why he did
not need or want a housekeeper. Each one seemed logical,
complete, and adequate when he argued with the bishop
and Father Pat, but not even the whole set of reasons carried enough weight to contend with Anna's need.

"You can start tomorrow."

"Wonderful. Full-time?"

"Did you want part-time?"

"No. Full-time is good."

Anna uncocked her knees, rose from the chair, and pointing to the wall above the priest's head, said, "That's a beautiful picture. Did you paint that?"

"No. Botticelli painted that."

"Botticelli. An Italian?"

"Yes."

"What's it about?"

"It's about Venus, the woman. She was a goddess. The story is she came out of the foam of the sea."

"I guess that's why she's standing on a clamshell."

"Yes."

"An Italian goddess. It's nice to know that something beautiful came up out of the sea."

After Anna left, Father Pat Mancini called. "I think we're in for a tussle down in the pit yard," he told Father Rod. "The rumour's around that Tomassio murdered Ump and the Mounties have captured him. The word is the miners will refuse to go underground unless they pull the Italians."

"How can they do that? There's too many of them. The pit can't operate twenty-four hours a day without them. The company wants more production as it is."

"I know. It doesn't make sense. But that doesn't mean it's not true. Some of them are mad because of Ump and they're blaming it on the Italians. They're talking sabotage. The Italians blowing up the mines. They've already invented three people who are sending signals to U-boats at night with information about coal shipments. As if it were some sort of secret that we're shipping coal. It's all nonsense but it's dangerous. Somebody is liable to get hurt."

"Is the bishop doing anything about this? These people are all Catholics. Is he the shepherd or not?"

"He says he is."

"Has he talked to the apostolic delegate?"

"He was up there, in Ottawa. I imagine he talked to him. I don't know what they said. And who's to know what side the apostolic delegate is on. You know those Italians. Pretty slippery."

"Very funny. Are you coming with me?"

"Yeah. That's all they'd need. An Italian priest telling them what to do. Look, if anything is going to happen, it'll likely be when the shift changes this afternoon. Or maybe tomorrow."

"Okay. I'll take a run down. Is the bishop around? I might want to talk to him when I get back. If he doesn't do something soon, it'll be too late."

"He won't talk on the phone. You'll have to come in. Give me a call when you get back."

Father Rod crossed the schoolyard to where he had left his car. The school kids were all out for afternoon recess. He stopped to watch some young skippers and listen to their chant. Two of them swung a double rope and sang, two others took turns, jumping in and out of the twirling ropes, their dresses and their braids swinging and swaying with the innocent music.

"Red, white, and blue, your mother is a Jew,

"Your father is a curly-head just like you."

He waited until one of the children missed a beat and tangled the rope. "Hi girls."

"Hi Father," they chanted.

"Are you having fun?"

"Yes, Father," they chanted.

"Where did you learn the song?"

They all looked at him and pursed their lips, and looked at each other. "We don't know, Father," Gina said.

"Could you sing it for me, the four of you?"

"No, Father," they chanted.

"Why not?"

The three girls looked to Gina. "It's not a singing song, Father," Gina said. "It's a skipping song. You have to skip."

"Okay, I'll skip. You sing."

"But you only got one eye," Gina said.

"That's okay. I can still skip."

"Okay, we'll only turn one rope," Gina said kindly.

"Okay. Here we go."

"Red, white, and blue, your mother is a Jew,

"Your father is a curly-head just like you."

Father Rod made it through one verse before he tangled the rope.

"See," Gina said. "You can't skip with only one eye." A nun came out on the school steps. She waved to Father Rod and started swinging a bell up and down, clanging the end of recess. She waved again and disappeared into the building. Gina was coiling the ropes around her hand and elbow.

"Gina," Father Rod said, "do you know what a Jew is?"

"No, Father."

"What about a curly-head? Does anybody know what a curly-head is?" He scanned their little faces. They looked at him and pursed their lips, and looked at each other again.

"What grade are you in?"

"Grade four, Father," they said in unison.

"Okay, I'll come and see you some day and we'll have a little chat. Would that be okay?"

"Yes, Father," they chanted.

TEN

How good bad music and bad
reasons sound when we march
against an enemy.
FRIEDRICH NIETZSCHE

JIM MCMAHON LEFT HIS HOUSE by the back door
and walked toward the mine through the sunshine, pit
can under his arm, hands in his pants' pockets. The
heat of the sun spread comfort over his neck and shoulders, but beyond the pit bank, out over the Atlantic, a menacing storm cloud crouched like a patient, ugly grey dog,
woolly hair hanging down, covering the eyes and hiding
the teeth, ready to pounce on the land as soon as the south
wind relented.

Jim heard droning from above and stopped to watch the
Lysander, "the flying carrot," a single-engine, top-wing
reconnaissance aircraft, as it flew inland from its mission
over the Atlantic. It dipped down in front of the storm to
five hundred feet. He could make out the bombs on the
wheel caps and the four-circle red, white, and blue insignia
of the Royal Canadian Air Force beneath the two-man

cockpit. The pilot banked and circled the Coaltown colliery several times.

Jim knew the pilot and he knew the photographer, who waved to him as the aircraft finished its final circle, gained altitude, and sped off to the airport at Reserve Mines. For Jim, it was not a good omen that these two took time at the end of their mission to take pictures in Coaltown. He knew this photographer had a nose for trouble. He had been on hand to take a picture of the Royal Canadian Dragoons, their tents, and their horses encamped in Sydney at the steel plant when the federal government sent them to Cape Breton to suppress the labour movement in 1923. By good luck or good management, he'd been in New Waterford in 1925 when the police shot Bill Davis in the crowd of protestors.

Jim watched the small plane diminish to a dot in the sky and then drop out of sight. The memories of his turbulent past appeared to him like photos. His wife had teased him about it just this afternoon.

"Oh, Jim, why are you always on the unpopular side of every dispute? Not that I mind, now, don't get me wrong, I only married you because you got on the wrong side of my father."

"Your father is a capitalist lackey."

"I know. It's his one redeeming quality."

"You watch your tongue or I'll ship you back. That's if he'll take you in, which I doubt, he knows what kind of an appetite you got."

"Listen to what's talking."

Thinking of his wife improved his mood a bit. He never knew if her joking was self-prescribed therapy to alleviate the anxiety of being married to a troublemaker, or if it was camouflage to conceal her irritation at the frequent disruptions in their life together. She had never laughed much before they were married. She'd little enough to laugh at in her father's house, he thought. Since then, she thought everything but his work in the pit was funny. Even during the strike when someone torched their house and they came home from a union meeting to a heap of ashes, she couldn't help but quip, "Well, Jim, I guess we finally got rid of that ugly chesterfield."

"Will we go live with your father? Or my brother?"

"Let's go talk to your brother, he's got a spare room now Joey's married and gone." Janice grabbed his arm. "C'mon, we'll walk. It's a long way and by the time we get there we'll feel better. But listen here, Jim, once we have kids, we can't have people burning down our house."

"Are we gonna have kids?"

"I can pretty well guarantee we're gonna have at least one. So don't lose your job. And don't you dare go in the army."

After they burned down his house, he and Janice moved to Low Point, where they lived with his brother while he rebuilt the house. He got a job with the *Maritime Labour Herald* as a reporter, and his first assignment, doing a story on the gypsies and the local toughs who were harassing them, allowed him to spend extra time in the public library, where he'd met Leda Perenowsky, the tallest woman he had ever seen, and her daughter Helen, already lanky at three years old. They were gypsies, and he featured them in his article for the paper and consequently singled them out for even more harassment. Leda and Ty, her husband, generously forgave him, but it was an ugly memory and a bitter, useful lesson.

He had thought he could change public opinion by telling the truth. His editor published the story but warned him, "There are two things that won't change public opinion, bombs and the truth. Neither will work."

"What will work?" Jim asked.

"Money. If you want people to believe something, either make it profitable to believe or make it expensive to disbelieve. And remember, Jim, if you have a family to support, it's probably better to stick to the pick and shovel—you won't make enough money with a pencil."

In those days Jim was not so easily discouraged. When he worked for the *Maritime Labour Herald*, even as a delivery boy, he was labelled a communist. When he started in the mines and got active in the United Mine Workers of America, he was labelled a rabble-rouser. The bitter winter of the '25 strike, police brutality, starving, shivering children, a humiliating, ignoble settlement, left him angry and feeling strangely guilty. Working conditions were worse. More overtime, more back shift, more accidents, more pressure to produce, more maiming and needless deaths, but how can you complain now with men dying overseas, some who thought they would be safer in the war than in the pit?

"At least in the war you're allowed to shoot your enemy," his nephew had said to Jim and Janice as he waved goodbye after his last visit.

Blacklisted after the strike, Jim had no steady work until the blacklist disappeared with the advent of war. He was still angry and frustrated. He knew the men, too, were still angry and frustrated, and although mollified by wartime prosperity, they continued to look for somebody to blame for their woes. And now Mussolini had given them an excuse to blame their Italian neighbours. Overnight they had transformed their buddies into "enemy aliens."

Jim bent his head and began to walk, and his grumpy eyes watched his new shoes lead him toward the wash house. His new belt strained against his expanding girth. Prosperity squatted at the back of his mind, replacing the space vacated by poverty, haunting his days, spoiling the happy moments with buddies in the pit, with Janice at home. And now the mines working full-time, miners working overtime, there was too much pit, and not enough home.

But worse than the haunts of his days were the spooks of his sleep. Last night he woke up screaming from a dream of J.B. MacLachlan, whose naked body, made of straw, hung from a rope around his neck in the doorway of his newspaper office, the *Maritime Labour Herald*. J.B.'s hands clenched a copy of *Sartor Resartus*, covering his phantom testicles. A phantom soldier thrust a bayoneted rifle at the book. Suddenly straw man and soldier turned into flesh. Jim woke up with Janice's hands holding his head.

"It's a dream, Jim. A nightmare. Wake up."

Jim turned onto the pit yard road and walked toward the slag heap. As he approached, he studied the crowd of men in front of the distant wash house. A car pulled up beside him as he walked. He stopped and put a foot on the running board when Father Rod rolled down the window. His two hands clutched the lowered window.

"*Ciamar a tha thu?*"

"*Chan eil ach meadhonach. Tha thu fhein math?*"

"*Chan eil dona, tapadh leat.*"

Jim and Father Rod always began their conversations in Gaelic. Both understood the ritual as acknowledgement that in spite of their differences, they still had in common what they regretted losing. Neither of them could speak to their own fathers in a communal mother tongue. They courted each other, Catholic priest, lapsed Protestant, like two male dogs from the same mother, separated at birth, then brought together in adulthood, occupying adjoining yards separated by no physical fence, but lacking a language that would be almost as rich as blood. They managed fairly well, however, with English.

"Warm for June."

"Yes, Padre. As long as the south wind lasts. But if she turns nor'east, look out. But she'll be warm and then some in the pit today. If anybody goes down."

"You're late. Want me to drive you in?"

"I'm in no hurry."

"What do you think?" Father Rod asked.

"Trouble."

"For sure?"

"These Italians," Jim said. "They're all Catholics. Right?"

"Yeah."

"So. What's the church gonna do?"

"I don't know."

"You do know what they did in the strike in '25."

"Yeah. Nothing," Father Rod admitted.

"I wouldn't say nothing. They told us to go back to work. They told us we were nothing but a bunch of communists. I'd say they did a whole lot less than nothing. They undermined the miners. Well, maybe I'm contradicting myself. A kick in the arse is not what you want, but I guess you can't call it nothing."

"I guess they can't call the Italians a bunch of communists," Father Rod commented. Wanting to leave the subject, he asked, "How's Janice?"

"She's good. She's worried. Maybe I'll take a lift in after

all. But take your time. Trouble won't run. It'll sit there and wait."

Jim rounded the front of the car and got into the passenger seat. The pattern of their relationship was familiar to them, and Jim smiled as he realized it once again. Once they had chatted for a while, they realized that their mutual hostility was as artificial as food colouring. In their hearts and in their bones they were allies. The differences between them were not much more significant than the difference in their clothing. Jim got into the passenger seat and opened his pit can. He took out his tea bottle and handed it to Father Rod with an egg salad sandwich and a date square. "Here, let's take a break, Padre. My guess is I won't be going down to work today so I won't be needing my lunch."

Father Rod accepted the bottle, took a swig of tea, a bite of the sandwich and another swig of tea, and passed the bottle back to Jim. "Thanks, Jim, good tea. Good sandwich."

"Yes indeed. Janice can turn a pit can into a banquet table," Jim laughed. "So what are you up to, Padre, you gonna go to work in the pit? War wasn't bad enough for you?"

"Father Pat called me. Said there might be trouble for the Italians."

"There's no 'might' to it."

"Pat thinks they might listen to me."

"MacPherson won't listen to you. He's the ringleader. He's having too much fun. He's been fighting with his own priest since a year over his wife."

"What priest? He's after his wife?"

"No. MacPherson is beating his wife. Father Danny is telling him to stop. He put her in the convent with the nuns for a couple weeks, but in the end she went home. What else could she do? He beats the kids too. She's waiting for her brother to come home from overseas. He'll look after it all right. Of course, he might not come back. My nephew, Joey, got killed last week, eh."

"Yeah. I'm sorry."

"There's not a miner in the pit made a decent living till the war started. Now we got enough money and too much work, but our boys are over there getting killed."

"There's a lot of Italians working in the pit," Father Rod said. "If they don't let them work, there's not gonna be enough coal for the war."

"I know," Jim smiled. "I guess that makes it interesting."

They passed the bottle back and forth and chatted for a while, watching the miners stirring in the pit yard, small groups forming, breaking up and reforming in what seemed an atmosphere of quiet confusion. Jim clipped the bottle back in the top chamber of his can and snapped it shut. Father Rod put the car in gear, drove in a little farther, and stopped.

"I think this is as far in as I'm gonna get the car. Is that MacPherson up there on the cart?"

"Yeah. He looks normal, eh. Wait till you get a whiff of his tongue."

"Nasty?"

"Ever see a slime eel?"

"I don't think so."

"Looks like any other eel. But it sweats slime. Put it in a pool and it fouls the water for ten feet around it. Every living thing in the water gags. It stinks so bad it can't stand itself. It ties itself in a knot and runs the knot up and down itself until it wipes itself all off."

"We'll have to hoof it from here. Let's get there before things get too heated up."

"Watch your step, Padre. She's kinda mucky."

"I'm used to muck, Jim. This is not the worst of it."

Father Rod and Jim walked single file across an intermittent causeway of round and flat stones where the wetted slag of the pit bank met an ancient bog called Frog Hollow, a playground for the local children and birthplace of marine life. Rivulets of water blackened by coal dust curled around a thousand fiddlehead stems holding their furry crosiers above water like a thousand worried bishops.

MacPherson was standing on the back end of a dump cart. The horse stood docile between the shafts, its head held up by the reins wrapped around a stanchion on the end of a plank that served as a crude seat. About forty or so miners stood in a semicircle watching and listening to MacPherson's performance. About two dozen more were on their way from the wash house to the lamp house to pick up their lamps and check numbers. More miners drifted from the lamp house. Everyone stopped to listen and joined the crowd or watched from where they were. Father Rod and Jim joined the crowd at the front end of the semicircle.

MacPherson was at the height of his harangue. "I'm not saying they're all dangerous. I didn't say that. But they're all Catholics. They all obey the Pope. Don't think the Pope and Mussolini are not in cahoots. One couldn't operate without the other."

"Are you crazy?" somebody in the crowd yelled. "Most of us here are Catholics. You don't have to be an Italian. You're a Catholic yourself, you stupid arse."

"Crazy. I'm not crazy enough to take a chance on them blowing up the pit. Like I said. They're not all dangerous. But it only takes one man to blow the whole caboodle up.

They chased a German submarine out of Sydney Harbour last week. What d'you think of that? Dropping off spies, likely. One man, that's all it takes. They've arrested a bunch already. They must have their reasons. They arrested Tomassio. And now he's escaped. What does that tell ya? There's a war on, you know. We have to do our part."

"If you want to fight the war, why don'tcha join the army?"

"I'd be in the army in a minute if I didn't have flat feet."

"I don't think it's the feet end that's flat."

Everybody laughed and Jim whispered in the ear of his friend David LeBlanc. "I think now is the time. Dave, see if you can knock him off that cart. Kick the horse or something."

Dave slipped around behind the semicircle of men and poked the horse between his legs with a sharp stick. The horse leaped ahead two feet and stopped. MacPherson fell face first to the ground, and by the time he'd scrambled to his feet Jim stood in his place on the cart.

"Listen, men, listen to me, listen to me," he chanted, and after the laughter died down, the men listened. "Who are we talking about here? These Italians are the same people who stood with us in the strike in '25. They arrested Tomassio. Yes. What for? Who knows? Tommy was my buddy in the pit for years. I'd trust my life with him. These people are friends. We work with them, we play ball with them, hockey, most of you go to church with them. They're neighbours. They're buddies in the pit. Our buddies."

"Maybe they're your buddies," someone yelled from the crowd, "they're not everybody's buddies."

"Listen, you," Jim pointed his finger. "How's your memory? Do you remember the strike in '24? Do you remember

'25? Do you remember hunger? Do you remember how many Italians brought around food from their gardens? I'd bet there's not a man standing in front of me whose family didn't get at least one armload of vegetables. And what about the winter of '25? Pickles, preserves, dried fruit, salt meat, fish. What about you, big mouth? Did you eat Italian vegetables in '24? Or did you eat enemy alien vegetables?"

Someone yelled, "Mackenzie King wants them arrested. He must know what he's doing."

"Mackenzie King," Jim yelled back. "Remember in the winter of '25 when we were all starving? We asked Mackenzie King for potatoes. He sent us soldiers. We asked for carrots. He sent us bayonets. We asked for bread. He sent us machine guns." Jim drummed his finger on his temple. "Now think, think, think. Who gave us potatoes? Who gave us carrots? Who gave us meat?"

Someone shouted out, "What if he's right, Jim? It only takes one of them."

"One of them," Jim said. "It only takes one of anybody."

"That's right," somebody yelled. "Get rid of the Polacks too."

"You're nothing but a communist, McMahon. You'd stand up for any of your rabble-rousers. Get off that cart or we'll knock you off."

"What's that, MacPherson? Am I supposed to be scared of you?"

"You're worse than a goddamn Chinaman."

"I'd rather be a goddamn anything than a slimy snake-brain like you."

MacPherson lunged forward and, grabbing Jim by the legs, yanked him off the cart. Two miners jumped on MacPherson and peeled him off Jim, then two more miners stood in front of MacPherson and backed him off.

"We'll settle this later, McMahon," MacPherson shouted at Jim, "when your comrades are drunk or asleep or gone for a visit to Moscow."

"That's fine with me. But while we're here, why don't you tell us which one of them is the one you think is gonna blow up the pit, and himself and his buddies in it, you idiot?"

"I said, nobody knows who. Maybe nobody will. But who's gonna take the chance? Some of them don't care if they kill themselves. They're fanatics. Like you and your communist friends."

"Hey, maybe it's Giovanni," Jim suggested. "His brother is with the Cape Breton Highlanders. Maybe they're in it together. Giovanni's gonna blow up the pit, and Romano over on the battlefield is gonna start shooting his own men in the back. Between the two of them they'll win the war for Italy, one at the front and one on the home front. You think maybe that's it, you senseless slug?"

Already some men were drifting away. Some to the lamp house to return their lamps and check numbers. Some to the wash house to change back to their street clothes. Some, still in their street clothes, left for home. By the time the mine manager, George MacDonald, came on the scene, it was too late to save the shift.

"Everybody go home," he said. "We'll work something out tomorrow, and we'll send word."

Father Rod and Jim watched the crowd disperse. Horse and dump cart disappeared behind the wash house and the pit yard was empty.

"What exactly happened here, Jim?" Father Rod asked. "MacPherson is an obvious son of a bitch. Why would they follow him?"

"They're not all following him. Some of them are stunned enough to think he might be right. Some of them are jittery in the pit anyway and this just makes them worse. Some of them are not fussy about work and any excuse is good enough to bring home to their wives. They don't need a good reason. A bad reason will do for an excuse."

"What about the Italians? They're not saying much."

"What are they gonna say? 'Hey buddy, I'm not gonna blow up the pit.' A lot of these Italians are really good miners, big producers loading coal, so the underground manager puts them in the good places because that boosts his production. So you get these other guys who aren't that good and they're jealous. They got themselves convinced that the other ones are producing because they got the good places and not the other way around."

"Jealousy?"

"Yeah. Good old-fashioned jealousy. And they're thinking, if the company kicks the Italians out, well, somebody is gonna get to work the good places. The Italians can't speak up. Just make things worse. The war is an excuse for everything, no matter how miserable. The Italians are just gonna try to keep low. Wait for it to go away. It's up to us. And what can we do? And what about the bishop? Like I said before, these guys are all Catholics. What's he doing about it? Sitting in his office?"

"C'mon. Let's get in the car," Father Rod said. "I'll run you home. Or maybe you'd like to drive. Have you driven the new Ford yet?"

The two men sat in the car. Jim put his two hands on the steering wheel and revealed the fact that he had never driven a car in his life. So they opened the lunch can and finished off the sandwiches and date squares and tea while

Father Rod explained the theory of car driving, explaining the choke, the throttle, the clutch, the gears, the brakes. Jim was an adept student and after a few aborted starts, unintended stops, and a bit of lurching and gear grinding, he managed to find his back yard, where they sat and chatted again for a while.

"Jim, bishops are like generals," Father Rod explained. "They're trained to think, not do. They don't like to make a move if they can't predict the outcome. The right thing in the short run doesn't interest them much. Sometimes they just wait. They like the long run."

"During the strike," Jim said, "Father Damien up the road there took in all the families that got kicked out of the company houses and put them up in the church. He wasn't scared to help out a bunch of communists. But he was the only one that I know of." Father Rod nodded to acknowledge what Jim was saying, and raised his hands, palms out, both conceding the point and changing the subject. They talked a bit of small talk until Jim got out of the car and went into the house. Father Rod drove to the ball field.

At the ball field Gelo was sitting in the dugout waiting for his bantam team to arrive for practice. He was repairing a set of catcher's shin guards when Father Rod arrived. Sadie was stirring a bucket of whitewash and using a ladle to paint the baselines. When she saw the priest talking to Gelo, she dropped the bucket and ladle and came into the dugout, splotches of whitewash already drying and flaking off her dress. Both of them appeared to Father Rod to be content in their busy work, but he knew they must be anxious. They seemed too composed and serene in the midst of the turmoil in their families and in the town. Perhaps they were enough for each other, he thought, but he was wary and tried to keep an eye on them. Sadie gave him a bit of a smile.

"I'm sorry about your father, Sadie."

"Thanks, Father. It's sad. We never got along, though. He was good to me, but we never got along. Everything I liked he didn't like, including people. I don't know if he liked anybody, except me. And he gave me a hard time. I don't know what happened out there, but Tomassio didn't kill him. Tomassio is full of jokes and fun, but he wouldn't kill anybody, especially Daddy. He's not stupid, he'd know they'd try to pin it on him. Anyway, he liked me, he wouldn't kill my father."

Father Rod got back to the glebe house after dark. Fatigue. His back hurt from bending over talking to little kids at the ball field. A band of mud lined his pant leg from demonstrating to bantams the ways to slide into second base. His shoes were covered in mud. He pulled his eye patch down, letting it hang around his neck, and splashed cold water on his stinging blank eye. He smiled at his mirror image. It reminded him of a Cyclops, one of Homer's giant shepherds of Sicily. Where is Odysseus now, he thought, with his hot stick? Cowering in his Trojan horse? Chatting up Circe? He poured a moonshine maple syrup hot toddy and headed for the tub.

When he put foot to stair to climb to the bathroom, he heard voices in the living room. He opened the door. Sarah sat with her back to him at one end of the table wearing a flowered housedress that seemed a bit too small for her, the buttons down her back straining to keep the panels of the dress closed. At the other end, across from Sister Sarah, sat Sister Mary, wearing what looked like a white gown with a blue mantle over her shoulders. Their heads were uncovered, Sister Sarah's hair roughly chopped around her ears and high at the neck, and Sister Mary's hair, a little longer, covering her neck. Sarah's elbows were on the table and her forearms made an inverted V over his initials carved in the table. One hand, raised over her shoulder, gripped the ace of hearts between thumb and index finger and it was clear she'd been about to slam it onto the middle of the table when she'd heard the door open behind her.

Sister Mary held her cards at her chin, covering her mouth, but when she saw the look on Father Rod's face when he opened the door, she dropped the cards to the table and started to laugh.

It was then that Father Rod saw someone else. Father Pat Mancini sat at one side of the table, Sister Sarah at his right, Sister Mary at his left hand. His collar hung loose down along his stock, his cards face up on the table, a gesture of surrender. When he heard the door handle turn, he'd looked up in hope. The card game was getting boring. Across the table from Father Pat, in front of the empty chair, a half-full hank of red wine waited. In front of the card players, like three fat thermometers, three water glasses, filled to different degrees with red wine, waited for hands to pick them up. An empty water glass sat on the table beside the hank of wine. Beside the empty glass an unopened letter with a foreign stamp rested on the table. Father Rod shut the door behind him, sat in the empty chair, stuck his finger in the ear of the hank of wine and lowered it to the floor. He put his hot toddy on the table beside the letter.

"Sorry, Pat. I forgot I invited you over."

"What odds?" Pat said. "I'm here. They're looking after me, as you can see."

"Quite the little ceilidh," Father Rod said. "I suppose I'm supposed to ask you two what you're dressed up as."

"We decided to take a little holiday from our habits and have a party," Sister Mary said, as she gathered the cards and put them aside. "We got the clothes from the costume room at the school. Sarah is dressed as Mother Normal in the very uplifting play, 'Everybody Loves Mum'. I am the virgin, Mary. It's all wrong, of course, because Sarah is anything but normal and I was married so if I were still a virgin I wouldn't want to admit it. And besides"—she pretended to confide to Father Pat, leaning his way and shielding her mouth with her hand—"I came close enough to the brink before I ever thought of getting married, what with visiting Sarah and Rod's house and sometimes only himself there to play hide-and-seek with. With me so poor at hiding and him so good at seeking, it's a wonder I wasn't married long before I even met Randy. And pity help the poor church then with neither me the nun, nor him the priest in it. Of course, we might have had a dozen or so priests and nuns for kids since that's a streak we got in us. He even asked me if I'd marry him. But that was after I was engaged. He didn't ask me to marry him, mind you, he just asked me if I would. 'I don't think so,' I told him, 'you're too much rod and not enough randy for me.' Here, pour me a bit of wine, Rod. Do you remember those rainy days in the attic, Rod?"

"How could I forget?" he replied, pouring the wine from the hank into her glass and not doing a very good job of it.

"You were married, Mary?" Father Pat said. "I didn't know that."

"Yes indeed. I was married to a nice boy, but he died."

"I'm sorry."

"Och, I'm all over it now. He was a nice boy, but it didn't look good for us. We were so young. The two of us foolish."

"What's that like, marriage?"

"Funny you should ask. I was rooting around in Rod's boxes of books just today and what did I find but *The Devil's Dictionary*. Of course, what else would you expect to find in a priest's library? Know thine enemy, right? It's only a small little book but it has all the good words in it. Here it is," she said. She reached down and pulled it from a cardboard box, opened it, and read, "'Marriage is a community consisting of a master, a mistress and two slaves. All in all, two people.'" She flipped through the pages and read some more, "'Love is a disease, curable by marriage.'"

"Speaking of love," Sister Sarah said, "your suitor arrived today with that hank of wine. Finish your toddy and taste it. It's the best wine I ever tasted, but you better try it out in safe company—it might be an aphrodisiac."

Father Rod smiled. He hadn't yet tasted his toddy and it was probably no longer a hot toddy. He put it aside in anticipation of the wine. He pulled the cork, put his index finger in the ear of the hank and with his left hand on the bottom carefully filled the water glass. He looked at the hank now with a new eye and noticed the label stuck on its shoulder, a two-inch-long piece of bandage tape with the words MASS WINE printed in pencil. Below it, bits of glue stuck to the clear glass where the previous label had been pulled off. The bishop will love this, he thought, homemade wine for the price of Harvey's Shooting Sherry. He took a sip and moved it around his mouth with his tongue.

"Mmmm," he purred. "That is some nice. Now what are you talking about, Sarah? What do you mean, my 'suitor'?"

"You know very well what I mean." Sister Sarah winked at Sister Mary.

Sister Mary said, "If it wasn't you who talked to her yesterday, then who was it? I understand she's coming here to work. Starting tomorrow, I understand."

"Well, yes, I talked to her yesterday. And yes, she's coming to work. So?"

"So you didn't notice the clothes on her? No?"

"Yes. She had clothes on her, I'm glad to say."

"Dressed to the nines," Sister Sarah put in.

"She didn't come to work. It was a job interview."

"Oh sure," said Sister Sarah. "The job interview. For a housekeeper. Mmm-hmm, I'm sure a person would want to dress pretty sharp for that. And the nylons, did you get a load of that? You can't buy those, you know. Every scrap of nylon is supposed to go to make parachutes, or to bribe prostitutes and spies in England. No ration cards for that stuff. You get it on the black market or you don't get it at all. Not cheap. Quite the investment for a woman with a growing boy."

Father Pat was chuckling, but he thought he'd better change the tone. He didn't want to spoil their fun but he didn't want to hear too much light talk about his cousin Anna, of whom he was very fond and who was not having a very good time. He picked up the cards and dealt out five cards to each and four in the middle for the kitty. "Let's have one game of 45's," he said, "and then I think I'd better get on the move. What happened to your husband, Mary?" Father Pat asked. "If you don't mind me asking."

"I don't mind. He was killed in the pit. The cable on the rake let go when they were almost up. They all jumped and they were all hurt, but he was killed. Hit his head. DOA, they called him." Tears rolled down Sister Mary's cheeks like little silver ball bearings and she wiped them out of the corners of her mouth. "I'm sorry," she said. "But I loved him, foolish as he was, and foolish as I was myself, he loved me. Marriage didn't cure us."

"I'm sorry, Mary, I shouldn't have brought it up. I made you cry."

"Oh no, dear, not at all. I need to cry once in a while, let off the pressure. When you're full of stuff like that, you have to drain it out once in a while, you know, like the radiators in the school, every now and again you have to turn the little wheel and bleed the steam out the spigot. It must be the wine. I shouldn't drink. It makes me think."

"You never thought of getting married again?" Pat asked. They studied their cards, but the game had stalled and the party mood dissipated.

"Oh, I think about it all the time. But I always wanted to be a nun. I got the idea from hanging around their house, you know, listening to their mother. It makes sense, you know, to be a nun. You get to live with other women, so you always have someone to talk to, unless you're a contemplative, and that wouldn't be me. And unless you're the cook yourself, somebody feeds you every day. Sometimes you have to help with the dishes. You get a good education free. You get a real job instead of working as a slave for some galoot and all his kids and maybe even his mother. You get two months' vacation in the summer, two weeks at Christmas, a week at Easter, you get a bungalow in the country, trips to Boston, Halifax, and Montreal. Next to being the Queen, what more could a person want? I knew all that. But I was one of those young girls who gets horny early but gets over it quick. It'd be nice to have kids, although God knows I get more than enough of them every day. But some of my own."

The telephone rang in the kitchen and Father Rod went to answer it. When he came back, he announced that he had to go on an emergency sick call. "Theresa Papadopoulos is in the hospital with T.B."

"Is she dying?" Sister Sarah asked.

Father Rod shrugged. "They called me. You enjoy yourselves."

"I've got an early Mass and a big day tomorrow," Father Pat said, taking advantage of the interruption. "But you girls stay."

"I can sit and talk to a nun any day of the week," Sister Mary said. "We might as well pack up tonight and get an early start in the morning."

"What?" Father Rod said. "You're leaving?"

"*Tha eagal orm*," Sister Sarah said. "Do you know what that means?"

"I'm afraid so," Father Rod replied.

"Exactly. I'm afraid so. Sister Superior called earlier today. She's not stupid, you know. 'I know what you two are up to,' she said. 'You get back here and when the bishop decides to grace the parish with his presence you can go back.'"

"The kids will forget everything you taught them," Father Rod said.

"We can zip out and give a refresher," Sister Mary said. "We'll be in the way here anyway," she smiled, "now that you got a housekeeper."

Looking down the table, Sister Sarah said, "You didn't open your mail, Rod."

Father Rod picked the envelope from the table and put it in his pocket.

"It's from London, England," Sister Sarah pointed out.

Father Rod didn't respond. He stared at his sister.

"It's a woman's writing. Looks like a Danish name. The return address."

"Yes," he said.

"I guess the party's over," Sister Mary said.

"*Oichie Bhath*, Rod," Sister Sarah said and gave him a big smile. "Good night, Pat."

"*Buona notte* sisters."

ELEVEN

I feel the need of some imperishable bliss.

WALLACE STEVENS

A TWIN-ENGINE CATALINA soared over the church steeple toward the yellow morning sun as Father Rod walked from the glebe house to the church. The plane's bulbous shape and its jaunty, avuncular demeanour cloaked a lethal power and deadly mission. The amphibian aircraft looked like a winged cruise ship, but in fact it was an arsenal housing two .30 calibre machine guns in front and one in the rear, two .50 calibre machine guns midway on either side, and four thousand pounds of depth charges. Its mission, to find and destroy German submarines operating off Canada's east coast between Cape Breton and Newfoundland, throughout the Gulf of St. Lawrence, and along the convoy routes between Sydney and Great Britain. From the airport at Reserve Mines, it could range more than a thousand miles out over the Atlantic with enough fuel for the return trip.

Father Rod entered the vestry for seven o'clock Mass, the half-filled hank of wine hanging from the index finger of his left hand, his breviary in his right. The altar boys, Gelo and his buddy Réal AuCoin, usually late, were already dressed in their soutanes and sitting in the two wooden chairs beside their vestment closet. The jaws of their intent faces moved in muted, grave conversation. Father Rod put the wine and breviary on the table, opened his closet door, and pulled out his vestments: amice, alb, girdle, maniple, stole, and the green chasuble, and robed himself to say Mass.

"What's wrong with you guys?"

"What?" Gelo turned to him, frowning.

"You're early."

"Oh. We wanted to talk to ya, right, Rey?"

"Yeah."

"We can't go to school. Right, Rey?"

"What's goin' on?" Father Rod asked.

"They told me to tell him," Réal said, pointing his thumb at Gelo. "If he shows up in the schoolyard, they're gonna put the boots to him. They mean it. So he can't go to school. And if he can't, I'm not goin' with him."

"They? Who's they?"

"Bernie and them," Réal said. "They're only in grade nine, but they're big as boats. Older than us, too."

"Bernie and them," Father Rod laughed. " Who in hell is Bernie and them?"

"Bernie Murphy."

"And them?"

"Johnny Cusak, Bernie's cousin. And Angus Poirier, Johnny's buddy. Them anyway. Some of them I don't know who they are. Another bunch, up at the Protestant school, said they're gonna put the pucks to Sadie too if she keeps going with him. Gonna rip the dress right off her. Right in the schoolyard, they said. I'd like to see them try it. She got a knife on her."

"A knife!"

"Yeah," Réal said. "She got a knife on her. Don't blame her. Right in her school bag."

"Okay. You guys come to the glebe after breakfast. No, wait, hang on. After Mass, come with me. We'll grab a bite in the glebe and the both of you come with me to the hospital. I'll drive you back to school after that and we'll check it out. C'mon now, let's get out there, we're late. Some of these people gotta go to work. The wine there in the hank, put that in the wine cruet. Use the funnel. Don't spill it. Make sure you put the cork back. Did you light the candles?"

"Yeah. Rey did. Hey, that's Mama's wine."

"Don't tell anybody, eh?"

"What? It's a secret?"

"Réal?" Father Rod said and waited until Réal looked him in the eye.

"Yeah," Réal said. "My lips are sealed. Loose lips sink ships."

All in green, attended in procession by Gelo and Réal in black soutanes and white surplices, Father Rod strode out to the bottom of the altar steps. On the way he noticed that attendance had increased from the dozen or so regular daily Mass goers to almost two dozen. That's a sign, he thought. Trouble coming or trouble already here. He turned to face the tabernacle, bowed, and with Gelo and Réal crouched on their knees behind him, he began to say the Mass:

"*In nomine Patris, et Filii, et Spiritus Sancti,*" said Father Rod, crossing himself.

"Amen," chanted Gelo and Réal.

"*Introibo ad altare Dei*," said Father Rod.

"*Ad deum qui laetificat juventutem meam*," chanted Gelo and Réal.

"What's he mean, 'check it out'?'" Réal whispered.

"*Adjutorium nostrum in nomine Domini*," Father Rod said.

"*Qui fecit caelum et terram*," they chanted.

"Search me," whispered Gelo.

"*Confiteor Deo omnipotenti...*" Father Rod began the Confiteor.

"I hope he's not gonna squeal on me I told him about Sadie's knife."

In the few short weeks he'd been in the parish, Father Rod hadn't given a sermon at daily Mass, but after reading the Epistle and the Gospel for the day, he decided to speak briefly:

"Today is the feast of St. Barnabas, and as you can see from the Epistle, Barnabas spent a lot of time preaching Christ's message to people in countries where he was an outsider and where he was often persecuted. Christ's message was simple but not welcome. He insisted that there is no such thing as an outsider. That message makes people uncomfortable, because we like the comfort of believing that we are insiders, that we belong. Of course, you can't have insiders unless you have outsiders. Even some of the Apostles thought only Jews should be included in their group. It took Jesus a while to get that straightened out.

"In the Gospel we see that Jesus himself addresses the same problem. At the beginning of the Gospel we read, 'Jesus said to his disciples, Behold I send you as sheep in the midst of wolves. Be ye therefore wise as serpents, and simple as doves. But beware of men: for they will deliver you up in councils, and they will scourge you in their synagogues.'

"Jesus warned the people that not only in the government but even in the churches there were people prepared to persecute them. And later in the Gospel he warns them that even among themselves there would be people prepared to persecute them. Remember his words: 'The brother also shall deliver up the brother to death.'

"These days, here in Coaltown, we have good reason to pay attention to St. Barnabas, because we share some of his problems. And we have good reason to pay attention to Christ's warning. Notice that Jesus has only one word of advice: 'Persevere.' We know from other things he said that he doesn't mean just to sit back and take it. We have to do everything we can to help. I want you people here this morning, when you leave Mass, to spread the word that everyone must do everything possible to help the Italians to persevere to the end of these troubled times. And spread the word that if anyone in this parish does anything to harm our Italian brothers and sisters, it will be a very serious matter for confession. And that goes particularly for our Italian brothers who are working in the mines, as hard as anybody, to produce coal for war to help our brothers overseas. If anyone has a problem, or knows of anyone with a problem, come and see me."

After Mass, Gelo and Réal put their altar boy regalia on hangers in their closet and Father Rod got back into his black suit, stock, and white collar. He returned to the altar and took a consecrated host from the chalice in the tabernacle and put it in the pyx to bring to Theresa Papadopoulos in the hospital. He put the pyx in his breast pocket and locked the tabernacle.

"Father," he heard a timid voice behind him. Two women he hadn't yet met, their heads covered by kerchiefs, stood behind the altar rail, their fingers knitted together in front of their sweaters. "Father, could we speak a minute?"

"Sure. You want to talk here? Or come to the glebe—about an hour? I have to go to the hospital for a little bit but I won't be long."

"This is fine, Father. We have to get back to the kids."

"Okay. Let's sit in the front pews then." Father Rod opened the gate of the altar rail, let himself through, and led the two women to the second pew. He sat in the first pew and turned to face them over his arm along the back of the bench. "What can I do for you?"

"My name is Lucia Gato."

"I'm Maria Goretti. We're losing our homes."

"What do you mean?"

"The Mounties took our men. They said if we don't have men in the pit, we can't live in the company houses."

"The Mounties said that?"

"No, not the Mounties. We don't know who it was. Some man came around. Said we got a week to get out. Where we gonna go? And they're gonna cut off relief. We'll have no money to pay rent. Or buy food. We got kids. We can't go to work. Even if there was work."

"Who said they were cutting off relief?"

"The man said. Said it was coming up at the town council."

"Okay, Lucia, Maria. Go home and don't worry. First we'll find out who the man is. Could be just rumours, you know. But if it comes down to it, we'll find a place for everybody."

"Where?"

"We can make room in the glebe house, and probably the convent. Even the school, we have a kitchen in the school. And maybe some people in the parish have extra space. But hang on. Let's make sure what's going on first. Don't worry about it for now."

"Are we gonna hear from our husbands?"

"I'll look into that. Don't worry. We'll find a way."

Lucia and Maria walked down the wide middle aisle of the church arm in arm and out the main doors. Father Rod went back into the vestry and out the back door. He walked across the driveway between the church and the glebe house, trailing Gelo and Réal behind him. Their spirits were soaring. The day was filling up with promise. Riding around in the priest's car and going to school with a bodyguard was a good start.

Father Rod winked at his car and smiled as he always did when he passed in front of it. The bishop had arranged a deal and ordered all the priests who didn't have a fairly new car to buy a 1940 Ford. The car plants now were only making vehicles for the war, and who knew how long the war would last. Soon cars might be unavailable even for essential services.

The car amused him. The engineers who designed the car seemed to think vehicles should look like people. The 1940 Ford's headlights were perched on either side of a nose-like grill above the smiling mouth of a bumper, making it look like a metal scholar with steel-rimmed glasses and a hood of slicked-back black hair. He called his car Thomas Aquinas.

As he rounded the front end of the car, Father Rod touched the left fender with reassuring fingers as if brushing the shoulder of a friend he hoped would be faithful through thick as well as thin.

When Father Rod came into the kitchen of the glebe house with the boys, he was surprised by Anna's presence.

She stood by the stove, stoking the coals, announcing her authority with a series of clanks of poker against stove, her face afire with the reflection of the flames. He'd forgotten he'd hired her the day before. "Start tomorrow." He remembered now.

"What do you eat for breakfast?" Anna asked.

"Cornflakes," he said. "But I haven't got time today. Got to get to Saint Joseph's. Would you make us each a peanut butter sandwich? And we'll take some apples, the boys are coming with me."

"That's not good enough," Anna said. "The table's all set. You go in there and read the *Post*. I'll feed these two out here. This'll be faster. Only take a minute. It'd take too long to make a peanut butter sandwich."

"Too long? How could it take too long to make a peanut butter sandwich?"

"There's no peanut butter. I'd have to send the boys to get some."

Father Rod was certain Anna was lying, but before he could protest again, she propelled him to the dining room table with the end of her index finger in the small of his back. He slipped off his jacket, and hung it over the back of the chair and sat down. For a blurred moment, he wondered where he was. Anna had dressed the table in a white tablecloth with a MacDonald tartan border. Several back copies of the *Sydney Post-Record* were stacked at the side of the table. Anna came in with toast and an omelet crammed with onions, garlic, carrot shavings, and cheese. She put the plate on the table between his arms. When she withdrew her hands, the hairs on their arms mingled and sent electrical charges all over his skin. She stepped back to the wall to watch the effect.

"Taste it, why don't ya?"

Father Rod closed his eyes until the shock subsided. Then he broke off a piece of omelet and forked it into his mouth. It filled his head full of flavours.

"How is it?"

"It's not cornflakes. Is that garlic I taste?"

"Yes, of course. You can't make food without garlic and olive oil."

"Good. The smell of it should keep the women away from me, anyway, I won't have to worry about that. Where did you find all this stuff? Not in my cupboards, I don't think."

"At the Co-op on my way over. I put it on your bill. Except for the cheese. And I made the cheese."

"The Co-op doesn't open till nine."

"I know, but the manager gets in early. He lets me in. How is it?"

"It's delicious, Anna. Out of this world, as they say."

"Good. Your tea is ready," she said, and disappeared for a moment, then reappeared and poured the tea.

"You got a visitor, I'll send her in."

Sadie came in with her school bag hanging by a strap from her shoulder and a tall cardboard box held in her extended arms. "Here's your cats."

"My cats?"

"Gelo said you wanted cats. These are cats."

Sadie put the box on the floor. Three calico kittens slept on a folded blanket in the bottom of the box. Sadie gave the box a tap with the toe of her shoe, and the three little heads lifted.

"Cute, eh?" Sadie asked, and gave him a lecture on cats, explaining that the mother couldn't come because she got killed on the road, but the kittens were off the mother,

200

they can walk and they drink milk but you had to stick their noses in it. They should stay in the warm kitchen until they were really on their own. They won't mind if nobody was there as long as they were together. She offered to come over every day and check them out. She could do her homework and keep a watch over them and house-train them.

"I want to put them in the bedrooms," Father Rod said.

"Once they're house-trained," she said. "It'll take a while. I'll come after school. This is not that far from school. It's shorter for me than going home. I can just dash down the road, cross over the Catholic schoolyard and over the fence. Don't worry about it. I know about cats. As long as I can come here when I need to. In an emergency."

Sadie suddenly stopped talking as if she realized she said too much. She backed up against the wall and clutched the school bag hanging from her shoulders and pulled it over her middle. For the first time he saw worry in her eyes, and for the first time she avoided looking at him.

He bent to the box and picked up the kittens one by one. "Fluffy, Duffy, and Ruffy. At least until we can think of something better. Oh, yeah, Sadie. I wanted to ask you something. Is somebody after you? I heard some boys are laying for you and Gelo."

"I'm not scared of those galoots."

"I know you're brave, Sadie, but I want you to be careful. Have you got a knife in your school bag?"

She put her hands behind her back. "No," she said.

"Have you got your fingers crossed?"

"No." She held her hands out, fingers splayed.

"Have you got a knife in your school bag?" The hands went back behind her.

"Okay. Sadie. Tell you what. I'm going to the hospital. The boys are coming. You come too. I'll bring you back to school later."

"I want to ask you something," Sadie said.

"Yes."

"I want to be a Catholic."

Father Rod looked at her standing against the wall. She was smiling now but her face was a mixture of uncertainty and determination. She dropped the school bag to the floor and Father Rod noticed her dress. She wore a navy blue dress with an A-line skirt, the top buttoned down the middle, with pink epaulettes on the shoulders and matching blue belt and shoes. It looked to him like a dance dress. Her nylons too gave her an air of going somewhere. Her shoulder-length hair was curled. She held her hands together in front of her waist.

"Perhaps," he said, with his disarming smile, "you should sit down for a minute and tell me why you want to do that?"

She pulled out a chair and sat at the table and she explained that she had wanted to be Catholic since she'd been twelve. At first it was just to spite her father but now that didn't matter. But since she'd started doing her homework with Gelo and studying the catechism, she was getting more and more interested.

"What would your mother say?"

"She wouldn't give a care. She used to be a Catholic herself. She turned to get married, which I might have to do if I don't turn before that. If me and Gelo get married."

"How is your mother?"

"Oh. She's pretty good, I guess. I'm not home that much. We get along. But she's always looking at me like something's wrong. I didn't go home much when Daddy was there, and when he wasn't there, she didn't seem all that fussy about me being around. So all in all I just stayed away or went to my room."

"Well, now that she's alone . . ."

"Yeah. I should. Maybe Gelo could study at our place. She wouldn't mind. Daddy would've blown a gasket."

"You and Gelo are going steady?"

"Yeah. I thought you knew that?"

"I guess I did, Sadie, but I'm new here, you know. I have to check things to make sure I've got the right information. It's tricky, eh, you two going steady when you're still in school and a long time before you get married. You don't want to end up like Romeo and Juliet."

"Yeah. We're taking that in school. Pretty stupid if you ask me, ending up killing themselves because their parents can't get along. I'm not letting anything like that happen, believe you me. Me and Gelo get along just great, but I'm in charge. I know what you're talking about. But I'm not gonna get married because I have to get married. I'm gonna get married if I want to get married. But I'm not gonna give up a good boy now and end up with some jerk later on."

"But what if you and Gelo don't get married? What if one of you changes your mind? People do. You wouldn't want to get married if you didn't want to, just because you were going together a long time."

"Well, no. But if we don't, we don't. And that's another thing. If I was a Catholic, I could be a nun. I'd be a teacher."

"Well, we'll talk later. I hope you know what you're doing."

"So do I," Sadie said, and smiled. "I gotta go now. Enjoy your cats."

They both got up from the table and went to the kitchen. In the kitchen Anna was handing out molasses

cookies to the boys and she offered the plate to Father Rod
and Sadie as they came out. Father Rod took a handful and
Sadie took one and nibbled at it. While the boys stowed
their pockets full of cookies, Anna ate the omelet leftovers.
"More tea?" she said to Father Rod.

"No thanks, Anna, I've got to rush now. Sadie, why don't
you leave your school bag here and come with us?"

"What are we going there for?" Sadie asked.

"To visit Theresa Papadopoulos," Father Rod said. "She's
got T.B."

"Is she going to die?"

"I hope not. She nearly died last night."

"Aren't you gonna read the newspapers?" Anna asked.

"Yes. I better. When I get back."

For Gelo, Réal, and Sadie, the hospital was a new
world. It was full of uniforms. Nuns in long white uniforms and hoods. Nurses in shorter white uniforms and
hats with different coloured bands rimming the tops.
Gelo and Réal knew the Sisters of Charity, the teachers in
the Catholic school. And Sadie knew about them. But the
Sisters of Saint Martha were a new experience, bustling
up and down the hall and in and out of rooms, their
starchy gowns flapping and snapping like flags. They
directed and redirected the nurses, who looked not
much older than Sadie. But in their white shoes and
stockings, white uniforms, scrubbed faces and hands, little watches hanging from lapels, they seemed caught up
in some awesome enterprise beyond the ken or compe-
tence of ordinary mortals. Sadie saw them one evening
walking in pairs down the sidewalk of Commercial Street
in Glace Bay in their navy blue capes, and she stopped in
her tracks and watched them out of sight. Now she still

couldn't take her eyes off them as they hurried about their mysterious agendas.

Father Rod, Gelo, Réal, and Sadie walked in single file over the polished floor, down the centre of the hallway, while nurses moved up and down along the walls bearing trays of breakfasts and medicine, pushing wheelchairs, gurneys, bed lamps, carrying sheets and pillows and various pieces of equipment full of tubes and wires. At the end of the hallway they entered a solarium walled with windows divided into squares. With the drapes pulled completely away, the morning sunshine streamed into the space, warming the room and the two patients on either side of the doorway.

On the left lay a patient completely covered in a sheet. On the right Theresa smiled at her visitors. She was covered in a cast from her neck to her ankles, lying on the bed on her back on the sheet. The blankets and top sheets were folded over the rail at the foot of the bed. Her feet, sticking out the bottom of the cast, her arms out the shoulder holes of the cast, and her head above the neck were the only parts of Theresa Papadopoulos enjoying the sun. The rest of her body sweltered in the fusty ambiance of her papier-mâché prison.

"You're smiling. You're feeling better?"

"Yes, Father. A lot. You must be a miracle worker. They thought I was a goner."

"You were in a coma when I left."

"Yeah. I went into a coma. They didn't think I'd come out. But here I am. Still alive. But as you can see, they half buried me anyway. Who's this you got with you?"

"This is Sadie . . . Gelo . . . and Réal. They're off to school, but we thought we'd come and visit first."

"Well, it's great to see people. They're shipping me off to

the San in Kentville tomorrow. God only knows who'll visit me there, if anybody at all. Be a long trip for my mum and dad, although I imagine they'll do it anyway. Geno could take them but he has to work most of the time. Of course, who knows, he might not be working at all, the way things are going these days. Isn't it awful?"

"Indeed it is."

"See those two nursing students in the door there?" Father Rod saw two young nurses looking in through the doorway. They smiled, then walked back down the hallway.

"Cute, aren't they," Theresa said. "And as innocent as daylight. They come every half-hour, to check on me. They seem happy enough to see that I'm still alive. But the first time they came, my eyes were closed and they came up close to make sure I was still breathing. 'She's okay,' I heard one of them say as they walked away. Then the other one said, 'We're sure getting a lot of them these days, pretty soon there won't be any beds for white people.'"

"White people?" Father Rod repeated.

"Yeah. Can you believe it? Of course, they think I'm an Italian because my name isn't Murphy or MacNeil. They don't realize what they're saying, they're so young, but you can see what's in the air."

"You're good enough for the trip tomorrow, you think?"

"That's what they say. They don't want me here anyway, contaminating everybody. Can't say I blame them. I'd like to go to confession."

"Will that be okay?" Father Rod whispered. "Is Mrs. Polegato asleep?"

"Oh, you don't have to worry about her, Father. She's dead. She died half an hour ago. The chaplain gave her the last rights. They're looking for the family now."

Father Rod looked across the room. The sheet was pulled over the woman's head. He had talked to her last night and she was cheerful and optimistic about herself, but worried about her husband. "Good Lord, she was lively last night."

"She was. They didn't expect her to die at all. She just had a touch of T.B. She took a heart attack."

Father Rod suggested Gelo, Réal, and Sadie take a look around the hospital. They were happy to move away from Theresa, who was making them nervous because they couldn't think of anything to say to her, and they were not used to saying nothing. And they were not used to standing in a room with a dead stranger. They eased out of the room and scoured the hallway with eager eyes.

Father Rod took his stole out of his suit pocket and draped it around his neck. He found a chair and placed it beside the bed so he could sit close. He closed the solarium door and sat down beside her.

"Never mind the 'Bless me, Father,'" he said. "Just tell me what's on your mind."

"Okay, well, Father, it's just that me and Geno, well, we sort of got carried away. You know."

"Yes. Well, that happens. It's normal. But you know, it could be a problem if you get pregnant. Especially if you're sick."

"Yes. I didn't know I was sick at the time. I'm scared to death he might have caught T.B. off me. But I don't think I'm pregnant. I'm pretty careful about that."

"That's good. Don't worry about it."

"No. I'm not worried. Of course, you can never be completely sure. God forbid."

"In order for me to give you absolution, there has to be sorrow for sin."

"Ah, hah," Theresa said. "I'm sorry it's a sin. But I don't know if I'm sorry I did it. Unless he got T.B. Might be I'll never see him again. Might be that was our one and only."

Father Rod laughed. "It's only a venial sin anyway. Just think of some sin in your past, even if you already confessed it."

"How about the time I hid my mother's false teeth because she wouldn't let me go to the dance."

"That's perfect. *Ego te absolvo ab omnibus censuris, et peccatis, in nomine Patris, et Filii, et Spiritus Sancti, Amen.* Now would you like communion?"

"Yes, Father."

Father Rod took the pyx from his suit coat pocket, opened it and extracted the consecrated host, and returned the pyx to his pocket.

"Theresa, this is a little different. I'm going to say a few words in Latin which mean 'Sister, take this food for your journey so that the body of Jesus may guard you from the wicked enemy and lead you into everlasting life.'" Father Rod said that much aloud. Then, silently, he added, "But not right away into everlasting life." Aloud, he continued, "Then after I finish saying that, I say the usual thing, 'Body of Christ,' and you say 'Amen,' okay?"

"Sure."

"*Accipe, soror, Viaticum Corporis Domine nostri Iesu Christi, qui te custodiat ab hoste malingno et perducat in vitam aeternam.* You say amen."

"Amen."

"*Corpus Christi,*" Father Rod said, and placed the host on Theresa's extended tongue. She swallowed the host and responded, "Amen."

"Okay. That should get you as far as Kentville, Theresa."

"Father Rod," Theresa said, "do you really believe there's a heaven?"

He replied, "I think what's important is what you believe."

"I can't picture what it would be like, but it would be nice to think that one way or the other I'll get better and be comfortable again."

"Look at it this way, Theresa. If you die and go to Heaven you'll be comfortable and happy. If not, you'll go to sleep and be comfortable at least. Let's just say you'll soon be cured and comfortable."

"You're not too sure yourself, are you?"

"The truth of it is, we don't know. We believe. You can't have belief without doubt."

On the way out of the hospital, Sister Michael Mary stopped him in the hallway to ask if he could come back later in the day and talk to Mrs. Polegato's husband, whom the Mounties were bringing back from Truro. "They were just putting him on the train for Petawawa. When they told him his wife had died, he went berserk. Popped the Mountie on the jaw. They're bringing him back. What a mess."

After the hospital visit, Father Rod got the kids back to their classrooms and warned the teachers about the danger they might be in. Sadie asked to be dropped off at home but he went to her school and talked to the teacher. By now, the morning was about gone.

Back at the glebe house, a pot of tea was warming on the back of the stove and a plate of baloney, lettuce, cheese, and tomato sandwiches sat on the table beside the newspapers, today's paper added to the top of the pile. He poured his cup of tea and began to look over the papers. There was no sign of Anna.

Since his brush with Anna at breakfast, she had never quite left his mind all morning. When she had come to look for the housekeeping job, wrapped in her party dress and silk stockings and high-heeled shoes, he was unaffected, or thought he was. But today in her housedress, in spite of her authoritarian stance in the kitchen, she seemed vulnerable, needful, inviting. He ate his sandwiches and scanned the papers, starting with the *Sydney Post-Record*. On the front page, two Mounties in their Sam Browne belts, yellow-striped breeches, and high leather boots were crowding through the door of the Italian Consulate in Toronto. Someone is holding open the outside door and the two officers are on the steps in full stride. "MOUNTIES START ROUNDUP."

The cut line explained: "With Canada's declaration of war on Italy, Dominion authorities immediately cracked down on possible centres of enemy activity. Above, two Royal Canadian Mounted Police officers are pictured raiding the Italian Consulate in Toronto, as was done in other cities."

In another day's edition the headline blared: "NO. 16 COLLIERY IS AGAIN TIED UP BY ALIEN QUESTION." The story underneath continued: "Production of coal in the New Waterford district was further impeded when the miners at No. 16 Colliery refused to enter that mine with an Italian miner. The first tie-up occurred on the day shift and on the five o'clock shift the mine was only able to work at half speed because the walls had not been prepared on the day shift. The miner in question is said to be of Italian origin but Canadian born."

It was getting warm in the house, and Father Rod was beginning to sweat. He got up and took off his coat and refilled his cup. Sadie's school bag was still on the floor by the wall. He continued to read and finished browsing through the papers. Another story informed him that five cars manned by Mounties had driven a number of Cape Breton Italians to Truro and put them on a train for Ontario.

Father Rod decided to relax in a bath, and finish reading the newspapers there. If it were suppertime he would head for the ball field and tire himself out, if there were people around, and then go for a swim in the cold ocean. But for now, he'd have a bath. He tucked a newspaper under his arm, went to the kitchen, and made himself a maple sugar moonshine hot toddy. Upstairs, he ran a hot, sudsy bath. He undressed, put his eye patch on the chair beside his toddy, and submerged himself under the foam. He folded the paper so he could hold it in one hand.

The sudsy bath, as it always did, brought him visions of Erica, and now her recent letter, coupled with the plethora of nurses at the hospital this morning, seemed to intensify and clarify the vision. He closed his eyes. He was back in the hospital and the beautiful, vivacious, provocative Erica was taking away his pain.

But now his dream was intermittently confused by a competing vision of Anna in her housedress and her hairy arms. The army anthem, "Mademoiselle from Armentieres, Parlez-vous," sang in his head. He distracted himself with the newspaper.

Headline in a trumpet mode: "SEVERAL HUNDRED ITALIANS ARRESTED. OTTAWA. June 12—An intensive drive is on to round up those persons police have listed as possible saboteurs or espionage agents, said the Commissioner in charge of guarding Canada against fifth column elements...."

He soon wearied of the background story. He took a sip of moonshine and shuffled through the paper looking for answers to the questions that had been puzzling him in the past few days. Who created the list? Who was on the list? How to explain a list that seemed to include Canadian-born Italians with immediate relatives serving in the Canadian army, some of them already overseas? He could find nothing. No explanation in the background stories. Nothing on the editorial page. Nothing but excited head-lines, enthusiastic cutlines, and hardly concealed approval singing in every sentence: "IL DUCE PLUNGES ITALY INTO WAR."

ROME, June 10—(AP)—Italy joined Germany tonight in war against Great Britain and France. Premier Mussolini made the announcement to Fascists gathered throughout Italy, that the fateful declaration had been handed to the Allied ambassadors. The formal welding of the Rome-Berlin axis in the steel of war was officially set for tomorrow, but Berlin reports claimed Italian troops already had entered France through the Riviera.

Mussolini's announcement of the long-deferred decision from his balcony above black-shirted thousands packed in the square, and to millions at loudspeakers over the kingdom, came only as a partial surprise. It long had been anticipated....

Rejecting all appeals to stay out, Mussolini overrode the advice of both the Pope and President Roosevelt in their vain effort to prevent the spread of bloodshed.

Father Rod folded the paper and put it on the chair beside his moonshine and eye patch. He took a sip and sank again beneath the foam. Above the sound of the breaking bubbles, he heard the stealthy squeak of a foot on the stair. The bathroom door was open. Hope and fear welled up in him like a sweet and sour fruit.

TWELVE

✝

An errant woman that would live alone,
No husband there, her honour to defend,
Must study to be bloody and betimes.
ANN-MARIE MACDONALD

RED CEIT COULD NOT BELIEVE her ears. She could not stop laughing. After the initial shock of Anna's revelations, the two of them bent over in their chairs laughing and snorting and couldn't straighten up for more than a few seconds at a time to blurt out a few words. Over black tea at Anna's kitchen table, they laughed the giddy laugh of two women anticipating danger. Dust motes danced in the sunlight streaming between the kitchen window curtains, cheering the house. But fear crouched at the edge of the room like a surly cat, beyond the reach of hopeful laughter.

"Good God, Anna. Good God. The first day on the job and you slept with the priest in the middle of the afternoon."

"I didn't sleep with him, dear. I took a bath with him."

"Holy Mary Mother of God, Anna, and I thought I was brazen. How did you do it?"

"I just sat on him. Like a one-finger glove on a one-finger hand."

"Oh my God," Ceit squealed.

"And I stared into his good eye."

"Oh my God!" Ceit squealed. " Did he have his eye patch on?"

"No," Anna replied. "The eye patch was on the chair, on a book, by the tub. Next to his drink, or what was left of it. I think he had a pretty good snootful of moonshine. Imagine, drinking that stuff in the middle of the day. I had a couple myself, I found where he hid it. I was so nervous."

"Nervous my arse. Nervy would be more like it, if you ask me. Why did you do it? Do you like him, for God's sake? A one-eyed priest, for God's sake."

"Oh, I could like him all right. One eye is enough. He lost his eye saving my cousin Franco. If I didn't have a husband— and God only knows maybe I don't. If I do, where is he? I don't have a good feeling about that. But no, Ceit. I'll tell you why I did it. Not just for the fun of it, as you can imagine."

"But Anna, why are you telling me at all?"

"I can't very well go to confession, now, can I? To the priest?"

"I can see your point there. But still, what can I do? What's the good of telling me?"

"I have to tell somebody," Anna said. "You're the one I can trust."

"But why tell anybody? Keep it a secret. He's not gonna tell anybody, surely to God."

"No, you can't be sure of that at all," Anna said.

"He's a priest after all. He can't tell."

"I don't know about that. He'll have to go to confession himself, won't he, Ceit?"

"I never thought about that," Ceit said. "A priest going to confession. I didn't think they were supposed to commit sins. At least not the big ones. And didn't you jump him, for God's sake, what kind of a sin would that be for him?"

"Oh, he was expecting me. I started him off with a little tickle in the morning. I knew he'd be thinking about me. You know what they're like, they can't help it. Especially with a snootful."

"But my God, Anna, how could you be sure, weren't you taking an awful chance?"

"Don't you worry, I was pretty sure all right. He left the door open. I could see through the crack in the back of the door, his thing was sticking up over the soap bubbles. He was ready, all right."

"My God, Anna. I can't believe this." Ceit paused. "What kind of a thing did he have?"

"Circumcised. I only saw the tip. But it was quite the handful."

"Oh my God, Anna," Ceit blurted through tears of laughter, "stop it, you're gonna kill me. Honest to God, I can't stop laughing." But then she stopped. She folded her forearms on the table with her hands together and put her chin on her wrist. "There. I stopped. I'm not laughing. This is not funny, is it?"

"It would be funny if it wasn't me. But it is me. And like everything else these days, it's scary. But still, you have to laugh. Ceit, I have to tell you something else. Something even worse."

"Do I want to know this?"

"No. But I have to tell you."

"All right then." Ceit went to the stove and brought the teapot over and refilled their cups. A cloud passed over the sun. The sunshine stream and the dust motes disappeared. Ceit knew Anna was smart and practical, as well as wise and modest. But now she was beginning to wonder if the strain of the past week was bending her mind. Was she beginning to make things up? She couldn't imagine what was coming next. But she decided she would not laugh at this revelation, no matter what. She took a sip of fortifying tea, folded her arms on her chest, and waited.

"I have to tell you, Ceit. If I didn't have to, I wouldn't." Anna took a sip of tea. She took a deep breath. She bit her lower lip. She looked into Ceit's face.

"Tell me then. For God's sake," Ceit said, "get it over with."

"I killed Ump."

"Anna!" Ceit let the word hang in the air between them while she absorbed the shock. She stared into Anna's eyes without a blink. She could see nothing in them but truth and sanity. She closed her eyes and lowered her head, then took in a deep breath. "I know you have a good reason for everything you do. I can't believe you would murder anybody. Tell me the whole story."

"Yes," Anna said, "you have to know everything. I didn't murder him. I killed him. He jumped me down at the end of the baseball field. I kicked him off and he fell over the cliff."

"My God. He jumped you."

"Yes. He tried to rape me. When I was having a pee. Can you imagine? In the pitch black. I didn't know who he was."

"Nobody could blame you for that. It wasn't to kill him. It was to get away. Just tell them what happened."

"They wouldn't believe me. I was wearing Tomassio's pit boots. The Mounties think Tomassio murdered him. They found the boots in the house. They'll think I'm just trying to take the blame off of him."

"Why would they think you'd do that?"

"Because they'd hang him. They wouldn't hang a woman. Especially if I said he tried to rape me. My word against, well, nobody, I guess, there was nobody else there. Of course, they might do me in anyway, a jury, with all this anti-Italian stuff in the air."

"Tomassio wouldn't murder anybody. Why would they think he would?"

"Ump and Tomassio didn't get along."

"I know, but murder. Get out! Nobody would believe that. Tomassio?"

"It happened the night Tomassio escaped from jail. Somebody saw him start across the ball field around the same time it happened, give or take an hour. And then there's his boots. They took casts of the tracks the boots made. They found bruises the boot heels dug into Ump's chest."

"But so what? It doesn't mean he did it. He wouldn't. We know he wouldn't. They must know he wouldn't. Why would they think it?"

Reluctantly, Anna admitted, "Tomassio was carrying on with Cathy, Ump's wife."

"What!"

"Yes. I bet the Mounties know. I got that feeling. They know. They keep tabs on everything. You didn't know about it yourself, Ceit? You never heard a whisper?"

"No, Anna, not a breath."

"Good. Maybe nobody else knows."

"I doubt anybody knows if I don't, what with the hairdresser I got. Holy Mary Mother of God, Anna, what are you going to tell me next?"

"All right, now," Anna said. " Now this is the thing. I went to confession to the priest."

"To the parish priest, Father Rod. Did he know who you were?"

"Yes."

"My God. Why didn't you go to a strange priest?"

"Because I wanted somebody to know I did it. Somebody who couldn't tell. But then, if they pin it on Tomassio, the priest will know he didn't do it. The priest couldn't tell about the confession, but he could tell them he knew who did it and that it wasn't Tomassio. Couldn't he? They'd believe a priest. I don't want Gelo to be somebody who's got a murderer for a father. And what if Tomassio is dead? Then everybody will think he did it and he won't even get a trial. Then I'll have to tell them I did it."

"But what if they find out anyway?"

"If they find out it was me, you'll know the real story. I want you to write it all down, everything I told you, put today's date on it, tear the top off the front page of the *Post-Record* and put it in an envelope with everything I told you, and mail it to yourself. Don't open it unless we need it. And hide it where nobody can find it except me if I need it. Can you do this for me? I don't want Gelo to be somebody who got a murderer for a mother either. Unless I get caught I'm not saying anything. Because everything will come out. Gelo and Sadie are going together. Just imagine if they find out I killed her father, and his father was carrying on with her mother."

"Jesus, Mary and Joseph, what an afternoon. But Anna. You didn't say why you went with the priest, though. Why did you have to do that?"

"Just in case."

"What?"

"He'll think twice, won't he, if he ever gets tempted to let something slip. Maybe I'm crazy, but I can't take a chance.

I only got the one child and I don't want him ruined. I think that priest is a pretty safe bet. But you know, you can easy let something slip when you're not thinking, and somebody who hears it draws their own conclusion. And then, God only knows who's the priest he goes to confession to. I had a priest squeal on me once. But that was in Italy. Oh, I think I trust this fella all right. But it's good to know that we both have our little secret. Keeps a simmer on near the front of the stove. He knows I can tell."

"Indeed you can," Ceit said. "And you already did."

"And how about you, Ceit? Are you a pretty safe bet? Can you keep a secret?"

"Who in the name of God would believe me anyhow? I got a hard time to convince myself."

"I'm only kidding, Ceit. I'd trust you with my life. But I'm getting so cautious. It's so hard to trust anybody these days. I don't feel safe in my own kitchen. For that matter, is it even my own kitchen? I got two kitchens to work in now and I don't know if even one of them is my own. What's a woman to do, without a kitchen that a Mountie can't come into and haul off her husband, and some other galoot can't walk in without so much as a knock and hello and tell you if you don't have your man in the pit you don't have a claim on a house? The Mounties, for God's sake. We always thought we could trust the Mounties. And the priests. We got a good priest, but I heard some of them are talking against us. From the pulpit. The only ones I trust right now are the nuns. They don't allow any of that nonsense in the school. Gelo told me. Oh God, Ceit, what's gonna happen to my boy?"

The deserted beach, wild with the noise and motion of nature, seemed to Father Rod a place apart from space and time, a place of meditation uninterrupted by quiet and stillness. Nothing but ocean and the unrelenting pounding of waves slapping hard sand. In the infinite distance, toward invisible Europe, wedged between two phalanges of clouds full of rain for tomorrow, the top arc of the sun edged over the horizon. Only an eye that knew could make out the artillery emplacement and observation post on the Lingan headland. Any eye could see the puff of smoke flying from the stack of the *Cariboo*, with its cargo of passengers, steaming its way from Port aux Basques, Newfoundland, to its berth in North Sydney, Nova Scotia.

Purged of the smoke of war, the wind from the east blew sea salt over the land, pushed spume, seaweed, and jellyfish up the slanted beach. Later, when the sun climbed high over the horizon, the growl of Harvard Trainers and the scream of Spitfires and Hawker Hurricanes from Reserve Mines Airport, practising dogfights in the high air and low flying techniques over the water, would fill the bay with artificial noises.

Father Rod walked over the twigs of wood and sprigs of seaweed that marked the edge of the high water. Water sloshed up the incline to the edge of his sneakers, then swirled and retreated, carrying pebbles, broken clamshells, and periwinkles, bumping them down over the ridges of sand shingles, returning them to the next wave, ready for another run up the shore. Squadrons of squawking seagulls took off from the high tide mark in front of him as he walked. Spiralling over the turbulent water, the gulls dived in behind the breaking waves, grabbing the dislocated bits of body parts of fishes, lobsters, crabs, mussels, sailors, and merchant marines. From over the headland near Table Head, several streams of black smoke fled inland from the smoke stacks of the Glace Bay Collieries.

Father Rod walked the full length of the beach until he reached the bridge spanning the narrow harbour between the sandbar and the Lingan shore. Then, standing in the middle of the iron bridge, holding on to the struts, he leaned over and watched a thousand minnows in their urgent rush up the canal. He licked the sea salt from his lips and waited for his confessor.

Father Pat Mancini parked his car by a nearby sand dune, clomped over the bridge planks, and joined his friend, leaning with him on the black iron railing over the water.

"Watch your hat," Father Rod warned. "If it falls you'll have to chase it to River Ryan."

"What are you gawking at?" Father Pat asked.

"What does it look like?"

"Looks like a bunch of fish."

"Don't be so stunned. That's what it is. I asked you what it looks like."

"So. You're in one of those moods. Okay, I give up. What does it look like?"

"Did you bring your stole?"

"What do you think? Didn't you ask me? I got it on."

"That bunch of fish. To me, they look like a hundred thousand sperm looking for an egg."

"What have you been up to?"

"I screwed the housekeeper."

Father Mancini put his forehead in the palm of his hand. His hat fell to the water and sailed under the bridge. Although he barely noticed it leave his head, he instinctively grabbed for it, a good enough grab but doomed to failure because there was no hand on the end of his left arm. He smiled and thought, how nice, the River Ryan–bound hat would give him something stupid to worry about, a distraction from the genuine problems that loomed in his day, especially the two-legged problem beside him. He knew a story would come to clarify and complicate the simple statement of fact of Father Rod's confession. And he knew he had to hear it. But the story would not obliterate the fact.

The sun burned on the horizon and glinted off the top of his head while he hung onto the struts of the bridge and joined his friend in meditation upon the tiny fish fleeing like self-propelled torpedoes, under the bridge, running on the tide, up the canal, in a mindless rush to fulfil nature's imperative.

"Your hat's gone," Father Rod said.

"Yeah. That's good," Pat said. "It'll give me something to do. Hunting it down. You can meet a lot of nice people … hat hunting."

"Did you hear the latest Franco story?" Father Rod asked.

"Don't think so. Drinking again, is he?"

"No, not again. He's still drinking. Someone said they saw him standing in front of the pool room on Commercial Street and yelling across the street at the Salvation Army captain when the band was between tunes on Senator's Corner. 'Hey, Captain, you guys save bad people?'"

"We try, the captain said."

"'What about women?' Franco says, 'Save bad women?'

"The captain says, 'We try.'

"Franco says, 'Well, would you try to save me one for Saturday night?'"

"Doesn't sound like Franco," Father Pat said.

"I know. They're making the stories up now. There's a new one every week."

"He's your responsibility," Pat said. "You saved his life. You better do something. Try something. I suppose you're beginning to wonder if he was worth saving."

"I suppose we could wonder that about all of us."

"Isn't that the business we're in?" Father Pat said. "I suppose by rights we should all die trying to save somebody, or at least lose an eye."

"Or a hand," Father Rod said.

"Yeah, but I wasn't saving you. You were saving me. And don't try to suck up to me for an easy penance. But you know what?" Father Pat grinned. "Franco's story might have a good idea in it for you. Perhaps Captain McQueen could set you up every Saturday night. Then you wouldn't have to bother the housekeeper."

Father Rod fell silent. A swordfishing boat started up, slipped from the wharf, and sailed up the canal against the incoming tide. A fisherman coiling rope in the stern with his back to the sea waved to the motionless black figures on the bridge as his boat ploughed toward the sun. They watched until it disappeared around the Lingan headland under the silent, patient barrels of the anti-aircraft guns. A blonde young woman driving a motorcycle, with a blond young man holding on behind her, rumbled across the bridge boards behind the two priests.

"All right," Father Pat said, "What happened? Let's get it over with. My hat'll be wondering what's keeping me so long."

"It started in the morning. Anna was serving me breakfast. After she put it down, she dragged her arm across my arm."

"Hold on. In the morning. She served you breakfast.

She dragged her arm across your arm. Is that what you just said?"

"Yeah."

"You're blaming her?"

"No, I'm just telling you what I can remember."

"Okay, let's not make a song and dance about this." Father Pat spoke deliberately. "Let's keep in mind who's the priest and who's the parishioner."

"I know."

"And who's the master and who's the servant."

"I know."

"All right. Go ahead." Father Pat sighed. "And hurry up, my head is getting sunburned."

"To make a long story short, I went to the hospital, to the school, the usual stuff, got back in the middle of the afternoon and took a bath. She came into the bathroom and got in the tub with me."

"You took a bath in the middle of the afternoon. That's a good idea. She came into the bathroom. How did she get into the bathroom?"

"She walked in. The door was open."

"You mean unlocked open, or open open?"

"Open open."

"Why wasn't it closed? And why wasn't it locked?"

"I've been living alone. I'm not used to women in the house."

"You had two women living in the house all week."

"Yes, my sister and her buddy. I think that was safe enough."

"I guess now I know why you didn't want to hire a housekeeper."

"So what d'you think?"

"I think you're a fuckin nincompoop."

"What do you want me to do?" Father Rod asked.

"Why did she do it? She must have a reason. She has a husband, as far as we know. Or is she so fascinated with one-eyed priests she can't control herself? She's willing to risk her reputation and embarrass her family so she can take you on in a bathtub in the middle of the afternoon without benefit of a chocolate or a flower or a candlelit dinner. We're not talking about Betty Bimbo here, buddy. We're talking about Anna. How did she do it anyway? Did she flip you over and slide underwater?"

"I don't think I should answer that."

"No, you're right, you're right. Well then, why?"

"I think I know why. But I can't say."

"Oh…" Father Pat watched a seagull swoop under the bridge. "Is it a matter of confession?"

Father Rod did not answer. The minnows were gone. Now the canal was full of a school of hungry mackerel. A flatbed truck rumbled across the bridge, forcing the two men to straighten up to make room so the overhang of lobster traps could inch by them. Once straightened up, they stayed that way and faced each other.

"Okay," Father Pat said. "First, apologize to the woman. Good God. Is there any chance this can happen again?"

"Not a chance."

"I don't suppose there's any point firing her. She needs the money. If you can't keep out of the house when she's in it, at least keep out of the room she's in. Is she there all day?"

"I don't know. It's full-time. Whatever that means. We didn't discuss her hours."

"Tell her the mornings only. But pay her for the whole day."

"All right. Is that all?"

"No. I want you to spend from ten minutes to an hour a day thinking about what to do to help Franco and an hour a month actually doing something. He's a good boy and we're his only hope. And he's Anna's cousin. I'm heading for River Ryan—you want me to drive you home first?"

"No. I'll walk. I need a bit of time to think."

"I'm not surprised," Father Pat said wryly.

The two men walked together as far as Father Mancini's car. "By the way," Father Pat said, with a sly smile, "how's the state of your faith? Got it all straightened out yet? Got a new theory?"

"It's all a matter of transcendence, Pat," Father Rod replied. "Remember the first time you rode a bicycle? The thrill of freedom. No longer earthbound. And skates. Remember the thrill of lacing up the skates? Those machines got us off the ground and made us realize we can transcend our roots in the ground. That gives us hope, and hope gives us faith."

"Sure," Father Pat said. "Keep in mind that those fighter pilots we see every day training over Indian Bay, when they transcend Europe, will be trying to kill transcendent German pilots, and their transcendent brothers are going to be dropping bombs on the non-transcendent people on the ground."

Father Rod walked back along the sandbar. He couldn't keep the blond couple on the motorcycle out of his mind. He had never seen a woman drive a motorcycle. Who could she be? A woman driving a motorcycle would attract attention, would have a certain amount of local fame. And besides, like her blond companion, she seemed unusually tall. Who could they be?

✝   ✝   ✝

At Low Point nothing grew tall. Except Helen. When the Atlantic roared, it was good to be close to the ground. The salt wind intimidated everything but strawberry plants. They managed to survive, to blossom, and to bear fruit by hiding under the tents of the leaning grass that grew along the cliffs between Low Point and South Bar. Only Helen and, as far as she knew, one other woman came to pick the berries. The cliffs were too dangerous for children, the winds too annoying for their parents. A tall, skinny, pale girl, Helen roamed among the strawberries along the bank above the cliff. And she swam and walked among the rocks and along the brief sandbars below the cliffs. It was her territory, a narrow strip of cliff top, a scrag of beach, a narrow margin of sand along the edge of the water. Such a poor and isolated scrap of geography seemed safe, impregnable, even if only because it appeared so undesirable, and, like the harbour itself, so far at least, unassaulted, uninvaded.

She walked in front of, behind, and below the guns and the searchlights, a familiar distraction for the bored gunners and searchers who were forbidden by their captains to approach her or attract her attention. Helen was unaware of their greedy eyes.

When Ty and his wife had married, they lived in a tent on a piece of land no one else wanted on the bank of Sydney Harbour near Low Point. He dug a hole for a concrete foundation by hand with pick and shovel. He built forms for the footings out of timber discarded on a steel plant dump. He built the foundation walls seven feet high out of cement and beach stones. He made window frames from the timber pulled away when the footings were set. He found more timber and boarded in the top of the foundation with what he intended as the floor of their home but ended up becoming the ceiling. He covered the top with tarpaper. They moved in, and with the money he saved he made temporary rooms, a kitchen/dining room and three bedrooms, and he left a space for a future bathroom. He bought furniture with the remainder of his money and his wife bought dishes and bedclothes and towels with the money she saved from sewing and telling fortunes. She looked in her crystal ball and predicted a bright future. They had a child, a boy, and years later, a girl. They saved money to build the top of the house. When they had enough money to start, Leda dropped dead. He went queer. He never spoke English again and Helen understood little of the little he spoke except for the names of food.

Because her birthday was in October Helen didn't start school until she was nearly six, a year older than her classmates. She was already a head taller than girls her age and head and shoulders taller than the tallest boy in her class. By the time she got to high school her teachers would tilt their heads to look her in the eye. In high school her classmates, if they addressed her at all, called her Squint, because in the least bit of brightness her eyes closed nearly shut.

The day Helen started school her mother had dropped dead, and her father went queer. Became a ghost. He waked and buried his wife with the subdued aplomb of a professional undertaker. Then he retired to his basement home where he rocked like a pendulum, marking time but unaware of its details, conscious only of daylight and dark. He left his back-and-forth momentum only to go to work as a cook in a Ukrainian café in Whitney Pier, or to prepare meals for Beaver and Helen, and go to bed.

After her mother died, Helen continued school but she did not participate. The other children did not know what to make of her. Her milk-white skin, long white hair, and sapphire-blue eyes startled them. Her dresses, decorated with spangles, tassels, and furbelows, puzzled them. And because she was older and so much taller, she seemed like an adult. Her diffidence, her reluctance to respond, and her towering height made the children feel diminished, looked down upon. Sister Clare, sensing her discomfort, sat her in the back corner of the class near the door. When she found out Helen could already read and write, she gave her a book to read. Before the end of class, Helen indicated that she'd finished the book and wanted another one. After class Sister Clare took her to the library and introduced her to Sister Angela, the school librarian, and Helen was soon well on her way to reading every book and magazine in the library. From then on she had two friends. Sister Angela gave her support and comfort in school. Her brother gave her support and comfort at home. In between there was nothing but road.

Helen Perenowsky knew little about herself except information gleaned from mirrors and the attitudes of people she encountered in her scant life. A Mi'kmaq lady selling clothes props and baskets told her that her mother had lived with gypsies and made a living as a seamstress and fortune teller in Sydney until she married Ty Perenowsky. Helen had found a snapshot of her mother and father taken on their wedding day. Her mother wore an ankle-length, flared, white wedding gown, without a train but lavishly embroidered. In place of a veil she wore a hat with a big rim, jaunty, elegant, saucy, over her pale hair, which hung down over her shoulders. Her father, a head shorter than his bride, in a black suit with widely spaced stripes, wore a dutiful, grateful smile and looked like a consort. On the back of the snapshot someone had written, "Ty and Leda, Wedding Day." Helen had wrapped the picture in tissue paper to keep it from wearing out; she used it as a bookmark. She moved it from page to page, chapter by chapter of her voluminous reading, so that she looked at it many times a day and countless times a week. Her mother had saved the wedding dress, wrapped in tissue paper and mothballs, in a cedar chest, along with all the clothing she had made for herself over the years. Helen refashioned this clothing for herself as the need arose. When she was four years old, the year she waited to go to school, her mother taught her to read, to write, and to sew.

Helen's brother, whom she thought of only by his nickname, Beaver, seemed to know even less than she did about their family and showed no interest in learning anything. By the time she started school he was still in grade eight; he quit school after Christmas, when he was sixteen. After that, he left the house at dawn every day and never came back until bedtime. He didn't speak of his life but he must have been working because he constantly brought her gifts of candy and flowers and an endless supply of disposable trinkets. He bought a three-ton truck, a motorcycle, and a sailboat. On Sundays he taught her how to drive the truck and the motorcycle and how to sail the boat. When she became expert at the skills, he let her go off by herself, but only on Sunday and only on the back roads. He built a shed-like box on the truck and kept both the motorcycle and the boat in the truck shed behind padlocked doors, and wherever he went he took everything with him. When the war started, he had joined the merchant marine, and now he was shipping out. He had left home a week ago but he was not allowed to tell her when he was actually leaving. He was not supposed to know when he was leaving or where he was going or when he would be back, but he did know. He left her a sealed letter with the information and all of his money in it and a leather bag with the keys to his vehicles. If he was not back in two months, she was to open the letter and read it to her father and give him half the money. She knew by watching activity in the harbour that he would be going soon.

Sydney Harbour poked into Cape Breton Island from the North Atlantic like a thumb and an index finger with a swollen knuckle where the steel plant dominated the narrows between Whitney Pier and North Sydney. On the south side, from the lighthouse at Low Point near New Waterford to the military headquarters in Sydney, searchlights, signal stations, observation posts, anti-aircraft guns, and coastal artillery emplacements protected navy and merchant marine ships gathering for convoy duty. The organizing of the transportation of military personnel, equipment, and supplies for the war in Europe was growing through its frantic and frenzied infancy.

Since it began, September 1, 1939, the war had become more threatening. Canada had declared war on Germany on September 10. In December of that year the First Canadian Infantry Division sailed for Europe. When Germany seized Denmark and invaded Norway in April, British and Canadian troops withdrew. After Sweden and Holland fell to the Germans, defeat in France was imminent. France surrendered on June 22, 1940, and the expectation was that

England would be next. Great Britain was making plans to move the Royal Navy to safe ports in North America. With the United States still neutral, Sydney and Halifax were the closest available ports. Defences at Sydney and around the coast of Cape Breton were far from adequate.

When Beaver shipped out from Sydney Harbour, he left Helen a hundred dollars to buy a dress and whatever else she needed for the prom if someone asked her to go. Nobody asked her to go to the prom—the culminating failure of her social life at school. She didn't expect any boy to ask. Beaver had said he'd take her, but now he was gone. She did not use the money he gave her to buy a prom dress.

Helen wanted to go to the prom. She was reading *Kristin Lavransdatter*, and she knew that Germany had invaded Norway, and she wondered how Sigrid Undset was affected by the war. She never expected the faraway war would affect her, but now the ocean was a highway to the war, and her brother travelled that highway and could not take her to the prom.

"Do you think if I went to church and prayed?" she asked Sister Angela.

"Oh, I don't know," Sister Angela said. "Couldn't do any harm. But I think God expects people to find their own dates for the prom. Still, going to church might help. Sometimes men go to church, you know. Why don't you go to church in Whitney Pier? It's not far from your house. They don't know you there. You'd see some new people. Go and light a candle and see what happens."

"You think I should go to a different church? Where they're not used to me? I look so odd."

"There's lots of odd people in the Pier, dear. I'm one of them myself."

Helen went to Whitney Pier and lit a candle. The Virgin Mary looked benign but made no promises. Helen went back for Sunday Mass and the miracle happened. When she rose from her knees at the communion rail, swallowed the host, and turned quickly for a quick retreat down the aisle against the sea of wondering eyes, she almost crashed into him. She looked straight, horizontal, into his eyes. He was, like her, too tall, too blond, too skinny, too long in the face. He was perfect.

He followed her down the aisle to her seat at the back and knelt beside her until she blessed herself and sat back in the pew. He blessed himself and sat beside her. Her body and mind were in shock. Their clothes were touching. Her dress was touching his pants. Her sleeve was touching his sleeve. Her skin was alive with goosebumps. She wondered if she could stand and walk, but when the priest finally pronounced, "*Ite missa est*," the stranger stood by the pew while she entered the aisle as if he were her escort, and he accompanied her to the churchyard, and he began to talk, and she relaxed and chatted as if she had been doing it all her life. They chatted like normal people, unaware of the normal people who circled around them in wonder.

"What's your name?" he asked.

"Helen Perenowsky."

"So you're a Pole?"

"More like a stick," she quipped.

He laughed. She was not used to people laughing at her quips. Indeed she seldom got the opportunity to use the treasury of quips she invented for imaginary occasions, although she guessed from her reading that such occasions abounded in other people's lives.

"Not at all," he said. "Elegant. Tall is elegant. Trees are tall, and everybody knows trees are beautiful."

"I suppose you would think so."

"And so should you."

Helen unlocked her face and smiled. She was so happy it felt like pain. She wanted to go back in the church and make sure there was enough candle left to burn until she could get back and light another one. But before she knew it he was walking her home. They bought ice creams from Mariana at Padolskys' Dairy and walked out along the crescent of sand at South Bar.

They walked hand in hand, squinting in the sun. He told her everything, but told her nothing. His name was Colin MacDonald but he was not a MacDonald from Cape Breton. He came from a little town near Ottawa. He was in the navy, but he couldn't tell her any more than that. He couldn't tell her the truth. Everything was a military secret. Loose lips sink ships.

She told him the truth. She told him everything. About her mother, her father, her brother, Sister Angela. About *Kristin Lavransdatter*, the current book she was reading and hoped would never end. She told him about the stories she was writing herself.

"If you lend them to me, I'll take them with me and read them," he promised.

"But you're not telling the truth," she said. "You said so yourself."

"Sometimes I am," he said. "It's not a military secret that I'm going to read your stories."

"You're not telling me much of anything, are you?"

"I can tell you lots of things," he said. "But everything I tell you might be a lie. Unless I sing it."

"Unless you sing it?" Helen could hardly contain herself. She was actually talking to someone who was saying unexpected things and she was saying unexpected things herself. She felt these moments were more like one of her books than her life. "Are you going to sing now?" she asked him.

"Sure. My father is a farmer," he sang. "My mother raises chickens, my brother's in the army. The Red Sox are not happy with Dizzy Dean," he sang. "Is there anything else you would like to know?"

Helen didn't know any military secrets and she told him everything. They walked and talked and soon were walking hand in hand. She took him to her basement house and introduced him to her father. Ty looked at him and shook his hand and smiled. He said nothing. She showed him the house, her room.

"Don't jump for joy in here," she said. Between their heads and the ceiling there wasn't enough room for a small jump. He tried it and found out for himself. "I told you," she said. He looked out the basement window across the grass to the harbour. A corvette tracked across his vision, steaming to port in Sydney. A destroyer followed in its wake.

"Wonderful view," he said, and turned to her. "I'll come back tomorrow. We can spend the day together and tomorrow night we'll go to the prom."

"What'll we do all day?"

"We'll take a motorcycle ride. Then we'll go sailing."

"The motorcycle and the boat are locked up in the truck."

"But you have the keys to the truck."

"It's too late to buy a gown," she said. "I'd have to make my own gown."

"Why not, you've got all day today." He smiled.

"You think it's easy."

"Not at all," he said. "I think it's hard. But you can do it, because you want to do it."

"Where are you going?"

"Not far. Could you make a few sandwiches for tomorrow? We'll have a picnic. I'll be here at five in the morning. Wear long sleeves and slacks so you won't look like a lobster at the prom. I'll bring something to protect our faces and hands. Get up early, we'll leave at dawn."

First Colin drove. But when he discovered she could drive, he sat behind. His weight on the back made the bike seem lighter. She was a skilful driver. She felt transcendent. Rolling over hills, banking around turns, her hair flying behind her, she felt for the first time she was graduating from high school into life. In spite of her height, she'd always felt her long feet were stuck to the ground. Now the ground was an insubstantial blur.

They sped from point to point, but they stopped often, turning down every little side road to the coast, every once in a while eating sandwiches and drinking pop. He brought baseball hats and sunglasses for them both so they wouldn't have to squint into the wind and sun. They looked through his binoculars at the vast array of shipping that was gathering outside the mouth of the harbour. Colin made notes and drew maps everywhere they went.

At Fort Petrie, two QF six-inch "B" Mk II naval guns and two searchlights looked across the harbour to Chapel Point, where two 4.7-inch QF Mk VII naval guns protected the harbour from the north side. On the high bluff at South Bar, personnel tending the three searchlights and two six-pounder Hotchkiss guns had a clear view of the harbour from the steel plant at Whitney Pier across the water to where the Newfoundland ferry docked at North Sydney. Underwater, between South Bar and the Northside, the narrowest part of the harbour, the steel mesh gates of

Stubbards Boom protected the innermost part of the harbour from German U-boat penetration. Any ship going beyond this point had to wait for the gates to be opened. A magazine at Johnstown, three miles from Sydney as the crow flies, stored ammunition for the batteries.

"Are you writing a book or what?" she asked him.

"Exactly what I'm doing," he said. "I'm a writer too, just like you. After the war I'm going to be a travel writer. Everywhere I go, I write it all down so I won't forget. This is the first place I'm going to write about. You'll be in it. But you have to promise to put me in one of your stories."

"You didn't sing that, so I don't know whether to believe it or not."

"Sometimes I forget to sing," he sang, and they laughed as they laughed all day.

They followed the harbour to the ocean coast, sped through New Waterford to Lingan, across the bridge at Lingan. On the bridge they surprised two priests, who watched them in wonder. They fled over the sandbar to Dominion, Coaltown, down to Glace Bay, and along the coast to Louisbourg and then to Sydney. From Sydney they took a long side trip to Johnstown and on the way back went across to the other side of the harbour, through North Sydney and up the coast as far as the observation post and anti-aircraft guns at Oxford, across from Whitney Pier.

When they got back to Low Point, they made a new batch of sandwiches and they made the trip again, this time on the sailboat, hugging the shore and seeing everything again from the water. Their excursion took the rest of the day even though they moved quickly. Colin did most of the sailing. He seemed able to make the boat go almost against the wind, zigzagging along the coast, grabbing a puff of wind here, a rogue current there, skipping out on a western breeze for a long look through the binoculars, hovering in a cove for a picnic of pop and sandwiches. The day went by like a dream.

The prom was a dream come true. Everything in the cedar chest had been transformed once, twice, or more by Helen and by her mother. Dresses became skirts, skirts became blouses, blouses became underwear, underwear became scarves, scarves became furbelows. Everything in the cedar chest had changed over the years, everything but the wedding dress. It remained in its tissue paper perfectly preserved, milk-white. She changed it, mostly by subtraction. Off with ruffles, off with trim. But she left a flounce in the middle to express the appearance of hips. She dropped the hemline to camouflage the size of her feet. She built in supports to create a décolletage and a suggestion of breasts.

The metamorphosis was not entirely successful.

"Are ya getting married tonight, Squint?" Sally taunted her when her eyes landed on Helen's dress the minute she stepped into the hall.

Helen didn't care. She answered with a smile. Success was the best response. He had already told her she was beautiful.

"Beauty is in the eyes of the beholder," she said.

"Indeed it is," he replied. "I beheld you at Mass. I beheld you on the sandbar. I beheld you on the motorcycle. I beheld you on the sailboat. And now, let's go to the dance. Beholding time is over. It is time for holding."

No one had taught her to dance. But she danced. They towered around the floor like two periscopes undulating in a sea of hair, interrupted now and again by a curious classmate with spunk enough to cut in and steal Colin for a set. They were all curious, but only the girls wanted to cut in and only a few had the nerve. Who was the mysterious stranger? The boys, curious but unenthusiastic, went through the motions of dancing with Helen, staring at her breastbone. The girls tilted their heads up and asked questions. He told some he was from Ottawa; others, Moose Jaw; others, Trois Rivières. He was Colin, from somewhere. He was in the army, he was in the navy, he was in the RCAF, he was in the merchant marine, he was having fun.

Colin and Helen danced cheek to cheek, mouth to ear. He knew the words to all the songs and he sang them in whispers through the ramparts of her hair. "Sometimes I wonder why I spend the lonely night, dreaming of a song, the melody haunts my reverie and I am once again with you, when our love was new, and each kiss an inspiration."

Helen had never been kissed. "You know all the words," she said.

"Yes, I went to college in the States."

"You went to college?"

"Yes."

"Did you study music?"

"No. Languages."

"So how come you know all the words?"

"That's how I learned. First I learned all the songs. Then I translated them into languages. I memorized them and sang them. What's your favourite song?"

"My favourite song is 'Lili Marlene,'" she said, "but it's a German song. I only know it in English."

"Sing it. You sing a line in English and I'll sing it in German. Then you'll know both."

"You speak German?"

"Yes," he said. "And French. And Spanish. And English."

240

They ignored the orchestra and danced as they sang. "Underneath the lantern by the barrack gate," Helen sang by his ear.

"*Vor der Kaserne vor dem grossen Tor*," he replied.

"Darling I remember the way you used to wait."

"*Stand eine Laterne, und steht sie noch davor.*"

"That was nice," she said, after they went through the whole song. "But I only remember the last line, *Wei einst Lili Marleen.*"

"That's all you need."

"What's your favourite song, Colin? Sing it to me."

"I have lots of favourite songs. Do you know French?"

"Yes. But just from high school."

"That's all you need. Tonight my favourite song is a French song," he said, and he sang, "*Auprès de ma blonde, il fait bon, fait bon, fait bon, auprès de ma blonde, il fait bon, fait bon.*"

By the time he finished they were cheek to cheek, mouth to ear with not a hair between, and too close even for anything more explosive than a labial whisper. They left the dance and walked the glittering shore through the creamy moonlight, their clothes clinging desperately to their milk-white bodies.

Standing under the ceiling of her subterranean bedroom, Colin looked at his watch. "We have time for one last dance," he said. She took off her shoes.

"You sing," she said. He held her two hands in his. Their fingers coiled together. He sang, "I'm confessing that I love you."

"Can I believe everything you sing?"

They coiled their arms around each other's bodies and Colin sang. "My heart is sad and lonely dah dah dah dah, I love you only, why can't you believe me, I'm all for you, body and soul." Their clothing abandoned their responsibilities and shed the ghostly bodies.

An exhausting, climactic day. When her arousal subsided she fell asleep. Something woke her up. He was gone! He was gone! His clothing was gone. He was gone. She jumped up and dashed to the window and stood, a white, naked exclamation mark, looking across the grass to the harbour. She was in time to see his head and shoulders disappear as he climbed down Lorelei Rock to the shore below the cliff. She pulled her prom/wedding dress over her screaming skin and ran across the field. She stood on the Lorelei Rock and watched him row his dinghy out of the moonlight and into the fog.

Back in her bedroom, on top of her dresser, under *Kristin Lavransdatter*, she found the envelope her brother had left when he shipped out. When he gave it to her, she pasted it to the underside of the top drawer. Now it was torn open. Inside she found two thousand dollars. The letter itself was gone. The letter was gone. Gone.

"Oh my God. Oh my God."

She took off her dress and took her book to bed. She cried until she stopped. She read. Miraculously, she fell asleep. She dreamed of twins, unaware of the urgent sperm with their whip-like tails lashing their way up her fallopian tubes. Miraculously, she awoke. She pulled on her dress and went back to the beach. She found a baseball hat with strands of blond hair stuck to the sweatband. She put it on her head and walked the beach as far as Lorelei Rock. She found Tomassio, washed up, wrapped in seaweed, battered. Dead.

THIRTEEN

...The Ordinary forms the scaffolding
of the whole structure of worship
THE LAROUSSE ENCYCLOPEDIA OF MUSIC

W HEN MUSSOLINI JOINED forces with Hitler on June 10, 1940, the event produced no effect on the men's choir of Coaltown. Batiste Poirier, director, high in the choir loft at the back of the church, his back to the altar, the priest, and the congregation, elevated on his low stool, looked through steel-rimmed glasses at a collection of Acadians, Italians, Poles, Ukrainians, Germans, Russians, Irishmen, and Scots. About half of them worked, as he did, in or at the mine; the rest were shopkeepers, railroad workers, carpenters, policemen. Singing range was the acknowledged difference between them. Some were tenors, some altos, and some basses. Some, not sure what they were, simply sang along with whomever they contrived to stand next to. Deviant voices were tolerated with little more than half a frown and a smile from Batiste. Volume was his priority, unity a mere ideal. He raised his left hand, palm out, for silence. With his back to the altar and the congregation, he raised his right hand, fist clenched, index finger raised, his eye on the mirror where he watched the movements of the Mass celebrant, ready to strike the downbeat to begin the Introit.

Music was Batiste's passion. When he discovered Sister Sarah's library with its collection of books on the subject, reading about it became his pastime. When he read that the main parts of the Ordinary of the Mass, between the Introit and the Ite Missa Est, the Kyrie, the Gloria, the Sanctus, and the Agnus Dei were the basis for the major western musical forms, he became a student of the Mass. His favourite was the Mass for the Dead. It was never a pleasant day for the people in the church but it was a serious, solemn, passionate day, and it inspired him and he inspired the choir. He considered it an incomplete Mass because it did not include all the major parts but sometimes he would include them anyway.

The Introit.

Bishop MacNeil came to celebrate the Requiem High Mass. Father Pat persuaded him. "If you can't do anything about the Italian situation, at least go say the funeral Mass. Which reminds me, are you doing anything about the Italian situation?"

"What can I do?"

"What's the apostolic delegate say?"

"He said what I said. What can I do?"

"And what's the answer to that?"

"He's a diplomat. He asks diplomatic questions. They give him diplomatic answers. They don't trust him. He's an Italian. And he's not from Cape Breton, he's from Italy. You know about the war, Father Mancini, it didn't end when you left it. In fact it got bigger. Canada is at war with your ancestral fatherland or motherland, or whatever sex your ancestral land is. They're good buddies, the Nazis and the Fascists. The Germans shot your hand off because you and your buddies were trying to kill them. Remember? Nobody's in the mood for a chat. The apostolic delegate is a hair away from house arrest himself. It doesn't help much being a Catholic in Ottawa. Some of them would only wish it were the Pope so they could have a Mountie in a pin-stripe suit trailing behind him everywhere he goes."

"You have to do the Confirmation sometime," Father Pat said. "Why not now, and celebrate High Mass? Two birds, one stone. The people will see we're paying attention, at least."

"I don't want to provoke trouble. Not everybody in Coaltown is Italian. If it looks like we're favouring the Italians...it might hurt the church..."

"Hurt the church. The trouble is over. The killings have quieted everybody down. They need ceremony."

"Should I stay the night with Father Rod? That would make it my official visit. Kill three birds with the one stone."

"I don't think. No. He's got three cats. One on every bed in the house."

"What! Why would he take in cats to look after? And him with no housekeeper."

"Now he's got a housekeeper, and the cats."

"He hired a housekeeper?"

"Yeah."

"A married woman, I hope."

"Oh yes."

"Well. Someone to answer the phone, at least."

"Yes. At least that."

"*Requiem aeternam dona eis domine.*" The bishop intoned the Introit and Batiste's finger descended and set the choir in motion with Mozart's "Requiem." While the choir sang, the bishop mumbled along in Latin and Anna read from the English translation in her missal.

"Eternal rest give unto them O Lord, and let perpetual light shine upon them..." Anna felt as if somebody had ripped her husband from her body like an unborn child denied its chance to breathe. Her last meal was an egg, which her stomach refused to digest. All night she felt it trying to get back up to her throat. She looked at Father Rod in his vestments sitting at the side of the altar. Sex and eating, she thought. Why would we do them if we didn't have to? Why do we imagine they'll be fun? She felt she had done nothing but make mistakes all her life. What if she had stayed in Italy and repeated her mother's life?

She kept her eye on Gelo as he and his friend Réal attended the bishop. Would Gelo have happened in Italy? Who knows? She smiled. From the beginning of Mass he was like a little priest. An altar boy but no longer a boy. Lighting the candles, setting out the bell and the censer of incense, speaking carefully, solemnly, the Latin responses, his father's battered body behind his back, in the coffin in front of the altar rail. What is he thinking? Is he safe? Will he break down after the funeral? Him and Sadie, both their fathers dead, and they keep on an even keel. Do they talk about it, help each other? Is it enough? Will he join the army? Thank God, he's too young yet. Although I know damn well they let them lie about their age. Sadie? Will she keep him home? How long will the war last? What does she know about me and her father? What does she know about Tomassio and her mother? Cathy. Cathy crying. My mother crying.

"*Confiteor Deo omnipotento,*" the bishop intoned, and let the altar boys continue with the Confiteor.

"*Beatae Mariae semper Virgini . . .*"

Cathy read the Confiteor with them in the English translation in the missal. "I confess to almighty God, to blessed Mary, ever virgin . . ." Cathy was not crying, although she had started out crying. When the man in the black suit pushed the coffin up the aisle, between the two candles by the front pews, and into the bishop's belly, almost knocking him arse over kettle into the altar rail, she blurted something and she didn't know if it would sound like a laugh or a cry, and thank merciful God it came out crying. But now she stopped. She knew she would cry again when they sang the "Dies Irae." It was the piece of music she loved more than any other because it was sad and happy all at once, funny and scary like everything else in her life.

Like her wedding. She was so happy to get married, but when she looked up she saw nobody from her family, none of her friends. They excommunicated her, not only from the church, but from her family and friends. She expected it, she knew, but it never hit her until she looked up and saw nobody on her side of the church. Nobody. Row after row of empty pews. They didn't have to do that. They did it on purpose. And on the other side of the church, row after row of scowling strangers. And after that she never heard the "Dies Irae" again. She knew she'd cry when she heard it. Like the country music she listened to on the radio, beautiful music but sad things happening. Every time something good comes along, something bad comes along with it.

Tomassio. After all the battering he suffered they still fixed him up enough to open the coffin at the wake. And all the battering and fixing still didn't take the smirk off his mouth. Only her lips could do that, and not for long. She should have kept him in her attic forever. Oh, it was a sour wedding. And after, it turned out not to be marriage at all. Like living on a desert island with a tree.

She went to the wake. She was brave to go. The wake was too quiet. She left before the nuns finished the first rosary. She lasted through the Five Joyful Mysteries: the Annunciation, the Visitation, the Nativity, the Presentation, the Finding in the Temple. She lasted through the first of the Sorrowful Mysteries, the Agony in the Garden, although she kept thinking, the agony in the attic, the ecstasy in the attic. Why does death always make me think of sex? But when they started on the Scourging at the Pillar, her head filled full of baseball bats and Tomassio. She escaped.

When she came to the wake, she brought a ham and a roast of beef and five loaves of bread and offered them to Anna. She was afraid Anna might refuse. She was scared Anna might just stand there with her hands at her sides and never bend her arms to accept her offering. She'd have to walk out of the house with her arms full of bread and meat, and her back full of eyes. She knew Anna was capable of anything. It scared her skin pink. But Anna gave her a normal smile and raised her open hands and gathered in her gifts. The house was full of food.

"I don't have to stay, Anna," Cathy said.

"Stay as long as you like," Anna replied.

"I know it's hard on you, Anna."

"It's hard on everybody, Cathy. Thank you for coming. Thank you for the food."

So Cathy felt she had permission to stay and permission to leave. During the Scourging at the Pillar, she got off her knees and went to the kitchen and slipped out the back door and walked to the glebe house and went to confession.

"You can go to communion now," Father MacDonald told her, "even though it's not official until I contact the bishop. He has to do his thing to let you back in the Church. But you go to communion if you want to."

She didn't know if she wanted to. She didn't know if she'd be more noticed if she went, or if she stayed in her seat alone when everybody else went. She couldn't even remember if they served communion at funeral masses.

✝ ✝ ✝

"*Misereatur vestri omnipotens Deus*," the bishop cut in with the altar boys to finish the Confiteor, and Cathy read silently along with them, "May the almighty God have mercy upon you, pardon your sins, and bring you to everlasting life."

The Kyrie.

Kyrie eleison, Christe eleison, Kyrie eleison.

Lord have mercy, Christ have mercy, Lord have mercy.

For Batiste, when the Kyrie was over, the important part of the Mass was done. Mozart's "Requiem" and Kyrie he was sure of. The remainder of Mozart's Mass was sullied by deception, some of it written by Mozart and some by the imposter. Batiste himself could not tell the difference for sure, although he had his ideas. So he scratched out everything but the "Requiem" and the Kyrie and substituted the music of Palestrina. He knew nobody but Sister Sarah would know the difference. Tomassio would be pleased, but of course Tomassio knew nothing about music. Batiste did not like nor approve of the deceptions involved in the production of Mozart's Requiem Mass. But he understood deception, its uses and necessity. A person must live. A person must serve his loyalties, to work, music, family, to friends, and sometimes in order to serve Peter you had to deceive Paul. Batiste felt lucky that his dedication to celibacy and to the care of his aging mother combined to protect his deception from all but tolerant suspicion.

Father Pat sat while the bishop went to the pulpit and read the Epistle of St. Peter the Apostle (1, chap. 3): "Dearly beloved: Be ye all of one mind, having compassion one of another, being lovers..." As the bishop read, Father Pat's mind drifted back to the war, to his escape from the war with the gracious, courageous, loving help of the underground resistance soldier.

"All is fair in love and war," she said. "Do you know where that saying comes from? I think it's English. Who said that?"

"I don't know," Father Pat said. "But my buddy would probably know. He knows everything."

"Roddie would know?"

"Yeah. If it was written down somewhere. He reads everything."

"We'll ask him tomorrow. Right now, I don't want to go anywhere. I hope you don't mind. If I sleep alone I have nightmares, and that means I don't sleep much at all. And tomorrow, we'd better be alert or we'll be dead. Lots of sleep after we're dead, but I'd like to put that off for a while. Every time I doze off, the nightmare comes back."

"What nightmare?"

"It's a crazy thing. It wouldn't make sense to anybody but me. It's just a piece of paper, like a typewriter paper. And a pencil. The paper is suspended in the air and I control the pencil with my mind. My task is to make an inch margin around the four sides of the paper. I do a great job of it until I get to within an inch of finishing, and then I lose control of the pencil and it veers off into the middle of the page and it starts going every which way and I get completely frustrated and I can't get it back and I get terrified and I wake up."

"Where are you from?"

"I'm not supposed to tell you where I'm from."

"Your accent doesn't seem French. What's your dream all about?"

"Oh, I don't think it's too hard to figure out. We need complete control here. The Germans make lots of mistakes and we take advantage of them, and that's how we keep going. But if we make one mistake—pop, the bag is burst. And sooner or later ... "

"What?"

"Sooner or later we'll make a mistake. They'll shoot us. Life insurance companies don't welcome resistance fighters."

"Are you scared?"

"Oh no. I'd just love to get shot. Something to pass the time away on a quiet evening."

"Why don't you run?"

"I already ran. Where to now? I'm not what you'd call an experienced channel swimmer."

"Well, you're getting us out. Come with us."

"Sometimes that's an option. We'll see. It's something nice to think about. Especially this evening."

"You sound Swedish."

"Really. I thought my English is pretty good."

"Yes it is. Just about perfect. But now and again I hear something."

"I guess I wouldn't be too good a spy in Canada."

"Your name is Ingrid—is that Swedish?"

"It's not my real name."

"What is your real name?"

"Here," Ingrid said, "give me your hand. Put it here. Does that feel Swedish?"

"No."

"That's because in Sweden the mountains, even some of the small ones, have snow around their peaks all year. Here, take a look, not a trace of snow, not a flake."

"And does sleeping naked stop your nightmares too?"

"Not if I sleep alone. What's the difference in the dark? I can't carry pyjamas in my duffle. Not essential. I don't always get the chance to wash my underwear. Anyway, if I wore underwear you'd just have to peel it off. Will you make love to me if I tell you my real name? It's Marie Peut-Etre."

"Well, Marie Peut-Etre, I think my choice in the matter is now long gone into the history of love and war."

When he finished St. Peter's epistle, the bishop read the Gospel according to St. Matthew (chap. 5): "At that time: Jesus said to his disciples: Unless your justice abound more than that of the scribes and Pharisees, you shall not enter into the kingdom of heaven…"

The Gospel was the prelude to Father Rod's sermon, his eulogy for Tomassio. He had typed it out and now it rested on the lectern of the pulpit. He had memorized it but he put it where he could see it just in case. He tried not to think about what he wrote. He wanted it gone from his mind when he stood and walked to the pulpit so it would sound fresh, spontaneous, sincere, passionate. He let his mind drift through the drone of the bishop's reading. Last night Father Pat had stayed over in the glebe house, and they shared a drink before they went to bed. The end of a long day of a long week of a long year.

"Will the bishop stay the night, Pat? If he's going to do the Confirmation the next day he might as well. I've got a housekeeper now. Anna would prepare him a good breakfast. It would be a shame for him to miss the Chateau Neuf du Pape and the Ne Plus Ultra."

"He heard you took in some cats."

"Get out now. Where did he hear that?"

"The walls have ears," Pat said.

"I completely forgot the bishop is allergic to cats."

"Listen, Rod. Do you know where it comes from, that saying, 'all's fair in love and war?'"

"I do."

Father Rod's mind flipped to his latest talk with Sergeant Archimbault. Sergeant Archimbault was happy. Or, at least, satisfied. The "round-up" was over. His officers were back to normal duty, real anti-espionage, which was interesting, exciting. Already they had arrested a man with no identification walking in the woods near the airport at Reserve Mines. An amnesiac, according to him. And they were investigating suspicious activity at Low Point.

"Why?" Father Rod asked him.

"Because it's suspicious," Sergeant Archimbault said. "That's what we do. Fort Petrie is there. If the Germans invade England, Sydney Harbour will become one of the most important ports in the world, one of the few places the British Navy can retreat to."

"No, no. I mean why is the round-up over?" Father Rod asked.

"I guess they realized it was a stupid idea in the first place. We told them that. We're still watching a few people on their list but I think it's pretty well done."

"Is that what you do, watch people?"

"Of course. When something bad happens we like to have a pretty good idea of who did it. We can't sit in a box and wait for them to come and confess. That's a luxury for priests. We like to know ahead of time who's liable to do something."

"What about the men they took to Minto and Petawawa already? Everybody knows they're not spies or whatever it was they were put away for."

"I don't know. I guess they'll let them go sooner or later. But you know what bureaucrats are like, they can tie knots a lot faster than unravel them."

"What about Tomassio?" Father Rod asked.

"I'm very sorry about Tomassio," Sergeant Archimbault said. "Everybody knows he was a show-off. We know he was a tomcat, but he didn't deserve to die like that. I think we'll nail his killers. We're pretty sure who they are. Ump's cronies, likely. A little reward money will fetch them up. We have evidence, the murder weapon, footprints, we have a witness who lives across from the jail so we know how many. We have a description of the car. We'll get them. And when we do, we'll find out who smuggled them into the jail."

"But will his name be cleared? People think Tomassio killed Ump."

"We know he didn't do that. He wore sneakers when he escaped jail the first time. He still had them on when a witness saw him cross the ball field. He still had them on when we arrested him the second time and still had them on when his body was discovered in the harbour. His boots were in his kitchen all that time. Or most of that time. We think we know what happened. I suspect you do too. The case is on the back burner, at least until the war is over, likely forever."

"What about Tomassio's reputation?"

"We'll issue a press release. It'll clear his name. But you know what people are like. They believe what they want to believe."

"You owe him more than that. If it wasn't for your damned list, your round-up, as you call it ..."

"That's not what we call it. And it's not our list. They handed us the list along with our orders. We obeyed. It's war. With the war on, people feel they can justify anything. Look at you. You were in the war. What kind of work is that for a priest?"

"I was supposed to be saving souls."

"Yes, I'm sure. I understand you saved Franco's body, or most of it. From the looks of him, though, I think maybe he lost his soul."

"Yeah. Well. We're still trying."

"So are we."

Father Rod felt Father Pat's elbow in his ribs. The bishop was finished and already sitting down on the chair beside Father Pat. The congregation waited for his sermon. He walked to the pulpit. He looked down at the first word on the typed page, "Today"—and he looked up at the expectant faces. The entire Italian community from Coaltown attended the funeral and many came from the other coal towns. Steelworkers came from Whitney Pier and many came from Sydney, Sydney Mines, and North Sydney, and many from the countryside. They filled the pews, the back of the church, the choir loft, and spilled out into the porches and the churchyard. He began his sermon.

"Today, you heard the bishop read from the Epistle and Gospel of last Sunday, the fifth Sunday after Pentecost, so some of you have heard it twice now, or more. But I would like to repeat a couple of lines from Peter's epistle. In the first line he says, 'Be ye all of one mind, having compassion one of another.' And later he says, 'For he that will love life, and see good days, let him refrain his tongue from evil, and his lips that they speak no guile.'

"In Matthew's Gospel Christ says, 'Whosoever is angry with his brother shall be in danger of the judgement. If therefore thou offer thy gift at the altar, and there thou remember that thy brother hath anything against thee, leave there thine offering before the altar, and go first to be reconciled to thy brother, and, then, coming, thou shalt offer thy gift.'

"Our brother Tomassio, like me, like you, was a sinner." Father Rod paused a moment to allow his listeners to wonder where he was going. "Most of our sins," he continued, "at least the ones that matter, are betrayals. We betray our parents, our children, our wives, husbands, our friends, our bosses, our fellow workers, employees. Indeed anybody. Anyone who will give us half a chance. We become very good at it. We become so good at it we often don't even know we're doing it. A famous poet once wrote, 'Oh what a tangled web we weave, when first we practise to deceive, but after we've practised a little while, how vastly we improve our style.'

"Betrayal is what we most despise in others, and most easily forgive in ourselves. The second last thing we ever want to do is admit a betrayal to the person we betrayed. The last thing we ever want to do is forgive the person who betrayed us. When Peter says to be compassionate one of another, he means to be compassionate to those who betray us. Peter knew something about betrayal. Indeed, we know him as the apostle who betrayed Christ. And Christ picked Peter to be the rock, the foundation of our faith. He is the first priest of our religion.

"When Christ says go and be reconciled with thy brother, he means us to reconcile with those we betray, and with those who betray us. That's what he died for. And every time we say Mass we re-enact his death to remind us of what we must do. It is not easy. It is easier to pretend we are innocent.

"We are not seeing good days in Coaltown. Our friends and relatives are risking their lives overseas. On the home front betrayers and betrayed surround us. Each other. We have to remember that. We are the betrayed and we are also the betrayers.

"Tomassio, like me, like you, was a sinner. He did not deserve to be battered out of his life before he found and accepted the opportunity to reconcile with those he betrayed, and with those who betrayed him. Murder is the ultimate betrayal because it makes reconciliation impossible.

"My talk is blunt today because I want to shock you. And me. I want us to redeem Tomassio by allowing him to redeem us. Christ's death is a shock. Tomassio's death is a shock. His death must shock us into taking advantage of the opportunity his murderers stole from him. The chance to reconcile with the people we betray and the people who betray us. In that way we redeem Tomassio's life, sanctify it by making it useful; as the theologians say, efficacious. Useful in the sense that his shocking death will shock us into contrition for our sins, shock us into redemption. Then, like Christ, Tomassio will have died for the forgiveness of our sins, for our redemption, and Tomassio, like Christ, will be our redeemer."

Father Rod sat down in the wake of silence. Batiste's left palm held the choir at the ready. He raised his right hand, pointing his finger toward the top of the organ pipes. He prolonged the dramatic moment. Finally, he cut the air on the downbeat and the choir sang.

The Credo.

"*Credo in unum Deum,*" the voices began. The bishop turned and glared at the choir, but to no effect. The music swelled. The congregation watched the turmoil on the bishop's face and wondered why he was upset. The choir was two bars ahead of him, but that is not what annoyed the bishop. The choir annoyed him because the Credo, like the Gloria, did not occur in the Requiem Mass. Nothing to do but stand and wait until they finished. Gelo and Réal crouched on their knees on either side of the bishop and stared at the floor, once in a while glancing across and catching each other's eye. The bishop would have been even more annoyed if he had known that Batiste knew perfectly well the Credo did not belong in the Requiem Mass, but it was the piece his choir knew best and did the best job of singing, so he did it anyway.

Sister Sarah loved her brother's sermon. It was the kind of thing that kept her going. She knew it was the kind of thing that kept him going, too. She worried about him. She liked to worry about him because it kept at bay the worry about herself. *Credo in unum Deum*, she pondered. Is that what I believe? Or do I just believe in my own freedom? She frequently pretended to the others that, like them, she felt restrained and constrained and frustrated by the restrictive rules of the Order, except for Mary, of course, whom she could never deceive. But in truth she felt the rules protected her from distraction so she could devote her time to reading, studying, and music. It was true she wanted to be a music teacher but her superior had told her she had to go off and study Library Science. "Why?" she asked. "Because that is what we need," Mother Superior said, and that was the end of that. But now, she was glad. She didn't have to teach unwilling children the fundamentals of music over and over again. She could play her own music as much as she liked. She could help out with the choirs and with the Christmas and Easter concerts. But she could indulge herself in books every day—it was what she was supposed to do and what she loved to do.

Yes, she missed the thrill of sexual anticipation, but she knew full well the smell of coffee offers a richer flavour than the unfulfilling cup, the surreptitious taste of a morsel in the pantry leaves a more memorable tang than the distending meal. The thrill of expectation disguises the poverty of fulfilment. She envied Sister Miriam's undoubting dedication to knitting socks for her soldiers, although she knew her envy was as transparently hypocritical as the envy of the rich for the simple lives of the poor. She confessed her doubts to Father Pat. He laughed.

"Relax, Sarah," he said. "You're getting as bad as your brother."

"Roddie. I think the war made him cynical."

"There's always a war. If you can't survive surviving the war you have to wonder what you brought to it in the first place. So it's him you're worried about?"

"I suppose it is. I guess it's easier than worrying about myself."

"I suppose it is. Trouble is, worrying is a waste of energy. Why don't you do something instead?"

"Like what?"

"Tell him the truth. You know what it is?"

"You tell me."

"When you stop doubting, you stop believing. Do you think Thomas was any the better off after he washed his hands in Christ's wounds?"

"And what about me, smarty-pants, what should I do for myself? I suppose you got the solution for me too."

Father Pat smiled. "Yes. Indeed I do. Relax. Take a week off. Knit a pair of socks. Write your name and address on an envelope and put it in one of the socks. Send it to a soldier. It'll give you something to look forward to. And maybe take you down a peg or two."

"Is that my penance?"

"Why not?"

Sister Sarah now regretted the sour smile she had rewarded Father Pat with for his exotic penance. She fumbled for two weeks under Sister Miriam's guidance, hardly containing her impatience, but when finally she mastered the knit-purl rhythm she found it soothing and meditative. She began to think about trenches knee deep in water. She began to think about soldiers huddled soaking wet in bomb craters trying to keep their heads under the thunderous air and the debris flying through the stinking smoke. She wondered how their Credos were holding up as they suffered the real-life experience of their chosen profession. When she spread her first grey sock over the black habit covering her knee, it looked more like a mitt than a sock. She wondered if somewhere there was a one-armed thumbless soldier who might find comfort in her fortunate incompetence.

+ + +

The Agnus Dei.

The bishop waited to begin the Agnus Dei and kept time with his foot while the choir worked its way through the Dies Irae.

Cathy's shoulders in front of Sister Sarah were shaking with her sobs. The long white girl who had told Father Rod she wanted to become a nun sat beside Cathy and turned to her and bent down and whispered something in her ear. The choir sang, *Qui Mariam absolvisti, Et latronem exaudisti, Mihi quoque spem dedisti.* Sister Sarah translated, You absolved Mary Magdalene, you absolved the thief, there is hope for me.

Batiste gave up trying to follow the bishop and simply pushed the choir through its repertoire until communion. Cathy went to communion and nobody noticed. The tall blonde woman who followed her to the rail and back commanded the attention of every eye glancing in her direction. After communion it seemed no time before the bishop intoned final prayers over the coffin while Gelo swung the censer, sending spumes of smoke coiling through the air.

"*Ite missa est.*"

"*Deus gratias.*"

And the funeral men in black coats came, closed the coffin, and rolled the remains out of the church and into the hearse.

FOURTEEN

✝

AFTER HELEN LED THE POLICE, Father Rod, and
Anna to Tomassio's body on the beach below her
cliff, after they took away the body in an ambu-
lance, after she sat with Father Rod and Anna in her house
under her father's silent gaze and answered the policeman's
gentle questions, she was so distraught she packed a small
suitcase and went with Father Rod and Anna to the glebe
house and stayed the night. In the morning she went to
Mass and after the altar boys left she asked Father Rod to
hear her confession. She told him everything, about the
prom, the motorcycle ride, the boat, the sex. Everything. He
gave her absolution and told her not to worry, none of it
was her fault.

"What if I got pregnant?" she asked.

"If you got pregnant," Father Rod said, "you'll have
a baby."

Helen smiled. It was not the answer she was expecting but for some reason it satisfied her. They were sitting at the table in his study among the still unopened boxes of books. She sat back and felt her neck and shoulders relax against the long back of the wooden kitchen chair. "And then what?" she asked.

"I'll baptize it."

"And then?"

"Let's wait. If it happens there'll be lots of time to talk about it."

Helen folded her hands on the table. "I did the wrong thing, didn't I?"

Father Rod looked at her across the table and smiled. "No. You did the right thing. You just did it at the wrong time."

"I'm reading *Kristin Lavransdatter*, did you read that? You've got all these books."

Father Rod nodded and she continued. "She did the right thing at the wrong time, but she was a good woman."

"Yes, she was. Let me tell you about a wrong thing," Father Rod said, and he pointed to his initials carved in the table and he told her the story of his mother's gift to him of the tables and chairs. "That was a wrong thing to do at any time but it's a great reminder and sometimes it keeps me from making the same kind of mistake again. What you did is different. What you did might end up giving you a lot of trouble, but even if it does, it'll mean a new life with lots of beautiful possibilities."

When the Mountie came to question her, Father Rod had advised her to take her time, lots of time, and tell the truth but to dodge any questions that she didn't want to answer. And don't give them any information they don't ask for. He insisted on sitting in when they talked to her.

"That won't be necessary," the Mountie said. He was dressed in a grey suit, a blue shirt and a grey tie, a square haircut and a big smile.

"It may not be necessary," Father Rod said, "but it's the way it will be unless you want to lay charges and we'll get a lawyer and all that stuff. Do you intend to lay charges?"

"Too early for that."

"Fine," Father Rod said, and aimed his eye patch at the bridge of the Mountie's nose. "Let's get on with it then."

"Where is your brother, Helen?"

Helen gave him a long look. She turned and looked at Father Rod's smile, then she folded her hands on the table and stared at her thumbs. She explained that she didn't know where Beaver was. He joined the merchant marine and she thought he might have sailed about a week ago. He had told her he'd be going but he didn't say when."

"Who was driving his motorcycle?"

"I was."

"You were? Tell me about your friend. Who was he? "

She looked at him again. At his hat on the table. His notebook was open and his pencil was in his hand but so far he had written nothing. She looked at Father Rod and back at her folded hands on the table. She described her meeting with him at Mass in Whitney Pier. His name was Colin MacDonald. He walked her home from Mass, they made a date for the prom the next night, and the next day they spent on Beaver's motorcycle and his boat.

"What did you do Sunday afternoon and evening?"

"I made a prom dress."

"What did he do?"

"I don't know. He told me he was a sailor. From around Ottawa. He had something to do."

"Was he on shore leave, from a ship in the harbour?"

"I don't know. He didn't say. He told me he couldn't say anything about himself or what he was doing. Military secret."

"Did you believe him?"

"I believed him. But he didn't say much. He told me everything he said might be a lie unless he sang it." She looked at him and smiled.

"Unless he sang it?"

"Yes."

"What did he sing?"

"He sang 'Auprès de ma blonde,' 'Lili Marlene,' 'I'm confessing that I love you,' and 'I'm all for you body and soul.' And sometimes he sang talk."

"Just regular songs."

"Yes."

"Whose idea was the motorcycle trip?"

"He suggested it."

"Tell me about it. Where did you go? What did you do? What did he do?"

Helen described their trip. It was a picnic. They stopped and ate sandwiches and drank pop. They went all around the coast to Louisbourg and over to the Northside.

"What did he do?"

"He told me he was going to be a travel writer when he got out of the navy. He was taking pictures and writing notes for an article."

The Mountie smiled and made a noise in his nose. "When he told you that was he singing?"

She looked at Father Rod. "I think he knows the answer to that," he said.

"Did he take pictures of Fort Petrie, of the artillery

emplacements in Lingan, of the Marconi Towers in Table Head? Of ships in the harbour?"

"Yes. I don't know the names of all the places. He took pictures of everything."

"Did he take a picture of you?"

"No," she said, startled.

"No picture of the prom dress?" Helen looked at her hands. She didn't answer. In the silence the Mountie opened his briefcase and took out a snapshot and pushed it across the table to her. It was a picture of her and Colin at the prom, a long shot showing her hair and the back and side of her gown. He was smiling, his mouth frozen open, talking perhaps, or singing.

"Is that him?" the Mountie asked. She didn't answer. "You can keep it if you like, we have copies. Someone at the prom took it and gave us the negative." She pushed it back across the table.

"Did he take you home from the prom?" Helen nodded.

"Did he stay the night?"

"No."

"Did he come in the house?"

"Yes."

"Did you sleep with him?"

Father Rod coughed. Helen looked at him, met his eye. He winked. "You don't have to answer that, Helen." She looked the Mountie in the eyes, then averted her gaze.

"You took your brother's boat as well?"

"Yes."

"Where'd you go?"

"Same as on the motorcycle. Around the coast."

"Taking pictures and making notes? Where is the motorcycle now, and the boat?"

"We put the motorcycle back in Beaver's truck. He took the boat. That's the last I saw of him. He disappeared into the fog in Sydney Harbour."

"There was two thousand dollars on your dresser in a book. Where did that come from?"

"Beaver."

"What about a note or a letter?"

"He took it."

"Colin MacDonald took it? What was in the letter?"

"Just Beaver saying goodbye before he sailed."

"Did he say when his ship was sailing?"

Helen explained that Beaver told her he would say in it what he knew about where he was going and when he'd be back. But she wasn't to open it for a while, two weeks or so, and that she was to keep the money until he returned, and if he didn't return, she was to give half to their father and keep half.

"Does your father have a shortwave radio?"

"Yes. He listens to it all the time. That's what he does. And rock. And work. And get our meals."

"What does he listen to?"

"The news."

"In English?"

"In English. Sometimes in Polish. Sometimes French. And other ones, I don't know what they are."

"Does he ever send messages?"

"Send messages? On the radio? You can't do that."

"Does your father have a flashlight?"

"It's in my room. He never uses it."

"Okay, that's all for now. Will you be staying here?"

"Yes," Father Rod said. "She'll be staying here."

At the door Helen said, "Sir?"

"Yes."

"You leave my father alone."

The Mountie nodded. Smiled. He picked up his brief-case, saluted with his fedora, and put it on his head as he left the house.

✝   ✝   ✝

After the funeral, the bishop declined Father Rod's hospitable invitation to stay the night at the glebe house and went back to his catless palace in Sydney. His housekeeper was not expecting him and her boyfriend was in the kitchen. She hustled him out, rustled up some cheese and tomato sandwiches and a cup of tea, put them on the table, and was out of the house before the bishop realized there would be no supper.

Next morning he was back in Coaltown for Confirmation, not in the mood for a long day. While Fathers Pat and Rod played cribbage in the vestry, waiting for the bishop to get into his vestments, the children and Gelo, their sponsors, the parents and friends of the families, all gathered at the back of the church. They filled the space between the last pews and the confessionals and up the middle aisle to about the tenth pew. Helen Perenowsky moved among them, buzzing from one to another like an albino bee among flowers, fussing with their hair, their dresses, their ties, their shoelaces and straps, tucking in shirts, pulling the boys' white shirt cuffs below the sleeves of their suit coats or sweaters, primping the girls' veils and squeezing their lips into a smile with her thumb and index finger.

Sisters Sarah and Mary had given Helen the job of keeping order and she went about it by dancing constant attention on her nervous recruits. She could adjust Gelo's tie by simply bending her long body. But to fuss over the other children, she dropped to her knees and moved backwards, crablike, from child to child. She reminded each one, "You will become a soldier of Christ."

The children appeared ready for Confirmation. Father Rod came into the aisle at the front end of the church and motioned Helen to bring everyone up front. She led them to the front and, standing where Tomassio's dead body had rested during the funeral Mass, she dispersed them to either side of the aisle along the altar rail in front of the pews, boys on one side, girls on the other. The sponsors lined up behind each child. Father Pat stood behind Gelo, which made Gelo feel a little less diminished by the humiliation of lining up with a bunch of children. Of course, he was designated to make the responses to the bishop in Latin, which elevated him to the status of a celebrant once the ceremony got under way.

The bishop flowed out of the vestry door onto the altar followed by Réal with a big grin and a wink for Gelo. Réal opened the gate of the altar rail for the bishop and then took the bishop's crozier and mitre, and closed the gate as the bishop cleared the opening.

The bishop stood on the kneeling bench of the altar rail, but even so, when he looked up he saw that the long white girl standing in the aisle before him was a head taller than he was. He had to elevate his chin to look her in the eye. He seemed bewildered and he turned first to Sister Sarah and then to Sister Mary, who were guarding the ends of the lines to his left and right. Their faces looked back at him with amused, silent eyes. Finally he bowed his head, opened his mouth, and began.

"*Spiritus Sanctus superveniat in te, et virtus Altissimi custodiat te a peccatis.*"

As the bishop chanted his verse, Sisters Mary and Sarah came to the front of the groups of boys and girls and raised their right hands, index fingers extended, and when the bishop finished, their fingers cut the air and the children chanted in unison, "Amen."

"*Adutorium nostrum in nomine Domini,*" the bishop bellowed over the white girl's head. The mice huddling in the organ in the choir loft felt the pipes vibrate and scurried through their escape holes under the floorboards.

"*Qui fecit caelum et terram,*" Gelo responded, and flashed Réal a small smile.

"*Domine, exaudi orationem meam,*" the Bishop bellowed.

"*Et clamor meus ad te veniat.*"

The bishop scanned the line of boys and girls. "Does everyone know what the Latin means?" he asked them.

"Yes, Your Excellency," they chanted in unison. Sister Mary's raised hand and index finger descended and her group of boys did their little singsong: "Our help is in the name of the Lord."

Sister Sarah's raised hand and index finger descended and her group of girls did their little singsong: "Who made heaven and earth." And the boys: "O Lord, hear my prayer." And the girls, "And let my cry come to you."

"That's excellent, Sisters," the bishop said.

"Thank you, Your Excellency," Sisters Mary and Sarah chanted in unison, and by the smile on the white girl's face the bishop knew they were making fun of him. He couldn't think of a safe way to express his fury so he swallowed it and continued, but already he was beginning to think thoughts, such as, I wonder if it's a good thing for a sister and brother to be working in the same area. There is a crying need for missionary priests in China.

"*Dominus vobiscum.*" His bellow now carried an edge which engaged a different set of pipes in the organ.

"*Et cum spiritu tuo,*" Gelo bellowed back. The bishop glared at Gelo. Then he stared into the sapphire eyes of the long white girl staring down at him like a spectre, but her eyes betrayed no conspiracy.

Helen contained her smile. After two days living in the glebe house, she felt calm and comfortable. They were all busy with the wake and funeral, but still they took the time to find things for her to do. And they made her talk. She wasn't used to talking to people. She wouldn't talk at first but they had coaxed her into it. Sadie carried around a little three-legged milking stool and every time she talked to Helen she got up on it until they were both laughing so hard they couldn't talk at all. Gelo carried around a little mock megaphone he made out of a dunce hat, and every time he talked to Helen he bellowed through it, "Hello, Helen. Can you hear me?" If that happened in school she'd know they were making fun of her, but here she knew they were just trying to make her laugh. They'd say, "Hey, Helen, reach up there in the attic, will ya, and grab me down my wool sweater, I'm getting a bit of a chill." She felt they were like a brother and sister.

She spent a whole afternoon in Sister Sarah's school library reading when she wasn't busy and helping with the books and paperwork. Father Rod decided he didn't have enough room for his books in the glebe house and Sister Sarah borrowed them from him to fill her empty shelves. She gave Helen the job of sorting, marking, and shelving the books and filling out the library cards for the drawers.

Helen balanced a question on her tongue all afternoon until finally, when they sat at the table in the kitchen of the Domestic Science room for a cup of tea, she blurted it out.

"Could I be a nun?"

Sister Sarah took a long look at her across the table. She imagined her in a habit after she put on weight, when her shoulders and her hips grew wide, her bosom ballooned and her belly distended, those sapphire eyes pouring blue all over a classroom of tiny people.

Sister Sarah did not believe in recruiting. She felt most young girls harboured foolish reasons they never expressed, probably because they hid them from themselves as well as everyone else. Her strategy was simple. Discourage them every way you can and if they persist, let them try it under the severest conditions charity permits. If they last a year, take the next step.

"Why would you want to be a nun?" she asked and blew the steam off the top of her tea.

Helen sat silent. She knew lots of answers. She read them in books. They were not her answers. She felt she might be deciding something for the rest of her life. She wanted to do it for the right reason. She wanted to be honest.

"Is it because you think you're too tall for boys?" Sister Sarah asked.

"No."

"You're sure?"

"Yes, I've had my fill of tall boys."

Sister Sarah looked up from her desk, alert. "Is it because you don't like boys?"

"No."

"You have a boyfriend?"

"I did."

"Did you kiss him?"

"Yes."

"More than that?"

"Yes."

"A lot more."

"Yes."

"Did you like it?"

"Yes."

"Is it because you like the habit? Like to dress up like a nun?"

"No. I want to be a librarian."

Sister Sarah took a sip of tea and looked at Helen for a long time. Helen grabbed the table to keep herself from fleeing.

Finally Sister Sarah spoke. "Helen," she said. "You are a girl after my own heart."

The bishop sped through the rest of the Confirmation prayers, and taking the container of chrism from Réal he quickly went from child to child, and asking them in turn to say their names and dipping his right thumb into the bowl of chrism, he anointed each with the sign of the cross after first mumbling in Latin, "*Signo te signo crucis et confirmo te Christmate salutis. In nomine Patris, et Filii, et Spiritus Sancti,*" and then in English, "I sign you with the sign of the cross, and I confirm you with the chrism of salvation. In the name of the Father, and of the Son, and of the Holy Ghost."

"Amen," each soldier of Christ responded in turn.

It wasn't until the bishop returned to his empty house, got into his pyjamas, and into bed with a tumbler of Scotch that he remembered he forgot to have the children take the pledge.

EPILOGUE

✝

Human nature, Mr. Allnut, is what we
are put in this world to rise above.
KATHARINE HEPBURN TO HUMPHREY BOGART
IN *THE AFRICAN QUEEN*

1965

I N THE EARLY DARK, Sister Helen Perenowsky, coming back home to her convent, rode her purring
Harley-Davidson down the convent driveway and
over a bit of lawn to the doorway of the potting shed.
Sisters Sarah and Mary peered through the screen door as
she opened the shed and lifted the bike to the sill, pushed
it over, and followed it in. She reappeared in a moment,
shut the door, and snapped the padlock in its hasp. She
took off her gloves, removed her helmet, pulled the elastic
from her blonde hair, stood still for a moment, and lifted
her leather shoulders in a deep breath and a long exhala-
tion. A cloud uncovered the moon and its sad light
showed Sarah and Mary the question mark still hanging
down Helen's long pale face.

Once inside, Helen walked between the two nuns and
went wordlessly up the stairs to her bedroom. Sarah and

Mary went to the chapel to meditate and get their minds ready for next morning and breakfast.

Helen knew the secret of poaching eggs so she was always in charge of breakfast. Actually, there was no secret. She just poached them. Put in two cups of water and a squirt of vinegar, bring it to a boil, turn it down to three, break open each egg onto a saucer and slide it into hot water, and take them out the minute they won't fall apart. She tried to teach Sarah and Mary but they couldn't do it. So they suspected she was hiding the secret. Probably a family secret she got from her father, who had a reputation as the best Polish cook in a Hungarian restaurant in all of the Sydneys. Perhaps.

If Helen had a secret she didn't know what it was. She had watched her father cook but the only word he ever said to her about it was, eat. Helen suspected the secret was that, like her father, she liked to cook and feed people, whereas Sarah and Mary liked other people to cook and feed them.

When Sisters Mary and Sarah came into the kitchen from their morning prayers in their smart modern clothing, Sister Helen was dressed in her old habit, hood and all, a yard of rosary beads hanging from her waist. The table was set for three, with a plate of toast and a dish of marmalade in the middle of the white tablecloth. Helen served them each a poached egg on toast and tea, served herself, sat down, and smiled her uncertain long-face smile. Sarah and Mary smiled back.

"Well?" Sarah said.

"Well?" Mary said.

"What?" Helen said.

Sarah said, "You don't seem to be Attila, the tough little nun you appeared to be last night."

"It's a long time since I've been little."

Mary said, "What happened to the leather? Did you buy all those duds for one rip-roaring ride?"

Sarah said, "At least you're back. I thought we'd be stuck with poaching our own eggs."

"I just wanted to feel comfortable one more time," Helen said.

"Can we help, dear?" Mary asked.

"I hope so."

They finished their poached eggs and toast. Sarah poured them another cup of tea. Helen reached into her habit and extracted an envelope wrapped in plastic. She took a letter from the envelope and she began to read the blue pages.

Dear Mother,

I don't know where you are or what you are doing, but someone who does know promised me to bring this letter to you. I hope it will be welcome. By doing a lot of digging and with the help of a friend and some good luck I found out you are still alive. I promised to say no more than that. If we ever meet, with your permission and blessing, I will be able to tell you everything.

As you know I am twenty-five years old. I am a teacher. I teach modern languages at a university. I am so tall I have to marry a basketball player, not really, but I am going to marry a basketball player. Are you tall too or am I just a freak? My mother? said wouldn't it be nice if you could invite your mother? and your father? to the wedding. My father? said, yes, wouldn't that be nice. I realize I could be an embarrassment to you depending on your situation. But if you can't come to my wedding, or don't want to, would you be able to pass this on to my father? I don't know who he is. I couldn't track him down. I'll leave it at that. My phone number is written on the inside of the envelope so you don't have to look but it's there if you want it.

                                              Love,
                                       Susan Cadieux

*PS My parents are both five foot two. It would be worth the trip and
the time just to see us stand together for a picture.*

By the time Helen had finished the letter, there were
more tears in their cups than tea. They sat silent for a long
time until Sister Sarah got control of her vocal chords. "I'd
say," she said in a swollen voice, "that that is about as irre-
sistible as it gets."

They sat silent again for a long time as if in prayer.

Helen gave them a long look across the table and
reached into her habit again and pulled out another letter
from another envelope, this one wrapped in tissue paper
and cellophane. She read it to them.

Dear Helen,

*The war is over. Germany is disgraced. Some people do not admit it, but
I do. I deceived you. I betrayed your trust. I manipulated your inno-
cence. I do not use the excuse: it was war. There is no excuse. There is no
way to understand. I just read a story by a German writer about cor-
ruption. He ends it by saying: "It is beyond understanding." Forgive me,
if you can. I would like to come to Canada and talk to you. I told you I
planned to be a travel writer and that is what I am. It was the truth
even though I did not sing it. I enjoy it. It is a job that keeps me busy and
on the go and keeps my mind off the past, but I never stop thinking of
you. I am from Hamburg but I am never there. My entire family was
burned in the fire bombing and there is nothing there for me. But I have
this address there and any mail will be forwarded to me wherever I am.*

                                          Sincerely,
                                     Helmut Schmidt

The three nuns sat silent for a long time, like reluctant sponges absorbing acid. Then Mary went to the stove, boiled the kettle, and made more tea.

"When did you get that letter?" Sarah asked, after they'd sipped into their fresh cups of tea.

"A few years after the war."

"Did you answer it?"

"No."

"Why not?"

"He killed my brother. I told you all about it."

"He didn't kill your brother," Sister Sarah said.

"As good as," Helen said.

"Your brother was as good as trying to kill him," Sister Mary reminded her.

"Beaver was in the merchant marine. He never tried to kill anybody."

"What are we having for supper, Helen?"

"What?"

"What are we having for supper?"

"Ham. Why? What's that got to do with anything?"

"Did you kill the pig?"

"What pig? No, I didn't kill a pig. What are you talking about?"

"Well as good as, wouldn't you think?"

"What are you talking about?"

"If nobody killed a pig, nobody would eat a pig," Sister Sarah said.

"I don't know what to think," Sister Helen said.

"Listen, dear," Mary said. "Don't think at all. But if you have to think, think about this. Suppose Helmut took your brother from you. Suppose that. On the other hand he replaced him when he gave you a daughter."

"That's cruel, Mary, cruel. That's inhuman."

"But it's true. It's human to want to get back at somebody who hurt you. But we have to live. We have to live. But you don't have to think about it, really. All you have to do is do something. Don't think, dear. Do. It's easier. And it makes things happen."

"Do. Do what?" Sister Helen asked.

"That's the easiest thing in the world, Helen," Sister Mary said. "Call your daughter. She gave you her telephone number. Go see her. Tell her about her grandmother. Tell her about her grandfather. Tell her about what it was like to be a tall girl in a school that didn't have a basketball team. I'm sure she would love to hear about that. She can tell you what it was like for her. Tell her everything. Tell her you love her. See what happens. Maybe you'll take a trip together, before the wedding."